THE UNFLESHED
THE TALE OF THE AUTOPSIC BRIDE

By LISA VASQUEZ

Edited by A.J. BROWN & DONELLE PARDEE WHITING

For more from
STITCHED SMILE PUBLICATIONS
www.stitchedsmilepublications.com

This is a work of fiction. Names, characters, businesses, places, events and incidents are either the products of the author's imagination or used in a fictitious manner. Any resemblance to actual persons, living or dead, or actual events is purely coincidental.

Cover design by Darque Halo Designs, Lisa Vasquez.
Editing by AJ Brown and Donelle Pardee Whiting
Stock Images by ShutterStock, FlexDreams

ISBN-10:1-945263-08-3
ISBN-13:978-1-945263-08-8

© 2017 Lisa Vasquez, Stitched Smile Publications

One of the hardest parts of writing a book has to be the dedication. There are the obvious choices; my mate, my children, and my family. But sometimes, a book calls out for someone else. For me, this book blossomed when I began the journey with my mentor and editors. Without the guidance of Jeff and the nurturing of Donelle, I know this book would not be what it is.

Jeff, and Donelle–the two of you combined form my balance. Not only as an author, but for Stitched Smile Publications, and in life. I cannot thank either of you enough. This book is dedicated to you both.

I would be remiss if I did not also dedicate this book to my father, Michael Trocki (RIP), for introducing me to the profound possibilities writers have to turn imagination and dreams into reality. At the time when Mary Shelley wrote *Frankenstein* (the inspiration for this book, along with its counterpart, *The Bride of Frankenstein* written by Robert Florey) she could never have imagined the organs from a dying person would give life to another–just like my dad. Because of the generosity and selflessness of strangers, and my own mother who donated her kidney to him, my father lived above and beyond the projected life expectancy of 5 years at the time of his diagnosis.

And finally, last but certainly not least, this book is dedicated to the Stitched Smile Publications' staff. Stitched Smile Publications lives and breathes because of interns and volunteers who all believe in what SSP stands for. We are a

FAMILY, and all of you mean more to me than words could ever hope to express.

Contents

London: August, 1348

A plague is rumored to be moving through Paris, claiming the lives of more than sixty percent of the population. A war with Mongolia spreads stories of the Mongolian army, on the verge of defeat, catapulting their disease-ridden dead into the fray. King Edward III reigns over England, there is open trade with China, and Pope Clement the VI heads the Vatican.

***

CHAPTER 1: EVERY BREATH YOU TAKE

"If you could just hold still … " Pursing his lips, the doctor tugged on the strap which held the girl's wrist in place. Muffling her screams was the cloth he shoved into her mouth prior to her being thrown onto the table. All of her writhing loosened her restraints, and she managed to get one arm free. Flailing wildly, she fought for her life, despite having no use of her eyes.

"This will all make sense soon," he continued. "You won't be around to see it, but your donation will be the catalyst to reviving life. You just … have to remain still."

Sobbing, Analyn bucked her body, using her good leg to push her hips off the table. Where her eyes used to sit, were two gaping holes cauterized by hot pokers. She still had the scent of burning flesh in her nose. Her final thoughts were of her mother and father weeping over her pine box. *If they ever found her*.

Gripping the girl's forearm with one hand, Angus Wulfe, the village's doctor, wrapped his fingers around the hilt of the cleaver, "The more you move, the more it will hurt, girl."

Her pain didn't matter to Angus. What mattered was using what she feared to make her comply. Having already endured a week of being dissected, Analyn was losing the will to fight. She wanted it to be over. She wanted to die.

"Pleeee– " she begged around the cloth. She could form only a few syllables with it lodged deep against the back of her throat.

"There, there," he said softly, holding the cleaver six inches over his mark. Analyn was sobbing harder, soaking the handkerchief with her spit. When her gag reflex kicked in, her nostrils pinched and flared to her gasping for air.

Dropping back down to the table, she rolled her head from side to side resolving herself to her fate. She was a guinea pig in some sick experiment. With her heart beating so hard, she could hear ringing in her ears, Analyn tried to listen around it. The grip on her arm tightened, cutting off the blood flow from her fingers which were now tingling with pins and needles.

When her breathing returned to normal, she grew as calm as an Easter lamb sprawled out for the feast. The danger came when the mind wandered. She was lying there trembling, trying to recall the sound of her mother's voice singing on Sunday morning when the sound of the cleaver came down.

CHOP.

There was a split second when the sound preceded infliction. The sound of her wrist being severed from her arm going through her chest was like a wave of vertigo until the sickness caught up, followed by blinding, white-fire pain.

Curling into a fetal position, Analyn's body muscles contracted. *Insects do this, too*, Angus thought to himself. Smiling, he imagined her pinned to the table with wings spread wide. Parting his lips, his tongue curled up to sweep over the blood splatter from her radial artery.

He was pleased with the extraction. The hand was close to the perfection of its new mate. Morrigan's body was succumbing to the unquenchable hunger of the Plague at a rate even Angus had not anticipated. His cure would take time, and he needed to preserve her beauty. Finding parts wasn't easy but he stalked Analyn for weeks before he confirmed she was the closest match he could find.

If he could keep Analyn alive, he could save Morrigan.

***

Angus watched her. The sweet, innocent way her dimples curved inward making her cheeks seem more plump. Her smooth skin was like cream against a peach. When she laughed, the color spread down to her slender neck. The delicate hint of skin peeked over the young mounds of her breasts. All of it together made his lewd gaze feel that much more lecherous. The more he tried to look away the more he stared.

He realized his lower lip trembled as he sat there engrossed with the view. His jaw was like rubber in the way it fell open, and his breathing grew ragged. He wanted her. Desired her in every way.

The prominent physician, Angus Wulfe, pulled off his spectacles and rubbed his handkerchief over the lenses while standing between two vending carts.

It was easy to feign interest in the exotic fruit brought to the market that day. The doctor knew Morrigan visited every Saturday with her friend, which made picking this spot important. He could stay hidden while having a clear view of the all the vendors.

Across from him at the square's entrance, Geoffery Blake made his way through the crowd. He was young and tidy looking with his fashionable attire. The sign of his wealth was in the fairness of his skin, free from blemish. His thick mane of yellow hair gleamed like a golden crown. He smiled, flashing bright blue eyes, and the women giggled like children at his approach. Being the son of a prominent landlord also made him a prime candidate if an arranged marriage could be negotiated.

The thought of it made the doctor jealous, and his lips curved into a sneer. He convinced himself if it weren't for the undesirable appearance of age and the scars left behind from his bout with the measles, he'd have been married with children of his own by now. He reached up and looked at his reflection in a

barrel of water he was standing next to. His hair was disheveled from the wind. With self-consciousness spreading through him, he smoothed his peppered black hair into its leather strap. It was more comforting for Angus to believe it was *he* who held out for the perfect candidate—the perfect, untouched beauty by name of Morrigan Kingsley.

Morrigan was wispy and feminine with a waist cinched to a diminutive eighteen inches. Her hips flared out like an hourglass into a firm, heart shaped rump. Her laughter was infectious and carried to his ears now like the sound of wind chimes on the breeze. She was close and the smell of her soap filled his lungs. He took in a deep breath and held it for as long as he could. His lungs burned but he held on, closing his eyes to immerse himself in the fantasy. When he exhaled at last, the doctor opened his eyes. "His" girl walked right past him to the neighboring cart. The smell of poverty filled the square with a mixture of unbathed bodies, rotting fruit, and poor sanitary conditions. It didn't matter though because even at this distance, he could capture Morrigan's scent. *Vanilla and lavender*.

The market bustled more actively than usual that day. Women with baskets of breads, tarts, and wild flowers wove in and out of the people. Children laughed and chased one another. Men shouted over their competitors for attention. It made Angus uncomfortable, but he was grateful for the camouflage it provided.

Angus' hand slid over the firm orange on display in the vendor's cart before him. His palm cupped it and he allowed his fingers to curl around the fruit before bringing it before his face. The citrus was fresh and aromatic.

"G'day, sir!" the girl tending the cart said, "Picked fresh jus' this mornin'. Care for jus' one?"

She's a liar, The beast inside him growled.

Angus looked the girl over, allowing his eyes to travel without shame. She was plain and didn't have the stench of pigs or livestock like the others. The girl smiled and swayed side to side when she caught his eyes lingering too long across her ample curves. She turned at an angle and gave him more of a show that allowed for a better view of her cleavage. Angus' intense stare continued unapologetically. He was much too worked up from watching Morrigan and daydreaming about peeling off her clothing. The desire to get to her sweet spot was too powerful to stop himself.

The vendor girl in front of him was groomed for this kind of behavior. She was freshly washed, and the oils in her neat, braided coif filled his hypersensitive sense of smell.

"Good day, girl," Angus smiled down at her, concealing the wolf in sheep's clothing. He leaned in close so she could feel his breath against her skin.

"How fresh are they?"

Angus whispered the words with a shuddering, exhaled breath and with his free hand he brushed a runaway lock of fiery-red hair away from her cheek. The girl smiled more and lifted her shoulder a little. Her eyes of jade floated upward and met his gaze again.

"The dew is still fresh upon its flesh, sir."

The Physician knew this was a lie, but he played along. The citrus was sweet and aromatic, but the stench of import clung to it. *She thinks I am a fool.*

Angus' eyes flicked upward and caught the girl's father watching them. Just as the predator was stalking his prize, this father had his sites on the hunter, and the man's jagged smile offered his approval. Angus' stomach churned. Soliciting his daughter cooled off any burning desire Angus harbored, and

with that the doctor dropped his hand to his side with disinterest. *She and her father are trash.* He thought.

The physician placed the orange back in the cart and walked away before he leaned in again and hissed into her ear, "I do not eat rotten fruit."

The girl cringed and looked up at her father whose eyes had grown dark.

Angus glimpsed the girl's scars peeking from under her loose blouse. She'd been whipped, often. What small interest he had in the girl left him and he continued on to the next vendor. Morrigan's laughter rang out catching the doctor's attention again, and he saw Geoffery was whispering in her ear. Beneath the surface of the soft-spoken façade he portrayed, his rage boiled. He had to get away.

He covered his nose with his handkerchief and breathed the herb infused oil into his nostrils to clear away the stench of the impoverished and continued on his way. He reached the edge of the street when he heard his name being called.

"Mr. Wulfe, sir!" came the voice.

Angus turned around and searched through the bustling faces until he saw the young lad pushing through to him. "Mr. Wulfe, please. You must come."

He held the handkerchief to his face more firmly, and stared down at the barefoot lad. He couldn't be more than fifteen and scarcely had meat to his bones. His face was gaunt, and his eyes were shadowed. *Malnourished*, he thought to himself.

"What is it boy, I am in a hurry." Angus replied.

"Sir, it's the King's Herald," the boy panted as he bent over and placed his palms on his knees. "He's ill, sir."

"He's ill?" Angus grew impatient. "Speak, boy!"

The waif-like teen was still struggling to catch his breath when he lifted his eyes to the physician's again. "Fever with chills and stomach complaints."

Angus narrowed his gaze at the boy, disgusted by him. The boy was used to it, but it didn't ease the shame he felt, or the weight of the doctor's gaze on him.

"I must fetch my bag. You will wait outside for me and lead me to him," snapped Angus.

"Of course, sir," the boy muttered down at his feet.

The messenger reminded the doctor of himself at a young age; worthless and often rejected by those around him. The memory of those feelings brought back dark images of his past, and it made him want to lash out at the boy with a stick or branch for conjuring them. He wanted to destroy those memories and all the feelings that came with them. Instead, he kept the monster inside him on a leash and led the way to his home to acquire his tools. If memory served, they'd be traveling through the more downtrodden areas of London to reach the Herald. He wanted to be sure he had everything and another handkerchief just in case. If it weren't for the fact the patient was the King's Herald, Angus would've sent the boy to one of the midwives or charlatans.

Of course they sent for me, he thought. A pompous smirk spread across his face, *I am the best*. It was obvious his reputation preceded him and to ensure his appearance, he washed his face and hands and swapped the coat he had worn with a cleaner, higher quality jacket. Knowing the boy was standing outside didn't urge Angus to move faster or cause any sense of urgency in him.

The physician looked through his bag, carefully assessed his inventory and added a few more items. He opened the cupboard and pulled out several beakers, petri dishes, and

hoses and carefully lay them inside the bag. He gave himself a final once over and smoothed down the tailored wool so it lie flat. Satisfied, he picked up his medical bag and walked outside to the boy waiting on him.

"Let's go," he said.

The boy bounced off the wall he'd been leaning on and reached for Angus' bag.

"May I car—"

Angus cut him off sharp, "Do not touch me or my things, boy. Carry on."

The boy flinched but led the way, keeping a nervous distance. He'd been on the streets long enough to trust his instincts. The Physician had the same look in his eyes as some of the more brutal Lords he'd come in contact with. He had plenty of scars to prove it, too.

The sun was beginning its descent following the bells of the church. Angus peered up at the overcast sky and realized he'd be heading home at night. His lips curled into a scowl. At night was when the ladies came out, displaying their bodies and shouting out salacious promises for monetary return. On one occasion, Angus delivered a sound chapping to fend off their grabbing hands.

The physician sighed in annoyance and shouted at the boy who was still ahead of him, "Where is he, boy?"

"Just up the way, sir. Up there at Lady Bess' home."

Angus could only guess why a Herald might be holed up in this part of town but managed to turn his thoughts to business when he caught sight of the cottage and servants pacing outside. The physician lifted his chin a bit higher and cleared his throat.

"Calm down. Stop fussing, and show me to the patient," he announced briskly, building up his presence.

The lady of the home rushed to greet the physician in a panic, "Please, sir. He's quite ill. You *must* do something!"

The woman's tone caused Angus to pause. He turned and looked down at Lady Bess and she gasped at the change in the doctor's face. Though his body language was non-threatening, his eyes gave all the warning necessary.

"I—I mean, please," she stammered, "please help him."

Angus' grip on the medical bag tightened, and he took a step back to allow her past him, "Show me where he is."

Lady Bess pressed her back to the wall as she scooted past, aiming to put a good distance between her and Angus. Once there, she kept her distance.

"He's here," she said.

The stench of the infection assaulted him from down the hallway. *Death,* he thought, *it smells like warm, wet death encroaching.*

The closer he approached, the more the smell stung the inside of his nose. Angus brought the handkerchief to his nose to smother the stench and turned the corner into the room. The Herald lay in the bed, the sheets stained yellow with sweat and pus. Flies buzzed around his sickly body scoping a place to lay their eggs. Lady Bess inched her way to the door, anxiously. The tendons in her neck drew tight as she fought down the bile rising to her throat.

"Fetch me clean water," Angus said, "and send the servants with clean linen. It's disgraceful to have the King's Herald in such conditions."

Lady Bess swallowed hard before turning toward the physician, "Truly, sir, he has been changed twice since this morning. The women are washing and hanging the linens as fast as we can."

Angus eyed her to assess whether she was being truthful or not. Her worried look informed him she was. His brows rose ever so slightly before turning to the Herald again.

"How long has he been here in this condition?" he asked.

"Beval has been here for three days, sir," she answered.

"And you just now had the mind to call for a physician?!" he snapped.

"He wasn't like this when he came, sir! I swear it!" Lady Bess cried.

"So God send me, if this man dies from your negligence I shall inform the
King of your hand in it!" Angus shouted. "Fetch the water, girl!"

The woman clutched her neck with her hand and spun out of the room. Angus watched her leave before looking down to the table beside the bed. Watered down stew sat untouched with a piece of loaf beside it.

The Herald had been woken by the shouting and craned his neck to see who was there. Seeing the physician, he reached a thin hand toward him and mumbled a plea for help. The man was still reaching out for him when Angus turned away and looked for a space to set up. Truth be told, he didn't want to touch anything.

The doctor could barely stomach the sight of the man. Angus took in the room. Stained walls surrounded him. Light barely filtered in from the whiskey yellow glass pane of the window that was covered in dowdy material heavy with dust. Candles sat in various areas, some half melted and dripping onto their holders. The floor was filthy. He jerked his foot back from a wet cloth that had fallen next to the Herald's bed.

Frustrated, he called out for a servant. "Can *someone* please come in and give me a proper place to work?"

A young girl with her hair and face covered by a cloth rushed in, her voice muffled beneath the cloth veiling her mouth.

"Right away, sir."

She knelt on the floor and began to clean with the discarded rag, then dunked her brush into the bucket she carried in with her, scrubbing at the stain left behind. When she was done, she left to retrieve clean, steaming cloths, which she used to clean the table Angus would use to place his tools on. Waiting, he looked around for a place to sit. A dingy upholstered chair sat in one corner. It made his skin crawl at the thought of sitting in it. The other corner held the only suitable seating, a simple wooden chair.

The light from the window was enough to show him her eyes were young and bright with youth. Angus trailed his eyes down further to her small shoulders covered in a cheap, grey material rolled up at the sleeves. Her face held a strong resemblance to Lady Bess, and she looked healthy. *She must be family,* Angus thought.

The girl felt the physician's eyes on her and tried not to look at him. Her discomfort made his lips twitch into an ever-so-slight grin. He loved to watch them squirm. It gave him a sense of power. The tension in the room mounted, and she worked faster at her task. Angus clicked his front teeth together delighting in the way it set on her nerves.

"What's your name, girl?" Angus asked with an intentional boom in his voice.

"Annie," the girl said with a visible start.

Angus smiled at the desired effect, "Annie, I think you missed a spot. I can't have filth around my tools or the patient."

Annie straightened from her hunched over position but refused to raise her eyes. She seemed undecided as she stood

there and looked more closely until she found the stain. She bent over as cautiously as she could and scrubbed the spot. This position gave Angus the advantage to leer at her unobserved. Her body rocked with each forced push of bristle against the wood. Angus took in a deliberate, slow breath. Annie froze at the sharp inhalation of his breath, and tightened her back. The fear crept up along her curved spine. *Yes,* he thought, *she has been in this position before.*

Annie scrubbed with rapid, furious motions to remove the stain before straightening and turning to Angus. Avoiding his eyes, she curtsied then ran out of the room. *It's a shame,* he thought, *she was plucked far too young.*

Angus rose and checked the cleanliness of the table by running a finger along its surface. *At least she did a good job,* he mused.

Wiping his finger on a clean towel, he retrieved from his bag, he rolled out the pouch holding his tools. Each one was tended to with careful observation. Every blade honed with an obsessive eye to razor sharpness. Each petri dish glistening and squeaky clean. He lined them all up in order and set the hoses to the side.

The man in the bed behind him groaned and Angus' jaw tightened. "Patients must be *patient,*" he began, "This is science. It is precise. Please remain silent while I begin and speak only when prompted."

The Herald really heard nothing the doctor said. It was all jumbled and muffled behind the sound of blood racing in his veins and thundering against his eardrums. His entire body burned and his sight was blurry. When he turned his head to look at the physician tending to him, all he saw was a dark, shadowed blur. He knew he was dying, science couldn't help

him, now. All he wanted was the strength to say goodbye to his sister, Lady Bess.

"The woman," Angus spoke with his back turned, "Who is she to you?"

Beval tried to speak. Instead, it came out as a faint wheezing noise from his swollen throat.

Angus watched the man try to speak. His gulping mouth was like that of a large trout. Without a word, the doctor pressed his fingers into Beval's mouth and felt nothing. He leaned down and pressed the man's head back. The sick man let out a whimper in protest. Angus pushed his thumb down against Beval's tongue to look into his throat. It was already hard enough to breathe and the doctor's fingers in his throat caused Beval to jerk and fight for air.

The physician took his time before yanking his fingers free. Beval lurched to the side and vomited black bile against the stained sheets. Gasping for air, he clung weakly to the bedside when Lady Bess rushed in.

"What is it, Beval?" she shouted.

Seeing her brother's state, she dabbed ineffectually at the mess and glared at the doctor. "Your bedside manner leaves something to be desired. This man is extremely ill!"

"Madam, you called for me, and I answered. If it please you, I can still make it home before sundown," He responded.

Lady Bess' eyes lowered in concession, "No. Please, stay and help him. Can't you see the state he's in?"

Angus used the clean rag to tidy the lenses of his spectacles again, then let out a sigh. "I believe that my knowledge in this field qualifies me, yes. But if you believe you're more qualified, I could leave you to it."

"Please stay,." she whispered, staring down at the floor.

"Then give me way, and fetch me a pot of boiling water," Angus began, "I'll need more cloths and a posset bowl to prepare him some medicinal drink. I'm sure a lady of your standing possesses these items?"

"Add to your list ale and fresh milk." Angus checked off his mental list and took a step back waiting for her to go.

The woman stood up and bunched her soiled apron in her hands. She dipped into a short, half-curtsy and scuffled out of the room to acquire the things on the list. The sting of his curt words left her eyes watery as she walked past the rest of the household. Lady Bess threw her apron into the bucket and threw open her cupboards in search of the things he demanded.

With Lady Bess gone, Angus began further examination of the Herald. "Beval is it?"

Beval's eyes tried to open again, but the light made them ache and caused a pain to pull at the back of his head. He responded with a feeble nod of his head.

At this point, Angus was almost convinced this was a case of influenza. He walked to the other side of the bed and found the pot of urine and feces. Angus' nostrils flared in disgust, and he covered his face and tilted the container at a slight angle. The pungent smell of stale, infected waste just about knocked him back. He set the pot down and went to the man's bedside again, turning Beval's head to the side. A stretch of skin showed his neck was swollen and red. The doctor picked up the Herald's wrist and felt for his pulse, noting his heart rhythms were faint.

The doctor gave great consideration to his patient's care. To keep things in order and to care for the man, Angus went to his bag and pulled out parchment and ink. He'd have to write down any observations and deliberate on them for a moment. He dragged the chair from the corner over. Letting the wood scratch

upon the floor, he then covered the fabric with a spare handkerchief and sat. Out of his jacket pocket he removed his leather purse and unknotted the strings to remove his pipe and tobacco. He was already going through all the symptoms in his mind as he stuffed the leaves into the bowl. Using the candle, he lit the tobacco and leaned back in his chair to exhale the smoke.

When he picked up his quill, he made the necessary notations from his keen observations. His precision in doing this was startling to some. It was as if he could see right into them, leaving the object of his study feeling exposed and vulnerable.

- ✓ *Herald Beval. Last name unknown at this time.*
- ✓ *Patient's age is approximately 19 years.*
- ✓ *Patient's appearance is yellow with red splotches along his neck.*
- ✓ *The Patient is too weak to speak, and wheezes out words in whispers.*
- ✓ *Patient's excrement is noxious and black.*
- ✓ *Patient's health has rapidly declined according to Lady Bess of whom the patient has been in the care of.*

"Where are my items, Lady Bess!" Angus bellowed out in a mouthful of smoke.

Lady Bess called from the kitchen in response, "I'm almost done, sir!"

Cursing under her breath at the man caring for Beval she said a small prayer to ask for forgiveness, afraid her unkind thoughts would bring more punishment to her brother. She made the sign of the cross and picked up her basket of supplies, and then headed back up to her brother's room.

"Punctuality is not one of your virtues, madam," Angus snipped.

Lady Bess bit her tongue and shoved the basket into the doctor's hands, "Will ye be needin' anythin' else?"

Angus noted her mocking tone and chuckled. "The slang of a Bawd does not suit you, *Lady* Bess."

Angus snatched the basket and clenched down on the bore of the pipe and blew out another puff of smoke. The acrid cloud stretched out to the woman's face, smothering her. The woman closed her eyes and held her breath, then opened them again with a slow rise of her lids. *She's biting her temper,* Angus said to himself, *smart woman.*

Lady Bess forced a smile. "Is there anything else I can assist you with, Master …?"

The woman let her words drift off, awaiting a proper introduction to the doctor.

"Angus. Angus Wulfe," he said. "And yes. I'd love a warm spirit. I'm sure you have something to standard."

Angus turned his back on the woman once again and set everything up to begin his preparations. He'd use the herbs and ale she brought to produce a medicine to reduce the fever. Once he had the proper measurements of the herbs within the mortar and pestle he pulled out a small jar and held it to the light. The leeches within squirmed and rolled over one another, having been forced in to a state of hunger so they were effective in their task.

With the jar set near the patient's bedside, he went to work grinding down the herbs and puffing away at his pipe until nightfall.

CHAPTER 2: I'LL BE WATCHING YOU

Morrigan gathered with Murielle and Eleanor in the market that day to round up supplies for Robert's birthday. Eleanor wanted to surprise him with a crustade lumbard she'd learn to cook from her aunt, who traveled quite a bit with her husband to learn new recipes. Each one called for ingredients that required rare and exotic spices. Some were so peppery compared to the bland dishes served in England, they would sting the tongue then spread through the mouth until it felt like every nerve was a lit fuse. It was because of these culinary experiences her family gained such favor in the elite and privileged circle. On every special occasion, they were expected to appear at private parties with a new culinary sample discovered on their ventures.

Most of the time these parties were dull and full of prancing ladies dressed and parading around the men in hope of gaining a husband, something her mother never grew tired of. If it weren't for Morrigan's friend, these parties would be unbearable. Just the thought of stuffing herself into an outfit to appease her mother, who talked about her like she was a prized sow, was enough to make Morrigan's mood turn bleak. When the girls were together, they always managed to turn a boring event into one full of secret commentary. They teased and poked fun at the haute fashions and ridiculous attire worn by the "hufty-tufty" around them.

Today, the girls walked around the market with their list and took their time picking ingredients from each of the vendors. Morrigan held up a small pouch of saffron for Eleanor to inspect and the two giggled at her impersonation of her Aunt Matilde's flamboyant hand gestures.

"What a lovely smell!" Eleanor proclaimed. "I'm positive this must've come fresh off the shores of Asia!"

Playing along, Morrigan sniffed the spice and nodded. "Oh yes. Hand ground with love and care just for you, m'lady."

Sauntering to the next spice, Eleanor picked it up and held it out to her friend, "And this? Oh, just divine. Salts from the farthest oceans ever to be sailed!"

The two carried on this way until Morrigan felt a chilling unease. She was being watched. Her smile disappeared and she looked around to find the source. When she wasn't taking part in Eleanor's antics anymore, her friend nudged her.

"Have you captured too much sun, Morgie?" She teased.

Morrigan's eyes passed over each face in the crowd until she spotted Angus, hiding between two carts across the way.

"No," Morrigan whispered., "It's him … Master Angus. He's here and burning holes in my new dress with his eyes."

Eleanor picked up an apple from the vendor's cart and brought it up to her nose using it as a guise to look over in the physician's direction. Turning forward again, she placed the fruit back on display where she found it. Pulling Morrigan to her she leaned in pretending to tell her a joke.

"He's absolutely frightening," Eleanor said against her friend's ear. "What's with all the scars on his face?"

"Shh!" Morrigan pinched her companion's arm and laughed. "You're wicked, Ellie!"

Eleanor grabbed a bundle of wild flowers from the next vendor and took in its beautiful scent, peeking over the petals past Morrigan. Her smile widened suspiciously and Morrigan spun to look. Geoffery was walking towards them.

"It's him!" Morrigan whipped back around, bouncing with giddiness "He's so beautiful I can't even stand it."

Eleanor still had that devious grin on her face when she tossed the flowers aside and winked at her. "Yes he is."

Before Morrigan could catch her, Eleanor ran up to Geoffery and slid her arm through his. "Geoffery I've been dying to introduce you to my friend. You must come straight away."

Geoffery didn't have a chance to protest as the insistent Eleanor tugged him.

"Easy girl, I'm coming!" he laughed.

Geoffery looked around and continued following Eleanor past the tittering women who surrounded him. "Who, Ellie?"

Eleanor stopped in front of Morrigan who smiled and curtsied before Geoffery. "Morrigan Kingsley, meet my cousin, Geoffery Blake."

Geoffery offered a bow to Morrigan taking her hand in his "M'lady Morrigan, tis a pleasure to meet you. Ellie speaks very highly of you."

Morrigan shot Eleanor a look then glanced over Geoffery's shoulder. The doctor was nowhere to be found. A feeling of relief washed over her, and she directed her attention back to the introduction.

"A pleasure, Geoffery. Ellie tells me many great things about you as well."

Eleanor danced behind Geoffery and made teasing gestures at Morrigan who did all she could to keep a straight face. The three of them continued together through the marketplace laughing and joking, but Morrigan could still feel the remnants of Angus' stare clinging to her. He was always watching her: at church, walking with friends, visiting the bakery, and now the market. The one time he did speak to her, he was puffing away at a pipe. The overpowering smell of mugwort

blew out in thick, grey clouds of smoke from the side of his mouth and made her choke. He seemed amused by her reaction and his apology insincere. The potency of the fragrance clung to her clothing and hair long after she excused herself from his presence. In a nervous, subconscious act she scratched at her arm as she remembered it.

***

On that day a year ago, Angus' eyes were glossy and his pupils dilated as he spoke in slow, exaggerated words. At first Morrigan suspected he was full of spirits if it weren't for the stench of mugwort on him. Later, she witnessed him smoking from a pipe as he talked to her father. She asked her father about the strange habit and device. He explained Angus was a physician who had traveled to places like Poland, Asia and other faraway lands. As a child he witnessed some of the men using different types of pipes to smoke herbs and resins, and as he grew older, he claimed he found medicinal purpose in the act.

Morrigan crinkled her nose and shrugged. "I don't see how inhaling a weed through the mouth can have medicinal qualities."

"There are quite a lot of strange customs we are unaware of, Morrigan," her father replied.

"It seems foolish to believe in such superstitions," Morrigan rebutted.

Paul looked down at his daughter and chuckled. "That sums it up rather nicely then, yeah?"

Morrigan smiled then drew her shoulders back with confidence. "Then you shall rule my favor?"

"I don't know of any sane man within a hundred miles who would discount such logic," her father mused.

The two continued talking as they walked through town. Morrigan waved to Old Lady Mariane who always gave her an extra piece of bread when she bought from her. The sky was greyer than normal, casting a shadowy hue overhead. It looked as though it might rain but rather than say something, Morrigan kept it to herself. She enjoyed spending time with her father as well as a good English drizzle.

She and her father spent a lot of time discussing philosophy, law, and current events in those days. It made her feel grown up when he spoke to her on as an equal rather than treating her like a child. Conversely, her mother treated her like a child, and talked to her about nothing more than cooking and clothing. Morrigan loved her mother, though, and loved sitting with her as the seamstress lay beautiful fabrics across their laps, but after an hour or so, her thoughts would wander. This aggravated her mother which resulted in countless heated exchanges.

"Honestly, Morrigan, your head is always up in the clouds someplace," her mother huffed and pulled another sample of silk to her lap. "A girl of your age should pay more attention to these things."

"I am, Mother," Morrigan said with a faraway smile, "I like the blue one with the embroidery."

Her mother's brows rose half an inch. I chose wrong, again. Morrigan sighed inwardly.

"This one?" she said incredulously, "Morrigan, feel this texture, you'll have it ruined within hours."

Morrigan's smile disappeared, and she lowered her eyes. Nothing she did or said was good enough for her mother. It forever felt as though the two were running some kind of marathon to see which one of them was better.

"You're so much better at this than I, Mother, why can't you choose for me?" Morrigan offered, trying to brighten the mood.

"Oh, so you'd like me to do all the work, too?" her mother huffed. "A party isn't enough; I must also pick out your clothing as if you were a small girl?"

"No, Mother. What about the wine colored silk over the gold tunic?"

Morrigan's attempt to make peace was squashed at once. Her mother shrugged her shoulders, "If that's what you wish."

Seeing it as a way out of hours more sifting through boring stacks of patterns, Morrigan seized the opportunity whether either of them were happy with the choice or not. "I think it's lovely. Actually … it's perfect."

Victoria looked at the untouched stack of patterns with disappointment. She had looked forward to spending a day like this with her daughter. The reality was, she never had days like this with her daughter, and she didn't know why she thought that would change, now. Enamored with the love and affection from her father it was common for Morrigan's mother, Victoria, to be left out of their conversations. It was foolish to try and compete over their daughter, but Victoria couldn't help but feel a sort of detachment. She carried and brought Morrigan's tiny body into the world but the moment her father lay eyes on her the two were inseparable.

"It's almost time for dinner," Victoria said, to change the subject. "Shall we drink some tea?"

Morrigan smiled but shook her head. "Thank you, Mother, but I have grown a bit weary. I think I will nap."

She stood and set the material down on the table then leaned in to kiss her mother's cheek before swooping off again. When she passed the foyer, she heard her father speaking to

someone. She remained extra quiet and snuck toward the door. Some of the company her father kept happened to be the upper echelon of society and didn't take kindly to others eavesdropping on their affairs so she had to be careful.

Peeking around the corner, Morrigan saw her father was engaged in casual conversation with Master Angus Wulfe, the local physician to the aristocrat society who was also the same man who stalked her. She was about to ferret away when she heard her one of them say her name. Morrigan paused and pressed her back to the wall chastising herself for listening in on them when she knew better. Most of the conversation she could not hear anyway, she justified to herself. Were they speaking at lowered tones on purpose? She pressed her ear to the wall and listened closer.

"No, I can't say that anyone, including Morrigan, has shown any signs of a cough or fever," her father said, "Should I be worried?"

"Not as of now, Lord Kingsley," Angus responded, "Perhaps I should set up a time for an examination of you and your family?"

Morrigan froze. The thought of Angus being intimate of contact with her made her skin crawl.

"I don't think that's necessary, Doctor," her father said with a lilt of lightheartedness in his tone. "I do appreciate the offer though and will let you know of any changes."

Morrigan felt a huge sense of relief and let out a soft exhale. She heard the shuffling of footsteps from the room, alerting her they were walking toward her, so she ran for the kitchen. Mrs. Frit, the cook, lifted her basket of fresh baked breads and called after her.

"Girl! You gave me a fright!"

"Sorry, Mrs. Frit!" Morrigan said, focused on the tarte lying on the table. When her father walked in with the doctor, she feigned attention on one of the loaves.

She could smell the mugwort permeating the air before her father spoke up to announce his guest. He was right there—in her home and standing in her kitchen.

"Ah there you are, Morrigan," her father said. "Say hello to Master Wulfe."

"Afternoon, sir," Morrigan said with reluctance.

Morrigan's father, Paul, watched his daughter, who hadn't lifted her eyes off the bread to give a proper greeting to his guest.

"Good afternoon, Morrigan," Angus said. His voice was soft but the dictation of his words cut with surgical precision. "You look lovely today."

When Angus stepped forward to take Morrigan's hand, she snatched a small tarte off the table and shoved it into her mouth getting the filling all over her fingers.

"Morrigan!" her father shouted.

"I'm so sorry," she said and put on her best apologetic face. "I was just so hungry, and father you know how I love Mrs. Frit's desserts!"

Angus' jaw tightened, and he forced a polite smile. He gave a curt nod of his head and pulled his hand back. "Forgivable, of course. Who can resist the temptation of such a delicious piece of work?"

Angus' eyes hawked in on her own as he spoke the two-edged words. The muscles in her legs felt like they would go limp and the dessert threatened to come back up from her belly.

"Go wash up, Morrigan," her father said in a disappointed tone, "and pray that Mrs. Frit doesn't give you a lashing for whatever that was."

Her father turned to Master Wulfe and gave a sheepish smile before raising his hands in surrender. "I've no idea what's gotten into the girl. You will forgive her on my behalf?"

"It's nothing, to be sure," Angus said and tore his sticky gaze away from Paul's daughter.

Morrigan gave a quick curtsy and dashed off to her room. When she got there, she spit out the dessert, which had soured in her mouth, into a cloth. She almost wretched as she recalled the way his eyes crawled over her. There was something wrong with him. She knew this deep within her soul. She slid down to her bed and nearly jumped out of her skin when Murielle, her neighbor and second childhood friend, tapped on the window with her palm.

"Morgie, come on! We've been waiting!" she said through the glass.

"I'll be right out," Morrigan said, trying to smile.

When Murielle ran off with the other girls, Morrigan took a few breaths to slow down her heart. Her face prickled with heat and perspiration began to bead on her skin. She pat her face dry with the back of her hand then stood and tiptoed to her door. She could still hear her father talking, and the sound of his laughter. Sneaking past them, she took quiet steps down the hallway, then turned left to the next hall and walked to the front door. She was still looking toward the other room and did not see Angus standing there. When she thought the coast was clear, she made a dash for freedom, running smack dab into the doctor's chest. Morrigan let out a shrill scream when they made contact and flailed her arms when Angus tried to steady her. Her father and another client, who had arrived after she left the kitchen, came running out, along with the entire house staff followed by her mother.

"Morrigan, are you all right?" her father asked then ran to her and wrapped his arms around her.

"I … I'm fine. I'm sorry. I just didn't expect …" Embarrassed now, Morrigan's cheeks were scarlet, not the soft pink Angus normally observed of her.

"I'm truly sorry, Morrigan. Your father asked me to wait in here while he consulted with Lord Dalton," Angus offered.

"It's fine. I'm fine. May I take leave, father? Murielle is waiting." Morrigan was still trembling when she looked up at her father.

"If you're sure you're all right. Yes." Paul's eyes looked down into his daughter's, searching for some answer she wouldn't verbalize.

Morrigan pretended to smile and kissed his cheek to assure him, even if it was a lie. She turned and offered a goodbye to everyone else then rushed out to meet Murielle and the others.

***

The memory of that day never left her. It still gave her a creeping feeling along her skin and Morrigan realized she was still scratching at it. Her stare drifted off into the market and she began to feel lightheaded when Ellie called out again to her.

"Morrigan!"

Morrigan flinched and looked at her friend, disoriented.

"I'm sorry, what was that?"

Ellie shot her a glare and gestured with her head toward Geoffery. Morrigan let out a quiet sigh. Her lips fell into a frown and her eyes welled with tears.

"Forgive me, I must not be well."

It wasn't a lie. It was true. The memory of the doctor made Morrigan's stomach sour like it did when she held the tart

in her mouth, and she dabbed her hand lightly at her cheeks which were now moist with sweat. She was nauseous, and she was starting to overheat. The world tilted on an imaginary axis causing her to sway with dizziness.

"Morgie, are you all right? You just lost all your color," Ellie said.

Geoffrey reached out with a quick hand to steady her but still kept his distance. Rumors of sickness had escalated in town and he didn't want to catch whatever was going around. Ellie caught on to his hesitation and gave him a shove.

"She's dizzy, not contagious. Help me get her home."

CHAPTER 3: WHEN IN ROME

Angus sat in the dark, dank cellar of his manor. He built this enclosed room when he'd arrived back from his tour through Rome and Paris. During the month he spent in Rome he learned the most about philosophy, medicine, religion, and some of the darker planes of gratification. The Romans were on a whole other level of sadistic pleasures, and Angus witnessed a great many of them. One of the things he brought back from his journey was his smoking pipe. He developed a fondness for it which led him to study different medicinal herbs—one of which he smoked now. Mugwort, his favorite.

Tonight, as he sank into his customized Roman bath, Angus gazed at the murals on his walls. Each of them depicted scenes of debauchery which he had been privy to. The memory of them, and most of all his participation, came rolling in like a dense fog. Facing him on the opposite wall was a mural of a woman bound by hands and ankles, adorned in glittering chains of gold. He'd crafted this image tile by tile, stone by stone, and painted each detail from recollection. It turned out quite beautiful, he mused to himself. Though he did not remember her name, which was of no consequence to him, he remembered her face due to her high threshold for pain.

Angus had given into his fury in the form of cruel lashings to her delicate skin. The harder he struck her, the louder she'd moan and beg for more. In the end, it was he who was spent. Like a satisfied, well-fed cat, he dropped the leather whip and the beast within him purred.

Taking a deep pull from the pipe, the acrid smoke coiled down his windpipe and into his lungs. Angus drifted into a sedated, meditative state. His eyes grew heavy, and he watched as the mosaic girl on the wall came to life, undulating under the

knotted, leather strikes of a whip. The young man standing behind her, who was tanned to a deep bronze and shaved smooth from head to toe, was a work of art itself. Each lash of the whip elicited twists and turns from her, and her glazed, jewel-colored eyes stared off into a world of pain laced with ecstasy.

Angus' head lolled to the side when the next scene sprung from the stone walls out at him. A man and woman entwined in a lover's embrace while their consorts let their hands roam freely, manipulating their audience into a rapturous wave of pleasure. Their moans echoed within Angus' mind and set his loins on fire. Sliding his left hand into the steaming water, he turned to the other wall. His favorite.

The woman was strapped to a table and surrounded by four men. Each of them stared down at her with insatiate want. The man at the head of the table had a funnel shaped object of which he held steady within her mouth. Beside him the other man held the pinned woman's head still. Water poured into the funnel, giving the girl the sensation of drowning. While her body jerked and convulsed the two remaining men had their way with her, using her for every carnal fantasy they could conjure. Each one more immoral than the first.

The illusion came to life through the plumes of smoke he inhaled, giving the illusion he was back in time and surrounded by this orgy of delights. Angus stroked himself to rigid attention, but he didn't finish the job. Just before he climaxed, with his fingers still clinging to the throbbing muscle in his palm, he inhaled, forcing his lungs to fill with oxygen. His panting slowed to controlled, steady breaths, and his fluttering heart resumed its normal measured rate. Angus stood out of the scalding water and went to the steps of sectioned-off portion to the bath where the temperature of the water was a stark contrast to the first. His skin contracted and horripilated. After taking a moment to acclimate

his body to the new temperature, Angus descended until his entire body was enveloped and his erection cured.

With his hormones once again in control, he emerged from the cold water and headed back into the main portion of the bath. The water welcomed him back into its warm, soothing depths allowing his skin to stretch. Angus moved through the bathwater to the edge where a glass of wine sat. Lifting the drink to his lips, he turned to face his mural again. Leaning in for a closer inspection of the mural, he could see Morrigan's face in each scene with astonishing likeness

Angus took a long swallow of his drink and sank deeper into the water, allowing it to cover his shoulders. The incense billowed and danced with the smoke of his pipe and formed a mist over the bath. This was his sanctuary. He could clear his thoughts and think here. He could fantasize about her here. Soon his other room would be complete, and one day Morrigan would enjoy it with him.

When his time with her was done, he exited the bath and walked to the wall. Reaching a hand out, he allowed the side of his thumb to trace over her painted lips then smiled. He was saving the best part of himself for his "Prize."

Getting her was going to be a slow process. His plan was to build rapport with her father in order to gain permission to court the object of his desire—his daughter. He had money, good social standing and now he only needed to solidify the trust between Paul and himself. He wanted there to be no hesitation when he asked for Morrigan's hand in marriage, and for her father to offer up his daughter, which would finally make her his ... His, forever.

The mere thought of it pleased him.

Angus turned his attention to the grains in the giant sandglass which sat in the far corner of his chambers. The pile

grew thinner in the top bulb, signaling an hour's time. Time …
Everything happens at the right time, he thought to himself.

Leaning over, he removed the large fur from one of the
beds—he had different beds for different activities spread
throughout the room—and tossed it around his shoulders. Angus
had work to do. There was a plague running rampant, and the
requests for his services were coming in from town at an
exponential rate. The filthy atmosphere of London was a
breeding ground for illness even among the aristocrat society.
Vermin, insects, infection, and more, were indiscriminate in their
choice of victim and the sickness, which found their shores,
showed its hunger for souls. Yesterday, a merchant confided in
him there was a ship which sailed in carrying with it roughly six
men who were consumed by coughs and blood filled blisters all
over their bodies. Angus was going to be a busy man, soon.

The bell above the door jangled, drawing him back into
the present. Angus walked past the room next to the bath and
paused. It was open a crack, allowing him to see into the
looming darkness behind it. He gazed into the abyss for a long
moment when the insistent bell rang out again, this time with
more urgency. From within the room a cold breeze reached out
and kissed his palm. He spread his fingers in acceptance before
curling them inward and took the stairs up from the cellar to
answer the caller.

Upon opening the door, he looked down and saw the
merchant, Marshall, he was just ruminating about

"What is it?"

The merchant pulled off his cap and curved his spine so
he looked like a hunched rat. His missing teeth left the man's
lips to pucker over one remaining central incisor.

"Please, sir. I've been sent to fetch you. Something—"

"Who sent you to fetch me?" Angus' tone bit off the rest of his sentence, insulated at the notion of him being fetched like a dog's bone.

"Paul Kingsley, sir." The merchant said, lowering himself even more.

"What is it? Is he ill?" Angus' voice changed from a crisp callous tone to showing a hint of concern.

"Not he, Master Wulfe," Marshall answered. "John Miller. Eleanor's uncle."

Angus left the door ajar and spun toward his bedchambers to redress himself. Marshall had followed him as expected. He did not have to turn to look; he knew the man would begin helping him to gather up his things, as he usually did.

"Hand me my stockings and fresh tunic," he ordered, pulling the one he was wearing off.

The tunic from his body was still wet from his bath and Angus hung it near the small hearth in his room to dry. He stood, bare and without shame, his nude body showing the scars of his childhood. Not only did he endure the measles, but he'd suffered through the Pox, Malaria and his father's heavy hand. Leather strap marks were left as a constant, distant memory across his shoulders. Marshall avoided looking at them and stretched his arm to hand Angus the fresh clothing.

Angus took it from him and slid it over his head before turning to face the merchant who already had his other items collected and in hand. The other man helped the doctor get dressed in silence. Marshall had become his assistant in an unofficial way. He accompanied Angus on so many of these house calls he knew the routine by heart. When he affixed Angus' belt, the doctor brushed past him without a word of thanks and hooked his fingers into the handle of his signature

black, leather bag. The two were out the door and fighting off the crowded streets.

It wasn't until they had walked a few blocks when Angus spoke again. "Where is John?"

"He's at home, sir. His wife discovered him coughing and shivering with fever this morning."

Marshall filled him in with the details as they walked side by side. His voice drifted to the background as Angus slipped away into his own thoughts. *This might be just what I need to get closer to Morrigan.* He didn't feel empathy for the woman or her husband. They were typical aristocrats, blind to everything around them until tragedy struck. They went on their holidays, dragging their small children around to stagnant dinner parties like dolls.

The thought of it dragged Angus back to his childhood with his mother and father carting him along on their own trips. All they wished to do was establish themselves with a higher society that cared little for anything but their personal gains. It was on those trips Angus learned how to say all the right things to get what he wanted. When his parents passed him off to caretakers, he would slip away unseen to explore. Doing this opened doors no child should peer into. He saw depravities that added scars to his psyche to go with the ones on his body.

"Master Wulfe?" Marshall said.

The physician stopped and turned his attention to the other man. Marshall had stopped talking and was walking up the path to John and Claire's manor. Angus was so caught up in his own memories he almost continued walking past it, unaware.

Nodding, Angus motioned for Marshall to carry on, which he did, both verbally and in the direction with which he was heading. It was common for Angus to "go away" like this. Marshall was accustomed to it after so many years of being in

service to him. It was better to call his attention back with a subtle nudge.

The Merchant, as he was called, was always cautious with Angus. He'd seen the darker side of the man a handful of times. The worst time was when Angus drifted off while researching. Old man Ridley came down with fever and an accompanying rash. None of the normal remedies seemed to alleviate his symptoms. Ridley was Angus' personal tailor at the time and the closest thing Angus had to a father figure. With his health failing, Angus would drift in and out more often than usual—much to the chagrin of Ridley's natural son, Tomas.

As Angus sat in the study amongst the piles of medical books, Tomas prattled on about petty issues like servants and social gatherings he'd have to cancel. When he got no response from Angus, Tomas thought it would be funny to slap his hand on the book in front of his father's physician. Angus grabbed his wrist and twisted it to the point of snapping, locking the joint with such strength that Tomas went to a knee in pain.

When he released Tomas, the man attempted to lunge at the doctor and found a scalpel pressed against the base of his jaw line. Ridley's son's eyes grew wide as he stared into Angus'; the doctor's pupils were over-dilated making the irises appear completely black. Tomas swore even the whites looked to be consumed by darkness. The doctor pulled him in close and whispered a threat so disturbing the man never spoke of the instance to anyone.

As Marshall recalled the experience, he grew quiet. Angus didn't seem to care or notice. The two men found themselves on the stoop, alone. It was unusual to see none of the servants out and about. The small torch outside the Millers' door flickered and danced in the evening breeze, lighting up the small area where they stood. Marshall knocked on the door and waited.

It took three more knocks before the door opened. John's wife Claire looked disheveled like she had just woken up. Her hair was in disarray, and she wore a wrap around her shoulders. Her face was drawn, showing signs of fatigue and stress.

"M'lady Miller," Marshall said, greeting her.

It took a minute for her to register the greeting and why they were there before she nodded. "Oh my, forgive me. Since my husband took ill this morning, I've been battling a little bug of my own."

Claire stood away from the door and opened it inward inviting them to come inside. Her eyes were glassy and yellow as piss, causing them to shine in the darkness.

"Lord Kingsley is in with him. Just down the hall to the right," she said, pointing them in the direction. "Care for tea, doctor? Marshall?"

Angus walked past the woman without a word, leaving Marshall to handle the small talk. The merchant watched Angus step in and make a direct path to John's room before he turned to Lady Claire.

"No, M'lady. Don't put yourself through any trouble," he said.

Angus was standing outside of John's room when Marshall caught up to him. The stench that rolled out of the man's bedchambers immediately brought Angus back to the Herald. Since the King's messenger came down with the illness that caused his entire body to turn on itself, there had been a striking number of cases to follow. Young and old were falling like flies dead in the streets. Homes were boarded and locked to fend off the "Black Death" as it was being called.

He knew without laying eyes on John the infection had moved in with a vengeance. He could smell the festering setting into the flesh, and the rancidness of it stung his nostrils.

"The herbs, Marshall," Angus said with a quiet voice that was clinical and detached.

Marshall reached into Angus' bag and took out the long mask and purse of his herbs. Angus had his own personal selection of ingredients dried out in his home and took a stash with him whenever he travelled now.

Taking a long pull from his pipe, Angus inhaled the mugwort deep into his lungs and then placed his makeshift mask over his face and exhaled. From two small holes, the fragrant smoke escaped and filled the hallway. It reminded Marshall of the censer boats used by the clergy. Sadness came over him when the symbolism of it set in; God had turned his back on them all. Marshall lowered his head for a small prayer before he retrieved the gloves from the bag and assisted Angus in pulling them on. The doctor placed a large, wide brimmed hat on his head, before he spread his arms and let Marshall double check his ankle length coat was entirely closed. The Merchant stared at it, taken in by its eerie and macabre appearance. Angus has been disappearing more and more each night, leaving Marshall to wonder about his mental state. Seeing the ensemble now gave the older man reason for concern.

"Stop gawking, Marshall. It's for protection from the sickness."

Marshall dropped his eyes in silence and stepped aside to allow Angus to pass.

With his attire fixed in place, Angus walked into the room where John lie motionless in a heap of sticky, sweat-stained linen. His shallow breathing whistled through partially opened lips and his coloring was a pale grey. John looked as though Death had already lay claim to him. If Angus hadn't heard the labored wheeze of John's inhalation he would've assumed the worst had come. The doctor set his bag on the table

and began the physical exam by pulling back the blankets to expose John's upper torso. The tunic he wore was soaked in sweat and clinging to his chest. Angus set the blanket down and leaned in so he could focus on grasping the thin material of the man's clothing with his bulky, gloved fingers. The thick leather didn't offer much dexterity, but it protected Angus up to the present from whatever this vile sickness was.

When Angus was finally successful in pulling the tunic away from John's skin he saw the angry buboes weeping with blood on his far side. John turned his head to look at him. In doing so he exposed his neck. He had a dark rash creeping up behind his ear and his neck was distended. John's hair clung to his temple on that side, caked with dirt and perspiration. Angus knew at this point Clair's husband's fate was in the hands of their God in whom Angus had no faith.

The two men stared at one another wordlessly. Angus was breathing in deep of the herbs and smoke and the effects of it made John's face twist in odd ways. John didn't need any of the aromatic concoction to have that effect. Angus' attire was odd and frightening in its own right. John tried to speak but the words would not form.

Knowing what he was trying to ask, Angus responded, "It has accelerated. Only time will tell if you pull out of it."

Angus didn't have an empathetic bedside manner. He was trained to be detached and not engage the patient or their family in a diagnosis, lest they try to enter into a debate or ask too many questions. The last thing a physician needed was for anyone to lose faith in their abilities. In this case, that was the best choice of action since no one, not even Europe's head surgeon knew what it was they were dealing with.

John's face grew more grim, and he turned his head before closing his eyes. Angus glanced over the buboes again and then returned the blanket to its original place.

"Get rest and eat well. The illness attacks all of your humors and pushes them out of balance. We'll begin bloodletting this evening."

When John did not answer, Angus turned and exited.

CHAPTER 4: THE BLACK DEATH

There was little time to sleep once the Black Death took its first steps on their soil. Angus deduced it was being carried in by the ships. When he'd voiced his concerns to the authorities he was granted permission to study every vessel that reached their shores. It was a tedious job but Angus took pleasure in it. He also profited from it. Ships were thoroughly inspected, which meant anything forbidden by the law of the land was confiscated. Having Marshall as his partner, the two formed their own clandestine market and used it to smuggle in other things.

Those things Angus collected for his "extra" room; filling it with them would fulfill his darker needs. He had a keen interest for interrogation pieces and began to amass a fine quantity of them. He stood gazing at the pieces and their craftsmanship. He had built the rack himself to display all of the instruments but it was the one in the center that held his reverence the most. He picked up the Heretic's Fork and held it in his hands. It had a long pole, approximately three feet long, with two spikes on each end he could use to turn the rope that made this both portable and small enough to conceal. Etched into its crude metal was the phrase "Quae nocent docent".

Angus smiled and translated it aloud, "What hurts teaches."

It was perfect.

He picked up the metal piece used to subdue whomever was unfortunate to be tied to his table. It had two large prongs that affixed underneath the victim's chin. After letting its weight sit in his hands for a bit longer, he placed the Heretic's Fork back on the rack and looked behind him at the petite girl whose family all died from the Plague. She was lying motionless, sedated, and missing her arm up to her radius and ulna, just below her elbow.

Playtime would have to come later. He had another house call to make. This time to the home of a baron on the far countryside.

Angus had Marshall prepare their horses while he readied himself, leaving the girl where she was until his return.

The death toll increased tenfold since John passed because of the Plague's ravenous hunger. Clair followed soon after by days, which placed Eleanor, Murielle, and Robert in the care of Paul Kingsley. His chances with Morrigan were increasing. The financial burden on the Kingsley home was growing, and Paul was feeling the pressure to marry his daughter off before her dowry dwindled away.

Marshall walked around upstairs. Angus heard his footsteps on the floorboards. Dust particles drifted down in the cellar where he stood. Angus locked the door and made sure it was secure before he went upstairs to begin his journey to the baron's home.

The baron was originally from France but moved here with the King's permission once the Black Death had claimed more than half of the population. Marshall relayed to Angus the baron was married to the king's fifth cousin, Amber, in an arranged marriage when she was barely fifteen. The baron was twice her age and rumored to be sadistic, even to his new, young bride.

Marshall stood at the front entrance. He was dressed in a long coat, similar to Angus'. Because he accompanied the doctor on so many calls, the two decided it was in the best interest of them both if he was also protected.

"The horses are ready," Marshall informed him.

Angus nodded and handed off the black medical bag to his partner then pulled his wide-brimmed hat out of the wardrobe. He placed it on top of his head and secured his spectacles around the back of his ears. Marshall was always

fascinated with the eye glass invention and watched as he affixed them. The thickness of the glass lenses made Angus' eyes appear larger and brighter than they were. The doctor stood there in silence and went through a mental checklist, then signaled he was ready. The two left the physician's home and walked out to the stable where the horses were tethered and waiting.

It was a half day's ride out to the countryside where the baron resided. When they arrived they noticed the property was already in disarray. Bales of hay lay haphazardly across the lawn and animals appeared to roam unattended. Marshall slowed his horse and peered toward the large stone country house.

"I'll ride up ahead and scout the area," Marshall offered.

Angus didn't argue.

The physician walked his horse in slow procession past the wooden fence, which established the boundary between the road and the grazing lawn. Angus heard the clopping of hooves from Marshall's horse when he trotted off, but the doctor's attention was on a dark spot about half an acre away. With reins in hand, he guided the horse around the fence and over to the area to investigate. Upon closer examination, he saw the bodies of five men piled on top of one another. They were the house servants. He could tell by their clothing.

Angus lifted his head with sudden concern for his counterpart and stared toward the direction he went. The doctor remained silent and scanned the property. He could not see Marshall, or anyone else for that matter. He gave a soft click of his tongue and pulled the reins to the side, guiding the horse toward the house. Marshall let out a shout. Angus' heel quickly found its mark in the horse's flank causing the horse to spring into a gallop.

"Marshall!" Angus shouted.

There was more yelling from where Marshall disappeared around the side of the house, but he could not see the man anywhere. A sudden glimpse of his black coat backing away from a man with a large sickle gave his position away. The man, who Angus assumed was the baron, was swiping at the air in front of Marshall, shouting at him in French. The doctor snapped the reigns again to goad the horse faster, arriving just as Marshall was backed into a corner.

"Baron Albret!" Angus yelled.

The baron held his sickle in the air and looked over at Angus wild-eyed and trembling.

"Baron Albret, I am Master Wulfe. Word was sent that you were in need of a physician." Angus gestured to the man to lower his weapon. "We are here to help."

The baron's eyes seemed to refocus, and he lowered his weapon. Marshall cursed under his breath and spit at the ground before he dusted himself off. The man bearing the sickle let his eyes search the ground, weighing his options, before conceding and dropping his weapon. When Angus saw they were out of danger, he dismounted and walked over to the man, offering a slight bow.

"Time is of the essence, Baron. Please take us to the patient."

"It's my daughter and my wife," the baron answered in his thick accent.

His voice sounded hopeless and filled with anguish. He looked up into Angus' face then turned, leading them both inside.

Angus kept an eye on their surroundings and took in every detail, "How long have they been ill?"

"Half of a week," the baron said.

"And the men outside?" Angus inquired with caution.

Marshall walked a few paces behind the two men, still put off by one of them trying to take his head. The baron turned and Angus caught the sight of the tears welling in his eyes.

"They were ill. First one, then the other." Albret's shoulders slumped, and he bit on his lower lip to keep the sadness hidden.

"How long has the sickness been here on your land?" Angus asked with measured concern.

"One month," the Frenchman answered as he opened the door to the bedchambers.

The stench assaulted the doctor instantly. "Wait, please."

Albret stopped, confused. Marshall walked up to Angus and began the ritual of dressing him. When the mask came out, the Frenchman let out a small gasp and made the sign of the cross over his chest. He watched as the herbs were stuffed inside the tubular beak of it and turned away when Angus placed it over his face. When the doctor was suited up, he moved into the room.

The tapestry over the windows were drawn and only a little of the late afternoon sun filtered in. Angus could see the rumors of the nobleman's sadistic nature were true. Upon first meeting, he had his doubts; the man seemed weak and insecure, but seeing the young bride lying in bed with a metal contraption strapped to her mouth, revealed the truth. She was meticulously clean. Observing her, she looked to be sleeping until her eyes flashed open and wide like a spooked horse. Without making a sound her body tensed until she was as rigid as a board.

Sitting in a chair by the bed was a nurse who stood quickly. In her arms was the baron's two-year-old daughter. Her skin was jaundiced and the hollows of her eyes dark. Beads of sweat dotted the hairline of both females. Angus looked from the child back to the shackled bride and her eyes followed his,

darting in between them both. The doctor looked to the wall and discovered the display of straps ranging in length and thickness. It was clear they were used to control her. Angus took a step forward, and she jolted so he stopped. The girl dug her fingers into the linen clutching them with her blackened fingers.

It's been longer than he's confessed, Angus thought to himself.

Looking over his shoulder, he called out to the baron in a stern, controlled voice, "What is your wife's name, Baron?"

The baron grew nervous watching the doctor take in the scene, but he fought to regain authority. "Amber."

Angus turned his attention back to the girl and spoke. "Amber, I am Master Wulfe. I'm your physician."

His words did little to relax the girl, so he continued. "I'm going to come closer and examine you and your child. Is that agreeable?"

The girl looked between her daughter, her husband, and the doctor.

With a lowered voice, he tried again. "I'm here to help you, Amber. May I proceed?"

Amber's eyes finally softened, and she nodded.

"Baron, I will need you to bring me some things. Marshall will assist you. I require privacy to examine your wife and child."

Marshall's eyes narrowed behind the doctor, but he pulled his gaze away to face the baron who had dropped his. The sadistic man was a mouse among men and took out his inadequacies on the weaker sex. Angus figured him out with little to no effort already.

"This way," the baron said, leading Marshall out.

Angus placed his bag on the end of the bed and noticed there was something heavy beneath the covers as well. He stared at it then looked up at the nurse.

"Madam, would you excuse us?" he asked.

The nurse was obviously uncomfortable leaving a woman alone with a male doctor. She felt it was considered inappropriate, but she had no grounds to contest it given her position. She gave a worried look to Amber before she lowered into a half-curtsy and left carrying the baby in her arms. This made Amber anxious, but Angus wouldn't give her time to allow those thoughts to cure.

"I need to ask you some questions," he began and nodded to her mouth piece. "Just nod yes or no. When your husband returns I'll order that device off of you."

Amber remained silent, staring at him. The uncertainty showed on her face; her brows furrowed and her eyes were wide.

"Have you been ill for longer than three and one half days?" he asked.

Amber nodded then stole another look at the door.

Angus took a step in front of it blocking her view. "More than five days?"

Amber considered her answer then shook her head.

The doctor nodded and gently lifted the cover from the bottom corner of her bed. She was shackled to the frame with leg irons. Oddly, Angus was not as angry as he should've been if he were a normal doctor; he was curious. Pushing back the distraction, he observed her toes had begun to darken. He slid his thumb over the large, outside joint of her big toe causing Amber's leg to jerk, but the length of chain did not give.

"You still have feeling in them. Good."

His clever, deceitful explanation disguised his curiosity, but the woman was still unsure and eyed him with suspicion.

When the doctor's vacant eyes rose from her feet and met with hers, Amber looked away with an abrupt swivel of her head. Angus moved up along the side of the bed, like a creeping spider and let his fingertips drag along the sheets until he was an inch away from her exposed skin. The girl took in a shaky breath, and Angus turned away, once again leaving her with the anticipation of some dark intention while he tilted the bed pan filled with excrement. Its contents were black and rank with infection.

The doctor covered his mouth with his handkerchief and walked back to his bag removing the oversized gloves, followed by a small metal bowl and scalpel. Amber began to jerk against her restraints again. Angus had to subdue the smirk threatening to peek from his stoic facade.

Her fear stirred him, and he could smell it curling under his nose like ambrosia.

The physician pulled out a few more tools and placed them on a small plate he took wherever he went. He walked the utensils to her bedside and lowered his voice when he spoke. Rather than being comforting, he fed the beast by instilling in her a greater fear.

"I'm going to make a small incision to your arm," he whispered, then leaning down he growled against her ear in a quiet, chilling tone, "and bleed you."

CHAPTER 5: DEATH BELLS

Angus' Journal Entry:

Last night I took it upon myself to collect more specimens for my experiment. I want to find a cure for the epidemic that has come through our city. Who else can save these poor souls but I? I suppose it is unfortunate for them that their "Savior" comes in the form of a "Wulfe", who cares little for the value of their lives but more so for the reputation it would bring me in accomplishing such a thing.

I devised a way to keep Marshall occupied with petty work; he'd be busy for hours with inventory of the medicinal supply. I keep a well-stocked pantry that includes hundreds of jars replete with herbs and powders from around the world. And so, with the cellar prepped, I was able to leave Ava alone. Ava's family suffered greatly from the symptoms of the Plague. She tried to care for them alone but found she could not move one morning having been struck ill herself. Without her to help them, her family died—some from starvation, some from the late stages of the illness.

When I arrived, the young woman's parents were frozen in various stages of decay, staring up at the sky through holes in their thatched roof. Flies and vermin had already taken up residence, and I could hear the vibration of tiny wings before I stepped over the threshold. In a basket on the floor was an infant, blue as the harvesting woad leaves the women used for dyes. I remember clearly, I thought the entire family had expired until I walked past Ava. Through the plumes of herbal smoke, and the sting of tears it brought to my eyes, I looked down to see that pathetic, impoverished lass still had fight left in her yet. She reached out to me with what remained of her strength.

It was easy enough for me to carry her to the cart of bodies I had attached to my horses and bring her to my chambers. From there, I nursed her to back to sufficient health. I noticed vast improvements in her skin tone and her fever had decrease significantly.

Presently, despite her being gagged, she remained spirited and filled with fire ... even when I amputated her arm. On several previous occasions, she'd been able to writhe free and scream for help, each time waking me from my sleep. This put me in a foul mood. Tonight was the final straw. I'd had enough of her disobedience and removed both of her legs as well. I used the tissues to conduct studies so I might have a better understanding of what this curious cloud of invisible death was capable of.

Unable to fall back asleep, I decided to sedate the girl making her more compliant. After sewing her mouth shut, the peace of quiet returned, and I went back to recording my notes.

They call this sickness "The Plague." Imaginative, but simple, just like the dalcops who gave it its name. While they were content looking to the stars or deluding themselves with superstitions and religion, the world was dying around them.

This is to my own advantage. I shall, alone, discover the cure and earn favor. Not only with His Majesty, but with Morrigan as well. Soon, she will see what she has put aside all this time. Soon she will see it is I who will keep her safe from the world we live in.

A bit of a curious realization has occurred as I write this. As I put the words to paper, something akin to an emotion taunts me. If I'm honest with myself I don't ever have such a feeling, nor have I ever been so inclined to inquire why that is. What lies within has always been enough for me ... until now.

The truth is, I rather prefer to see things preserved like the insects within my glass cases and jars. Emotions, to me, are like religion. The mad run through the streets speaking of Heaven and miracles, and here I sit in worship of one mortal girl. I must confess, I have a desire to possess her, and simultaneously, protect her. Some days I seek to watch her from afar—a silent observer—to see how she flitters and carries about. Alas, the wax grows low so I return to the story at hand.

I left the girl in the other room as I mentioned, sedated and restrained, to risk a trip to the graves. It took me hours to climb over the bodies and wedge myself a path to the center. Limbs stacked high all around me I was amused that—finally— the world matched how I my eyes envisioned it.

All those lifeless eyes staring at me, mirroring the dancing flame of my lantern like spyglass windows into Hell. Could the Devil be watching me as I watch Morrigan? The thought beguiled me until I pulled my cock out to piss on the upturned face staring up at me from beneath my feet. With the torchlight behind me casting its amber glow, the stream of urine appeared to be emblazoned with fire shooting from my bladder.

"If I could," I thought, "I'd soak the world and watch it burn."

With the concoction of death, infection, and now piss, breathing was hard. The mask, soaked in herbs and affixed to my face, did not ease the burden. Each inhale burned my nostrils and my lungs. Whereas I always carried a cloth in hand to ward off the unsanitary conditions of the infested rats that inhabited the city (both human and vermin, the same), others walk around exposed, oblivious to parasites and sickness. It is my belief, these rituals held me and the reason I never fell ill as an adult while others dropped like fodder around me ...

No matter. Tonight the dead were merely resources. For once, they would be worth something to me and would be instrumental in my experiments. Until this time, my concoctions had produced an array of results. Each one worth a pittance until at last, I had seen light! Ava would be my first favorable result of connecting limb to host. Though her arm had suffered massive damage from the buboes and the deep craters thereafter from the scraping, it made my stomach sour at her imperfection. There was thought in me to release her to death and start over with another.

Her strength and will to live saved her no matter my tortuous abuse. Even as I peeled back the layers of flesh and exposed the inside of her arm she never begged for mercy! This grew my interest. Men twice her size and known for their brawn had endured far less before their whimpering began.

The flesh of the dead, blackened and decayed, made up the walls of my church. Body upon body towered high around me, foul of stench. I had no doubt my Hell reached the gates of Heaven.

I turned my eyes toward the night sky and yelled until my throat burned, "Look at your children now!"

There was no answer. God had left his children alone with the "Wulfe" that walked among them, plucking them from their beds and spilling their blood. My heart raced with power I've never felt before. I looked to my feet again and pressed the heel of my boot into the head beneath it, crushing the bone. Its eye slid out on a trail of ooze. I reached down picked it up, then placed it inside one of my pouches.

After, I decided I would not take any more specimens. I wanted nothing but my church of death. In the darkness, I began pulling bodies from piles to make myself a throne. It was harder than I thought; having to break bones for the perfect position.

With the last body in place, I stood looking at what I created. It was a thing of beauty to me.

I settled into it for the first time as King when I saw a familiar face. It was the girl from the market. The one who tried to sell her rotten fruit. Her face grey and blue with patches of black decomposition around her mouth. I desired closer examination so I went to her.

I saw no signs of infection anywhere on her body, but I did see a bruise around her neck. I watched the ghost, following with mine eyes to her collarbone to where her tunic was torn, exposing her breast. She looked upon me with a cloudy, white gaze from her unblinking eyes. She was still fresh.

I know not the meaning of it, but I felt myself grow hard with arousal at the sight of her, and whit of her abuse. I removed the body that lie upon, setting it aside, and saw the stain of pooled blood on her skirts between her thighs. The liquid had darkened but contained drops of bright red.

"A gift." I thought.

Father Evil had rewarded, me so I accepted his gift by having my way with her among all the unloving witnesses. Her body was cold, but not like ice. No, not yet. And the heat of my body wrapped around her tickling something within me. I buried my face within the crook of her neck and smelled the blood mingled with lavender oil on her skin. My mind spiraled into a new high where I dreamed of being there at the moment of her death. I savored every moment, caressing her cold skin afterwards. I could not bear to discard her; she'd led my way to this.

When I finally left, I placed her into the wheelbarrow and brought her home with me. If I preserve her correctly, I can keep her for a length of time for my research … and my pleasure.

***

It had only been months since Death had come to visit their shores and with its arrival came the darkness. A plague ravaged the citizens of the otherwise dull, grey shores of London. Ships swayed back and forth, like empty skeletons on the water. Rats overtook the market and ate until their round bellies were bloated to double the sizes. Those who were left amidst the carnage, hid in their homes and stared out through broken shutters at the mass devastation. The church had all but abandoned them. The few priests who remained succumbed to heavy drinking and public debauchery; they didn't care enough to hide it any longer. Violence rose to a level of hysteria; the death toll was staggering and seventy percent of the population lay dead in mass graves.

The wind was louder these days in comparison to the silence covering the world. There was no one around. Marshall sat in an empty brewhouse watching the door swing back and forth on a broken hinge. At first, he reveled in the newfound wealth he acquired off the sick and dying. He had the pick of the existing women from any inn he visited. All he had to do was flash his purse, which hung low on his belt, indicating it was heavy with coin. The more he saw as he accompanied Angus, the more withdrawn he became. He lacked any theory of what the world was turning into but he was sure it wasn't something he wanted to be a part of.

Angus grew withdrawn as well. Though Marshall accompanied him on many of his visits, the new law stated physicians must be quarantined for up to forty days after taking care of patients confirmed to be carrying the illness. After each encounter the doctor was stripped of his clothing and provided with a new, clean tunic before being locked within his home.

Each time Angus emerged, his appearance brimmed with darkness. His eyes were colder, more distant, and he was more detached from reality. He rarely ever spoke and there was a difference in minute details such as the way he held himself and the way he walked. Marshall was deep in thought, categorizing his thoughts as he took another sip of his ale. He rubbed his calloused hand over his face, troubled by state of the world and the change that had taken over Angus.

After the first quarantine, Angus came out of the cellar acting like a lion pent up in a cage for too long being released into the wild. He ascended the stairs leading from the cellar to his kitchen, and instead of embracing the sunlight, he shied from it.

Marshall waited in silence, setting the table for breakfast. When most of the staff fled or died, Marshall never left his post. Once a week, Paul Kingsley sent rations over to help sustain the doctor during his lock-in, and Marshall sat there night by night talking through the door. Solitude did things to a man. The merchant had seen it many times during his service on the ships. He hoped by speaking to Angus during his quarantine he could hold some of the madness at bay.

By the second quarantine, Marshall noted a rapid decline in their conversations. In the weeks when Angus was free, Marshall witnessed him bringing crates down into the cellar and attributed it to him stockpiling for his next round until the crates grew larger … like the size of coffins. When Angus stopped talking to him after dinner, Marshall went about daily chores, and talked to himself. One of them had to keep from going crazy.

Some nights, Marshall would sit by candlelight at the table and read aloud from the books the doctor had stockpiled in neat rows in his library. The former merchant wasn't as educated as the doctor, but he could read well enough. Before Death came,

he had no reason to sit idle and read. There was too much work to be done with the ships. Now, however, he found himself enjoying the pastime.

Sometimes, out of the blue, Angus would correct a word Marshall mispronounced taking him off guard. He'd thank him to the sound of silence in return, then continue. There were days those infrequent exchanges were the extent of communication coming from beyond the cellar door. After a week of no response, Marshall wondered if he should go check on Angus. That's when he heard it—a faint tap, tap, tap. Pressing his ear against the door, he listened to hammering sounds coming from below.

What is he doing? Marshall wondered. He stayed there and listened, his face wrinkled with worry. The sounds continued deep into the night until the former merchant curled up on the floor and fell asleep.

When the morning light filtered through the window, Marshall's eyes pried themselves apart. Angus' voice caused him to jerk awake. He was right on the other side of the door.

"Breakfast?" Angus asked.

"Few moments," Marshall croaked in his morning voice. No response.

Marshall's bones creaked as he pushed to his feet and walked to the pantry. He pulled out a loaf of bread, two eggs, and dried meat strips. He gently lay the two eggs inside the water after placing the kettle over the fire. With more effort than usual because of sleeping on the floor, Marshall bent over and stoked the flames until they were burning large and bright. He looked at the door, and still hearing nothing, he walked out to pick some of the fresh dates from the tree in the back. By the time he returned, the kettle was boiling, and he went about prepping a small tray.

When he was done, Marshall used the thick cloth on the table to move the kettle off the fire and dumped the hot water into a pail.

The two eggs were placed in an egg holder with the egg eater beside it; the small spoon was set gently on a linen used to clean the doctor's hands. Marshall released a pinch of salt across them and picked up the tray. Careful not to tip it, he walked it to the door and set it on the floor. He knocked on the miniature pass door, then opened it and slid the meal inside.

No sound.

Adjusting the lock back into place, Marshall walked back into the kitchen, picked up his book and read aloud from where he left off. A short time later he heard the doctor's approach on the stairs followed by the sound of the tray sliding as it was pulled across the floor and then more footsteps as he retreated like a spider into the dark cellar once more. Marshall sighed looking down at the words etched across the worn parchment in his hands and continued. After reading out loud the first paragraph, Angus drowned out his voice with the sound of the banging hammer. Angus, who had assumedly had enough of his meal, went back to work.

Marshall tossed the book down on the table and shoved it away. I'm sick to death of this, he thought. Without a word, he snatched his coat and coin purse then walked out. He needed to find a brewery. If there were any left. He needed to get his head clear and be away from the "Monster in the Cellar.".

When Marshall got into town, he observed the fallout the disease had caused. Carts of bodies were being pushed toward mass gravesites. He stood off to the side to allow a funeral procession and watched the faces of those who passed by. The men who were carrying the pine coffin of their loved one each bore a mask of sadness and fear. The women's eyes were red and swollen from crying, and their mouths drawn tight to ward off

the infection in the air. The merchant took a step forward to cross the road and was stopped by a second procession that immediately followed. This time the pine box being carried was much smaller.

The mother walked behind the priest, hunched into her husband's shoulder, weeping with uncontrollable sobs. His face was lifeless and worse for wear as he held her to him. Behind them, the others followed in a slow, depressing march to the sound of a drum that trailed off near the end of the line. The bells were no longer allowed to ring—they would have never stopped.

Marshall's need for a drink overtook him, and he rushed across the road to the brew house. He peered inside and saw no one. Giving the door a solid push, he made deliberate noise to announce himself. He took a step in and waited. There was nothing. All dead. The smell from the neighboring butchery stung his eyes, but the need for an ale was greater than his repulsion. Marshall went to one of the barrels and helped himself. Once he had a fresh mug of ale in hand, he walked past the tables to an isolated corner in the back and chose a seat where he could watch the door. Sitting here was no different than sitting at the doctor's home, except there was ale. And that made all the difference in the hours that passed by.

Marshall realized the stream of sunlight that came in from the broken doorway had grown thinner and longer. It would be dark soon. The incessant drumming accompanied by the shadows of parading mourners reminded him of what was outside. He finished off his ale and stood with a noticeable lean then pressed his hand to the wall and steadied himself. Once the world ceased to tilt, he carried his mug to the bar and dropped a few coins on it.

Stumbling toward the exit, he raised his hand to shield his eyes from the light and emerged. Black smoke drifted into

the sky, smothering the rest of the midday sun lingering over their small, vanishing town. The acrid smell of burning bodies filled the air, amplifying the macabre scene with an eerie noiselessness. The vendors' carts were unattended and rotting fruit spilled over the edges. Flies swarmed over everything and no one bothered to swat them away anymore. Everyone's faces were covered with scarves, and some of the former wealthy wore long veils over them.

The buzz he got from the ale made Marshall's movements slow. He needed to get back home. He already missed giving the doctor his lunch and would receive a proper tongue lashing. He was sure of it. Twelve trips over his own feet and overturned cobblestone, and Marshall was through the door of the monster's home. He leaned against the wall inside the kitchen and looked over at the cellar entryway. The sounds of the saw continued on as if he never left. Marshall cursed under his breath and went to the pantry to make their dinner.

***

It was late when he awoke. Marshall could tell because the cool air slipped into his room and there was condensation on the thin window panes. The moon was drifting down into the horizon, making the night sky brighten just enough to see hints of blue and indigo instead of a canvas of ink black. Something startled him out of his sleep, but he didn't know what it was. A nightmare? A noise? Sliding out of the covers, Marshall slid his feet into the house shoes on the side of his bed and pulled a coat over his tunic. He sat on the edge of the bed and waited. The absence of anything stirring or disrupting the normal nocturnal sounds was both a relief and disquieting all at once.

Marshall lit a candle and walked to the door of his bedchambers. Pressing his ear to the surface he listened before exiting to investigate. The front door was still locked, so he walked into the kitchen where he could see the back entrance. Pushing the candle out before him, he studied the cellar door before proceeding. Both doors were still secure just as he had left them. *Am I going mad?* Not hearing anything else he decided there was no cause for alarm. *Must've been a dream,* he thought as he raked his fingers through his hair and walked back to his room. As a precaution, he locked the door before going back to bed.

When morning came, Marshall opened his door and shuffled into the kitchen to begin breakfast. He passed the cellar with a sleepy glance then continued into the pantry. He didn't sleep well after he was awakened in the middle of the night. He tossed and turned at every little sound. His actions now were more routine than conscious thought when he reached out to grab the dried meat. His fingers touched the shelf, but the pieces were not there. Perplexed, he rubbed away the sleep in his eyes. The meat had been moved. *How could that be?* he wondered, turning to look around. Everything else was in its place except for the basket of dates. It had been moved as well.

Marshall stepped out of the pantry and glanced around. Nothing else had been touched or was missing. Looking to the cellar door again, he walked over to it, testing the lock from the outside. He jiggled the handle a couple times, but it did not budge.

Marshall was about to walk away when Angus called from the other side, "Breakfast?"

"A few minutes," he called down.

Monsters don't sleep under your bed.
They sleep inside your head.
~Unknown

CHAPTER 6: THE DEVIL KNOCKS ONLY ONCE

February 1349

Paul Kingsley sat with the other men at the long, cherry wood table handed down for generations in his family. The gentlemen were served their ale, and after a long night of discussions, were dismissed. The last servant out turned and closed the door. Paul pressed his palms against the waxed surface in front of him. There were soft conversations during the secret meeting floating in both directions. Casual conversations that had nothing to do with the atrocities that were being committed on their very streets. The king's local magistrate abandoned their town, their baron fell with the disease, and their sovereign left them to their own devices for fear that he and his household would also fall victim.

Earlier, as he sat in front of his peers, Paul cleared his throat and took the lead. He had enough. Violence had increased astoundingly. Brother turned on brother, and chaos was the new rule. When the other men continued with their conversations, Paul stood and snapped.

"Gentlemen," his stern voice hushed them at once and they turned in his direction. "Let us begin."

The gentleman to his right was his best friend's son, Robert. When John died, he was left with the care of his children, and through a rough start, the two became quite close.

In turn, Robert and Paul were inseparable, and Robert began to show an interest in the law. Later that year, he began his apprenticeship. The men finally had all of their attention focused on Paul whose throat became dry all of a sudden. He lifted his glass and offered a toast.

"Let us start with a drink," he said. "To London, to justice, and to the strength to uphold it."

"Hear, hear!" they all chimed in at once.

Paul saluted them with the glass, then took the first drink. The other men followed his lead and waited to sit down until he did. Paul smiled, hiding his inward sigh. He didn't want to lead the group. He was content to fade into the background, but it was evident he was now the unspoken leader. Paul gathered his thoughts and began.

"We all know what's going on out there. I don't need to lace my words with a grandiose speech. What we do need is direction. We've come together to decide on a course of action. We may debate, we may disagree."

Around him, the men nodded. Paul knew in their hearts they felt the same as he so he seized the moment while it was hot. His passion rose up within him. A normally quiet and reserved man, he had an unquenchable desire to save what was left of their homes and their lands, despite the scourge that had overtaken them all.

"It is enough that we have to deal with losing our loved ones to a disease. It is enough that we are all scared down to our bones. But we cannot abide by the lawlessness of the land by our own people."

His words were met with a tapping of palms on the table and agreeable cheers.

***

From the hallway, Morrigan stood with her back to the wall and her head leaned down to listen to the meeting. She wasn't supposed to, but it was impossible not to overhear what was going on just outside the haven of their home. Soon enough, it wouldn't matter whose land was whose. People would force their way in and take what they wanted. Morrigan was frightened, but she was also sad to see her father and her adopted brother so stressed and consumed with the affairs. She and her father rarely even spoke anymore as a result.

Leaning in further as the men got down to business and began the discussions of how they would start regaining control, Morrigan was startled by a knock on the door. Not wanting to be caught, she spun and ran up the stairs crouching in a dark corner to peek through the rails. Len, the butler, emerged from the kitchen and made his lumbering procession to answer the caller. He finally reached the front entrance and opened it, greeting the man at the door.

"Please, it's urgent," was all Morrigan could hear.

"Wait here," Len said and walked into the meeting room.

Morrigan heard her father and the other men making inquiries before the crowd of them stepped out to talk with the young man who paced near the front of the house. Her father led the men, and Morrigan could see he walked with an air of authority that was not there before. She smiled with a sense of pride for him before shifting her attention once more to the messenger.

"They've found a woman. She's been …" the boy began.

He wasn't actually a boy, but in the crowd of distinguished gentlemen he stood out as much younger.

Morrigan guessed he was about her age. Crawling on all fours, she moved closer to the rail. She wanted to hear what he said.

The boy's voice dropped even lower, and he looked around to be sure his revelation wasn't received by any lady of the house, "... she's been *murdered*."

The gentlemen all gasped and looked at one another in astonishment. Her father pressed for further information.

"Murdered? How? Who made the discovery?"

"Yes, m'lord," he answered.

When he didn't answer Paul's questions, he pressed harder, "Come lad! Speak. Pray tell!"

The boy flinched and took his cap off, spinning it in his hands while he hesitated. "She was with child. It has been removed. She's been bled and discarded in the street."

The men leaned back in shock. Her father's face grew long, and he covered his mouth to conceal his disgust. He turned and spoke with a shaky voice. "Gentlemen we will continue this on the morrow. Robert, grab our coats. We must tend to this immediately."

It would be the first of many cases that showed up over the next three weeks, and Morrigan and her family were on edge. With the sickness taking over, there were less men to guard the women and the women were showing up dead with missing limbs. It was because of this, Robert and her father arranged for more servants and more torches outside the property. They collected more dogs, abandoned from a nearby farm to guard the main house, the servant house, and the stables.

Morrigan was afraid, but she knew her father would do whatever it took to keep them safe. It didn't, however, shake the feeling she was being watched; though she could never find proof of the claim. Without it, she couldn't go to her father with a mere speculation; it would be a waste of time. Her father liked

to have proof—facts that backed up claims—before anyone made accusations.

You're being foolish, Morgie, she said to herself.

After she talked herself down, she went to her room to dress for bed. With a fresh tunic on, she leaned over the bowl of water on her table to wash up when the feeling hit her again, a familiar creeping along the back of her neck. It stole her breath away. Morrigan spun around quickly and stared into the darkness outside the window on the opposite side of her bed. At first she saw only her own reflection looking back at her. Taking a few steps closer, she could feel her whole body trembling.

Waiting for her eyes to adjust to the darkness, she scanned from left to right with a slow pass of every shape. There was a shadow, blacker than the darkness behind it, near the fence line of the house. She couldn't make out what it was so she squinted harder, focusing in on it. As she leaned forward, she was able to make out a set of eyes. Morrigan jumped back and let out a scream, knocking her bowl to the floor. The water spilled out at her feet. The dogs outside began to bark and Robert burst through the door.

"Morgie?" he shouted. "Where are you?!"

"Robbie?!" Morrigan called for him. "Robbie, I'm here!"

She ran from the corner to his arms and sobbed, "There was someone out there! He was staring at me through the window!"

Robbie pulled from her and went to the open window, looking out into the yard. He heard the dogs but didn't see anyone. Slamming the shutters shut and locking them, he went back over to her and took her head in his hands. Morrigan trembled harder with the rush of fear and adrenaline.

"Shh ... it's alright. I'm here," he whispered. "I won't let anything happen to you."

A few seconds later, Morrigan's mother and father rushed in.

"What is it? Morrigan?" They shouted together.

Morrigan repeated the story and her father left to search the property. "Stay with her, Robert."

She could hear her father shouting orders to the men in the hallway and then continue outside. Torchlight illuminated her window as they gathered together in front of it. Her father organized a quick plan for them to spread out and search for the trespasser, then looked over his shoulder at Morrigan to give her a wave.

Morrigan's mother waited for him to turn around and lead the group off before she closed the heavy drapery to muffle the sound of the hounds. She came back to her daughter and took her hand. It was cold to the touch.

"Oh, Morgie you're like ice!" she exclaimed. "Let me get you some hot tea."

Her mother looked at Robbie who nodded assuring her he had it under control, and she left the room to boil water. Morrigan heard her shoo'ing the others away from her door telling them to get back to work. Morrigan's heartbeat finally slowed to its normal rate just before her mother returned with two cups and a steaming pot of water.

"I've added some chamomile to help you sleep," she said setting the tray down. "Martha is bringing you some brandy to add. It will help your nerves."

It was the first time in years Morrigan was glad it was her mother and not her father who was here with her. When Victoria wasn't grooming her for a potential husband, she was quite loving and warm. She smiled at her mother as she took the

cup. The hot water burned her frosty fingers, but it felt so good she clung to it tighter.

"Thank you, mother," she said, taking a careful sip.

Once Morrigan calmed down, Victoria kissed her forehead and handed Robert an extra blanket.

"It's alright," he assured her. "I will keep her safe."

Morrigan's mother smiled and nodded, pressing a kiss to his temple. "I know you will."

Having been convinced to leave, Victoria slipped out to check on the staff. The rest of the night, Morrigan slept in her bed, and Robbie stayed with her. He sat in the chair and stared out the window until finally falling asleep at dawn.

What the caterpillar calls the end of the world the
master calls a butterfly.
~ *Richard Bach*

CHAPTER 7: THE WULFE AMONG THE SHEEP

Angus' journal
*I couldn't sleep last night. The faces of the girls
continued to fade in and out of the mist of my dreams. Each
one's mouth open in a silent scream as I removed body parts,
leaving them an incomplete puzzle strewn across my table. The
pieces were all exact, but the faces were wrong. All of them
wrong! I needed them all to measure up to Morrigan, but their
eyes would never be the same. The shape of their lips would
never smile the way hers do. The pressure to solve the riddle was
swarming through my blood like an army of insects whose only
task was to devour me from the inside out.*
*My fingers were on fire, my brow sweaty, and my jaw set
in stone until I could not breathe without smelling her all around
me. I had to see her again to know she had not been afflicted yet.
I walked the miles to her home from the secret passage I dug
from my cellar. It mattered not that I could get caught. The call
was too great. It took over every bit of reason I had left.*
*In the cover of night, I could easily watch her like I
always did, from afar. Before Death came I could sit there for
hours outside her window. There were no servants guarding the
house, there were no pack of dogs to be concerned with. And
though they were there that night, I didn't care. I risked it all to
catch a glimpse of my bride-to-be. My angel of beauty and
perfection ... all I could never hope for myself.*

She appeared through the window, a vision of Heaven to a Devil such as I am. With her hair loose and free, it hung in waves of chestnut lit by the candle's glow like strands of gold. I could not move. I stood there, struck by the sight of her, immobile and rooted to the very ground beneath me. She moved through her usual routine: brushing her hair, fresh tunic, and washing her face, and I whispered her name into the night.

It was then she turned. She heard me! She heard me. I repeated it over and over in my mind until the roots in the earth released me. Just as I was to go to her, our eyes made contact. For a moment, our eyes touched and held on … and then she jumped back and screamed alerting the house and the dogs. My heart died and sank into the pit of my bowels.

Ashamed, I ran back to my dark hole in the cellar.

***

Angus' memory began failing him after the incident at Morrigan's home. Time escaped him for hours, sometimes days, at a time. The lapses were similar to the bouts he experienced when he was a young boy. The worst of it was when his father took him to his whippings, but continued up until he was in his early teenage years. Those years were when the magical transition occurred. It was when the older men lost interest; the years when those who took advantage of him considered him a man.

Angus didn't feel like a man. He felt empty.

The doctor looked down at his trembling hand and then down at his chest. He was panting in fear and anxiety, drawing in air so fast his head grew light and his fingers were numb. He couldn't stand being cooped up in the cellar anymore. Even when he was alone, he'd leave the secret doors open to relieve

the feeling of suffocation and claustrophobia. Angus stood there now, closing his eyes and welcomed the draft which made its way into his prison. No matter what he put in his pipe to escape, he could not bury the memories forever.

But a temporary escape is good enough, he thought. With a strong pull of the mouthpiece, he inhaled until the smoke filled his lungs and allowed the effect of the herb to pull him into his peaceful place.

Hours later, Angus returned, crawling through the creek and running through mud until he collapsed at the entrance of the tunnel leading back into his prison. Stumbling to his feet again, he navigated back to his chambers soaked to the bone and trembling from the cold. He looked around him and breathed a sigh of relief. There was no blood … *this time*. The knock at the cellar door caused him to jump. *Did they find me*?

"Angus? Are you alright?" It was Marshall.

He must've heard Angus stumbling into his room. "I'm fine!"

The words came out harsher than he intended. Most of the time he tried to keep a level demeanor with Marshall. It would not serve him well to lose his assistant. He cleared his throat and took a deep breath, regaining his focus.

"I'm just … I'm just hungry," Angus called out, again.

Marshall was silent for a moment and the doctor cursed under his breath. He was starting to spiral out of control. He was about to call out again when he heard the familiar shambling of the merchant's footsteps come close to the door once again.

"Few minutes."

Angus released a sigh of a relief and moved swiftly, rushing to clean himself off and redress in a fresh tunic. He threw the soiled clothing into the fire then stood in front of it to warm himself. His lips were still trembling when he heard the

pass door and the slide of his tray. Leaving the warmth of the fireplace, Angus trudged up the stairs and snatched a few scraps of food, shoving it into his mouth with one hand.

When Marshall shuffled away from the door again, Angus went back down to his bed chambers and fell asleep. The nightmares were becoming more and more vivid, and the visions in his head stayed with him long after he was awake. He tried to keep them at bay by tending to his "play toys"—the tools he amassed from his underground collection—working on each one until he collapsed from exhaustion.

At the end of his quarantine, his entire extra room of the cellar was filled with contraptions Angus saw firsthand as a child and some he only read about. His paintings on the wall grew more gruesome. Until, upon his emerging, he'd refuse to see patients for weeks at a time.

Marshall tried to talk to him and began taking notice of his changing demeanor. Angus, in turn, was growing paranoid of his assistant finding out the truth of his evolving madness. Sometimes in the middle of the night, the doctor found himself jolting awake and rushing to check that the cellar was locked. On one occasion, Marshall stood watching from the bedroom as the handle of the cellar door jiggled and turned. Without a word, he turned and went back to bed. What scared Angus the most, was in fact, his freedom. At least in the cellar, even with his escape route, it was difficult to get out. With the quarantine over, it was easier to come and go, making it difficult to avoid leaving his home.

His arrangement with Marshall was his best advantage. Most times, he could send him out to get whatever he needed. Marshall obliged, but often tried to coax Angus to join him. Angus used the excuse he was too busy with his work and trying to find a cure for the disease that was wiping out London. The

more noble he made it sound, the less his madness seemed like madness while whispers circulated that he was "consumed." Angus knew there was no line of distinction, it was merely to make others feel better.

It was a Sunday afternoon when Marshall called from the kitchen, "I'm going to town, are you coming?"

"I've got work to do. You go ahead. I've made a list for you on the desk," Angus said, emerging from his bedchambers below. "I placed extra in the purse. For your troubles."

Marshall looked down at the list and picked up the purse as he read through it. He could feel the weight of the coin in his hand and, rather than making a case for Angus to join him, gave a smile instead. He would never argue with a bit of extra coin, and Angus knew this. Responding with a grin, the physician went back down to the cellar, locking the door behind him.

He's gone stark raving mad, Marshall said to himself before leaving.

Below, Angus stood in the torchlight facing his playroom, which by normal standards, was a room of torture. He no longer cared he was being torn apart from the inside. His psyche was shattered down the center, and he could feel the glass cutting into his soul. Something, though, was left behind. A scratch of a nail at the base of his brain, hissing into his ear. *This is wrong,* it said. *What am I doing?*

The conflict bubbled until his rage spilled over, and he rushed at the table with the saw and the shackles. Using all his weight, he threw them to the ground, falling with them. He could hear the crack of a rib at the point of impact sending a shock of pain through him. Angus stayed there, too hurt to move and barely able to breathe. He curled into a fetal position on the stones and sobbed. His entire body jerked with each growing wave until his cries ripped out from the pits of his belly.

Hours passed with him curled against the cold stone before the voice within him spoke again, berating him and demanding he stand up. Angus rolled to his knees, holding the shackles in his clawed hands with spittle hanging from his lip in a line from his chin to the floor like an anchor. That fragile thread was all he had left holding him to this earth. Without it, he thought, he might fly off into oblivion.

I have to purge this.

Wincing in pain, he rose to his feet, uncurling his spine one vertebra at a time until he was at his natural height. Closing his eyes, he took in a deep, excruciating breath then released it with a slow hiss. In doing so, he cleared his mind enough to reign in the growing demon within him. When he opened his eyes, he focused his sight on the mural of the opposing wall. Morrigan's face peered out at him, twisted in torment.

Oh, God, he whispered inside his head.

I cannot do this to her. I cannot taint her with this wickedness.

The doctor looked down at his hands, still holding onto the shackles, and whimpered like a wounded animal. He grit his teeth, shaking as he tried to swallow the emotions. The swell of madness would not be contained. Every nerve was on fire, and his skull felt like it was splitting along the center. The crescent shape of his nails was embedded into his palms and the metal of the shackles bit into his skin allowing the trails of blood to slide down each link. *It's happening again. Please ... stop!*

Falling to his knees again, Angus' eyes went dark, and the inner demons spilled out unwilling to be bridled. Like a rat, he hunched over and skittered into the tunnel. His final thought before he blacked out was if he didn't purge the evil, he would end up harming the one thing he cared about, Morrigan Kingsley.

***

Hours passed, and nightfall came when Angus spotted the girl. She was a perfect offering to the abyss vitiating him. She had the same hair color, the same fair complexion, and though she was not as beautiful as *his* Morrigan, she was a comparable offering. With live hosts running low, Angus had no time to lose.

He pulled his hat down low and stepped out onto the street in close proximity to where she was "working." When he got close enough, he lifted his eyes up from the ground to make contact with hers.

She took the bait.

"Well 'ello handsome," she called out. "You look cold. Le'me warm you up for a spell."

Oh, she was vile, compared to his beautiful girl. Her mouth spilled poison with every word she spoke. Angus painted a smile on his face and stopped, turning enough to face her while keeping his face concealed from the others. Disinterested, the girls off to the side kept their eyes on other passersby in hopes of capturing their own *date* for the evening. Angus extended his arm out, offering it to the girl, who waved to the others.

"Have a g'night ladies! I'll be keepin' warm wi'this handsome gent," she howled out.

Angus concealed his disgust by lowering his face allowing the large brim of his hat to shadow his features. He walked toward a less inhabited street away from the seedy eyes. The less people who saw them, the better. When they were on a more secluded block, the woman draped herself over him. Her overbearing use of lavender made Angus' stomach flip, but the smell of the ale on her already rotten breath was worse.

"We're alone now," she said tugging at his jacket to push her hand within it. "Don't be shy."

Angus turned his face to her and she saw his features in the half light of the moon overhead. His eyes were rimmed in dark purple from lack of sleep, and his skin was pale from isolation and quarantine. He looked mad. And he was. She gasped softly then steeled herself, forcing a shaky smile at him.

A consummate actress. A liar. An odoriferous stain on the world, the beast prattled on.

Her smile slipped away before she could scream along with her hope for a safe night when the doctor shoved his handkerchief against her mouth. Thrashing under his grip, her attempt to scream was snuffed against his crushing palm and the chemical soaked cloth.

To camouflage what he was really doing, Angus leaned in against her ear and pretended to be embracing the girl. He pushed her to the stone wall and held her up with his own body weight, crushing her lungs, forcing her to take short, labored breaths. Her eyes faded from wide to heavy, and after brief struggle, she went limp in his embrace.

Angus' heart raced, exhilarated from the arousal of subduing her. He had to get her home before suspicion arose. Looking around him, he saw an older man had them in his sights as he walked by. The doctor laughed loudly and draped the woman's arm around his neck.

"Ah the lady cannot hold her wine!" he announced to those he passed by.

The man looked away in disdain and continued on. Most of the time no one bothered to look twice. Across the street, the other ladies-of-the-night glanced at the commotion but shook their heads, gossiping among themselves at her unseemliness.

Angus was astonished at how easy it was. An unfortunate advantage for him and his next attempt.

CHAPTER 8: THE TIDE DRAWS NIGH

The working girl, Tess', eyes began to open when the pain spread like lightning throughout her entire body starting in her legs all the way up to her widening mouth. A scream escaped from her throat and filled the thick air around her waking the silence. Even with her eyes wide, darting back and forth, she could not find light.

Oh God, I'm dead! she thought. *I'm dead, and I'm buried somewhere in the earth!*

Her immediate response was to lift her arms and feel around her for the pine box, but there was nothing. Just air. Stunned and confused, she froze to let her mind catch up and process what was going on. The pain shot through her in another electrifying wave causing her to scream out again.

"Help me!" she shouted at what she assumed was the ceiling. "Please help me! Someone!"

Angus watched her under the cloak of darkness. Observing the way she flailed and the way her body trembled. His eyes were used to this kind of darkness. They adjusted to it when he was a child and was held under the same conditions. Sensory deprivation was a key element in a lot of torture methods. Waking up in darkness set the mind on edge and heightened the other senses. A pass of a feather can feel like needles to a mind on edge.

"You see," Angus began as he walked out of the shadows, "torture is a two-part affair."

The woman stopped struggling, stopped screaming, and went completely still. The doctor heard her panting just a few

feet away from him. She strained to see where he was, who he was.

They all did this.

He took a few more steps, taking pains to step as quiet as he could. He wanted to watch her listen to guess his location. When she did, Angus smiled with deep satisfaction. He stopped where he was, remaining still. He took a pebble from the ones he carried in his hand, and tossed it across the room. It pinged against something metal, jarring her with the echo that reverberated. The girl let out a short yelp.

"I don't understand. Why are you doing this to me?" She began to sob.

Whipping her head around the girl searched in desperation for her captor. Angus continued to toss pebbles one by one in other directions, laughing to himself when she'd try to follow it. The girl wailed and begged to be freed, but he never responded. Isolation was all part of the game.

Turning on a heel, he disappeared from the room. Upon closing the door, a small hiss released from the cracks, sealing itself from light. The only air she would receive was from the grated tunnel access, which was secured. Angus hummed softly to himself and walked away.

Upstairs, Marshall was just getting in and smiled at him in a toasty, drunkard way before disappearing into his bedroom. He was accompanied by Ruby, a bar wench from whichever brewhouse he chose to lose his coins in that evening. The doctor offered a nod and continued on to his study. The merchant and his date for the night put Angus' worries to bed as they romped in theirs. He was quite confident no one would hear the girl's screams from below over Ruby's well-rehearsed grunts and howls.

The next morning Angus was sitting at the table when Marshall and Ruby appeared. He watched their quaint after-morning exchange before Marshall walked her out. It was still dark outside as the doctor sat picking at his breakfast. It was a challenge for him to keep from looking at the cellar door even as Marshall walked in and began talking.

"The Kingsley man had a gathering of the minds," he said, pulling some bread off the table and shoveling it into his mouth.

This meant Marshall wanted to gossip. Gossip was good, in Angus' mind, because it let him know what was going on. He lifted his head with interest and watched the other man flitter around the kitchen until he settled across from him at the table.

"Oh? What does Paul have up his sleeve, now?" Angus replied.

"Andrew, the old butler, tells me they were discussing getting chaos back to order. Someone must not have liked it too much," he baited.

Angus took the bait and asked, "Why do you say that?"

Marshall leaned in like he was telling a ghost story to a child. "Because halfway through it, there was a knock on the door. A dead floozy was found hacked in the middle of town." His voice lowered to his best spooky whisper. "Her baby was missing. Cut from her womb!"

Marshall sat back, smiling, waiting to see if his story had the desired effect on Angus. Angus' features barely changed. There was the lifting of one eyebrow which suggested he might have a deeper interest but Angus was still pondering it. Marshall's smile was fading when he held out his hands, pleading his case.

"Did you hear me? Muuurdered. Cut!" He made the slashing motion with his hands.

"I heard you, Marshall," Angus replied, "And what did they find?"

Marshall waved his hand at him dismissively for ruining his frightful story. He took his bread and sopped it in some broth before stuffing the wet dough into his mouth. When he talked, Angus could see the mastication process; each of his eight remaining teeth mashing the piece of food down. It took a great effort for Angus to push back the bile rising from his stomach.

"They don't know who did it. No witnesses. But it was true! She was pregnant. And only her family of miscreant street sisters knew anythin' of it!"

For a merchant, Marshall was usually well spoken. Of course, Angus was learning his little friend was like a chameleon taking on the manner of speech for whomever he was with at the time. For instance, his night spent with Ruby gave him gutter speak.

"Interesting, indeed," Angus added.

"And that ain't all of it," he continued speaking around another full bite of his bread. "A few nights after, there was someone watching Morrigan through her window!"

Angus was lifting the cup of tea to his lips when he stopped, perking a listening ear at Marshall. The aroma of the tea was warm and fragrant under his nose. One of the many advantages of having an old merchant as a partner was getting first pick of imports from the incoming trade ships.

"What say you?" Angus prodded. "What is the word on that?"

Marshall interpreted the doctor's sudden interest in the story as his cue to continue. The old boat merchant still had it in him, he mused. Hooked a big catch: Angus' attention. It only took a simple mention of Morrigan to reel him in. He had no idea the voyeur in the window was his business partner and "friend."

Letting out a laugh, Marshall continued to sop the broth up with his bread. Angus was beginning to squirm watching the man continue to dip, mop, and swirl with his dirty fingers. The doctor let out a small cough and covered his mouth with his balled fist, trying to keep from losing his own breakfast.

With another mouthful of food, Marshall shrugged, playing it off as if it were no big deal, "They chased the man but never found him."

When he was silent afterward and focused on his meal rather than continuing, Angus pushed again.

"No ideas on who would do something like that? Surely, they must have some clues."

Marshall was sucking the broth off his fingers, his lips making puckering and slurping noises as he did. Angus cleared his throat and stood, pretending to clean up so he didn't have to watch him.

"No. Nothin' that I've heard," he smiled at Angus' back then hid it when the doctor turned around.

"Well, that is just absurd," Angus said in a faraway voice.

"Oh? Am I missing something? Do you know who it could've been?" Marshall stopped and watched the doctor, who was still off in his own thoughts.

"Hm? No. Well …" Angus acted as if a thought came to him, "What of that boy? Geoffery, is it?"

Marshall thought about it and shrugged again, diving back into his meal. "I'll toss the name around the next time I speak with the butler."

Angus nodded. "Yes, do that."

The doctor grew weary of watching Marshall pack food in his cheeks and tossed him another purse. "I need more supplies."

Marshall's greasy hand dropped the bread and caught the purse, then glanced up at Angus.

"I need medical supplies," Angus said. "I am working on a medicine for this disease that is ripping souls right out of bodies and leaving them where they lie in the streets. I can't stop to make errands."

"You're close?" his eyes brightened somewhat with hope.

"Of course, I am. I'm The Physician, aren't I?" Angus smiled as he articulated his title.

Marshall began to chew again.

Dear God he looks like a cow chewing cud, the doctor thought.

"There are extra coins for your time and effort," the doctor added as a side note, "I will need the supplies immediately though."

Marshall reviewed the list. Strange herbs and concoctions he'd heard of before but knew little about. He was about to ask where to get them from when Angus cut into his thoughts before exiting the kitchen to the cellar.

"Apothecary. Friar Brannon," he called over his shoulder.

Marshall nodded, stuffed a piece of the loaf into his pocket and wiped his hands on his tunic before making his way to town.

Once Angus was certain Marshall was gone, he took his time and went over some notes in his medical journal. Kettles boiled on several of the tables, and he got to work with his mortar and pestle grinding down various herbs. In places like India and Asia medicine was more advanced, but here in London it was considered taboo. People put their faith in God before medicinal remedies. God must be punishing me, so I must atone

for some sin I may not have committed, was the philosophy most abided by. They'd flagellate, meditate, pray, pay tithes and alms; none of it cured them of the Plague that enveloped them.

Hours passed, and he realized the girl was still screaming in the next room. It was a faint cry which he could only hear because he was next door in his laboratory. He chuckled to himself and then let out a sigh. Guess I should go clean up.

He took his spectacles off and placed them on the table, then walked next door. Before he walked in, he leaned his ear in and listened. Her voice was gravelly from the strain her constant shouts had on her vocal cords. He could tell she was growing tired as each wail became less intense. Curling his fingers around the key, he inserted it into the lock and opened the door to let himself in. The girl stopped screaming at once and panted, listening for him in the dark.

"Please, sir! Let me go! I swear I'll tell no one!" she begged.

Angus stood in silence, escalating her panic. She started to weep again and he walked to the far table letting his fingertips brush over the tools he had laid out. It was still pitch dark inside the room so he lit one of the torches. She recoiled from it as expected. Excellent.

When she whipped her head to the side, her hair covered her face, shielding her eyes from the brightness of the flame. Angus stood directly in front of it, causing his silhouette to appear larger and more intimidating than he already was.

The girl trembled, causing her thighs to quiver. Angus stared down at her until she found the courage to look up at him. When she did, she shook her head in a silent plea.

Please, no. Don't hurt me. They were always the same words.

The doctor lifted his hand and brushed his thumb over her shackled ankle. She let out a shrill scream and her body arched off the table pulling at the chains like an animal trying to free itself from a trap.

She had soiled herself overnight. The doctor expected that because he planned it that way. Second phase of the torture process. Break the mind. Angus would bring her down to the lowest, basal level of fodder. Next, he'd erase her will until it was his own.

In his other hand, he held the scalpel. Raising it up, he remained patient and still until she had no choice but to drop back down to the table. Her adrenaline would flush through her system, and the lactic acid build up in her muscles would soon take over. After a few minutes of her thrashing and pulling, the girl fell to the table in exhaustion. When her eyes focused again she saw the scalpel, and it began all over again.

It was tedious work, and he spent several hours working on her in this way. When he was finished, he'd go back into his laboratory and make notes of everything he observed. Once that was complete, he'd go back to his work on his medicines.

The disease was spreading, and it wasn't inconceivable he might be afflicted. Or Morrigan. His job was to ensure they had a chance of survival. In his mind, it would be them to repopulate and rebuild the world once it was all struck down. Their world would be perfect.

Angus looked up to the wall where her images gazed down at him in angelic wonder. "This is all for you, my love. I will give you the world because you deserve it."

Suffering must be the inevitable tariff exacted from spirit for residing in human form.
~Mark Frost, *The List of Seven*

CHAPTER 9: WE'VE CREATED A MONSTER

Date Unknown

Young Angus could hear his teeth chattering so loud he thought they would crack in his mouth. He kept his eyes lowered and tried to control his breathing. The pain radiating from his knees set nerves on fire and they shot up and down his legs like lightning. Drool fell in slow, stringy drips off his chin and he closed his eyes. He needed to go away. Just disappear, disappear, disappear.

The switch snapped against his back again, and he sucked in the scream. He didn't dare let out a sound lest he be delivered twice the punishment. His father's voice came into focus again, penetrating the swirl of the world. A muffle at first, and then so loud it rattled his brain.

"Recite!" he screamed.

A spray of his father's spittle splashed against the side of his face. The young boy's body shook with violent twitches but he remained where he was, kneeling on the dried beans that were embedding into his skin and pressing against bone, cartilage, and nerves. The well of hatred was growing in the pit of his stomach, souring the soup of apathy he worked so hard to brew. The continuing punishment was serving no good other than to drive out Angus' humanity.

Another lash.

Disappear. Disappear …

"W-we are w-what we repeatedly do. Exc-cellence, then, is n-not an act, b-but a habit." Angus stuttered out through the excruciating pain.

His father walked around him, circling him like a shark. Angus knew more was coming. Never knowing from what direction was part of the game his father played. Angus' stomach churned. The pit of his stomach became the pit of a hell full of demons.

"One day," he thought, *"I will kill you. I will bleed you of your poison and breathe in your fire, demon."*

As soon as Angus found a dark cave in his mind where he could push the emotion back, where the pain would recede just enough to give him respite, his father's switch would come again to remind him of where he really was.

"Recite!" his father shouted again.

It was the way his father conditioned him. Strong, short orders barked in militaristic fashion. Repeated over and over until his only son knew nothing else but what he put inside of him.

"All m-men by n-nature …" That was all Angus could give for today.

His twiggy body gave in, and he fell to the side. His jaw clenched so tight he thought he'd dislocated it. Hyperventilating, he sucked in every breath until his vision was spotty. The shadow of his father crept over him, looming down from the sky. In reality his father was human; five feet and nine inches tall but right now he seemed as large as a giant. The boy peered up through glossy, tear-filled eyes without speaking a word, exasperating the demon he called "father." Tossing the switch to the ground, his father walked to the entrance of the house without offering an ounce of compassion.

Angus, feeling relieved from the cessation of his beating, lay his head on the stone and stared straight ahead. Once upon a time he feared his father, but now he fantasized about ways of hurting him. He wanted him to suffer more than he was ever made to suffer. He wanted him to scream from his soul. He wanted to consume him.

"Bathe him, feed him, then clothe him. We are leaving again tonight," his father stopped and called over his shoulder, giving a list of demands to the exotic nursemaid who happened to be male. Mostly, anyway.

Enuk, giving a dip of his head in response to Master Wulfe, rushed to Angus. His father chose Enuk because he'd been castrated, and his English was sparse. He had only a basic, elementary understanding of it. So his father thought. In truth, Enuk spoke English very well, and would speak only when the boy and he were alone. The doctor's young, impressionable son would find his only source of compassion in the androgynous companion his father bought for him in their travels. He felt it would compensate for losing his mother, who died during childbirth. When he was born, rumors had been spread, whispering of Angus who was born breech with a "veil" over his eyes. It is also said, seeing Master Wulfe's wife was unable to continue laboring without any assistance, the doctor chose his son over the woman and cut the baby out himself while leaving his mother to bleed to death.

If it was true or not, Angus had no way to know, but he felt in his entire being the rumors were not rumors but facts.

Angus' young eyes stared off into nothing as he recalled the memories. All he ever wanted was to live up to his father's expectation. One small moment of recognition or tenderness would add up to more than he had ever dreamed. Instead, he was discarded, and it made him feel empty inside. A well of darkness

with something swimming in the oil-slick waters below. It slithered and coiled around his heart, suffocating any chance of life to bloom from it. He did not know what love was, and so he did not long for it. When he witnessed his father's gentle touch to the women he paraded through the home, Angus felt resentment and hate. For both his father, and the women.

He was still lost in reveries when Enuk broke the silence. "Your father is wicked." Angus didn't respond. He sat in silence in the bath water. Enuk said this every day. Angus didn't need reminding of how wicked his father was. As he grew older, he wondered, *"If my father is wicked and I am the product of my father ... What does that make me?"*

As Angus grew older, it mattered less and less to him. The routine was always the same. Rigorous lessons followed by the thorough cleaning he received from Enuk, head to toe, and every nook and cranny. It compounded the feelings Angus had of being an object. He wasn't a living breathing boy—he was a "thing."

There was no place on his body the nursemaid wasn't familiar with. Once, as a young boy, Angus felt the sun-darkened one move his hands under the water until they were touching his genitals. Angus tightened his whole body. He may be just an object to everyone around him but he knew this was wrong. The eunuch's smile stretched across his face like a snake, enjoying the discomfort he was causing his charge, and pushed a finger between the tightly constricted crack of his buttocks. Angus tried to jump away, but Enuk laughed, and made fun of him as he pulled him back into the water.

"Don't be so shy!" he chided. "I just wanted to see if you liked it."

When Angus was older, the probing caused him a different sort of humiliation in the form of an unintentional erection.

He wanted to throw up the moment he felt it between his legs. He could feel his shame rise with the swelling of his penis. It was disgusting … he was disgusting … and it was wrong. Not knowing how to stop it from happening, Angus secretly used a leather strap at night to whip himself. He would stand in front of the window, staring at his reflection and bark orders at himself, just like his father.

"Dirty disgusting flesh," he growled, "You know what happens to dirty flesh? We cut it off!"

The first time he struck himself, he fell to the ground when his knees buckled. Every nerve burst into an electrically charged knot in his stomach. Angus curled into a fetal position and groaned, quietly. Holding it in as long as he could, he finally vomited on the floor beside his head.

As he continued, he became better at enduring such high levels of pain in silence. If his father heard him cry out and entered to see him as he was now, he'd be castrated like Enuk.

Over time, Angus persisted in the self-flagellation. Every night, every strike of the strap would sting his inner thighs and scrotum but he would keep going, verbally and physically abusing himself.

***

Because of his father's renowned skills as an apothecary and physician, Angus and he traveled quite a bit. His father was always busy with dinners and meetings on their trips. When his father was away it gave Angus time to revisit his mind and body.

He was eight when his father chose a new wife. The boy had no memory of which country they were in when he found her. There were too many countries, too many days and nights away. Callia would have nothing to do with her husband's son, anyway. She was young and simple, and cared only about the gifts her husband bestowed upon her.

There was one memory which stood out more than the others. One holiday, his father came home with a gift. He handed Angus a new tunic, handmade just for him. The fabric was soft and exquisite. Angus remembered this because the gesture frightened him. His father never gave him anything, and therefore, Angus fumbled for words. He had no experience on which to base his response.

"It is a handsome gift, Father," Angus finally said.

His father watched as Angus squirmed in discomfort. It felt for an instant … just a blink of an eye … there might be remorse.

And then it was gone.

"Yes, well now you can burn the one you've been wearing. Go change, Angus," his father said, then turned to Callia. "And for my wife …"

He handed her a large box to which she seemed disinterested in.

"Go on, then. Open it."

Callia opened the box revealing a handmade, brocaded dress. The needlepoint was meticulous. Each rose beaded and sewn one by one. Callia was so upset her husband had given the boy a gift she threw the box into the dirt and complained to her husband through tears.

"What is this?" she said with disgust on her face.

She reached down into the box and held up the new dress. Her face was twisted into a sneer as she looked at it.

"It is a dress, Callia. Made from the finest material to be found among the Silk Road," Angus' father snipped.

Callia grabbed hold of Angus' tunic and felt it. Huffing, she pushed it away. "His is better quality. A boy? With finer quality garb than your wife?"

Angus' father was confused. "What say you? You're comparing your garb to that of my son?"

"I cannot wear this!" she shouted and shoved the dress into his arms. "It is too rough. You know how sensitive my skin is."

Her shouts turned to a disgusting whine of ungratefulness Angus could not bear. He was anxious to be away from her and spoke in a soft tone. "Thank you, Father."

He almost felt sorry for his father as he waited for him to respond. He watched the two fighting, tuning out the high-pitched squeals of his father's entitled new wife. He was in unchartered territory, here. Did he stay and watch them? Or should he make a discreet exit. Angus felt sad for himself, realizing how blindsided he was by his father's gesture. He was so needy and pathetic. The moment his father showed an instant of acknowledging his existence, Angus became a bumbling idiot. Clenching his jaw, he closed his eyes and released a long exhale. When he had his emotions under control he gave his father a nod. He didn't care if he saw it or not.

His father didn't seem to notice. And so, Angus left to explore the markets

With his arms tucked behind his back like his father, he walked past the vendors perusing their wares. Behind him, Enuk followed, watching the slaves and other companions walk by. Angus was getting good at forgetting Enuk was a constant shadow. The nursemaid usually said little in public. Until now, he rarely showed an interest in anything.

The marketplace in this country was exotic and foreign to Angus. It felt like they were in another world with all the scents and colors he'd never seen before. Vendors sold food and wares like other markets, but the women were bold and held as equals to the men.

Two women had their eyes on Enuk, staring and whispering to one another. Angus looked over his shoulder at the eunuch and wondered what the appeal was. He continued to the next cart when the pair came right up to Enuk, fawning over him. Their hands were not afraid to touch him wherever they pleased without shame, even in front of the young Angus.

"He's so dark and lovely," one woman said to the other.

"He looks to be carved straight out of the mountain! He is so tall and hard," the other replied.

Both women were dressed in pristine, white tunics. Around their necks were thick bands of gold with matching bangles around their wrists and ankles. Behind the two women, stood several males. Compared to the women, Angus noted, their attire was boring and plain.

The first woman finally took notice of Angus as he stood off to the side waiting for Enuk to continue their walk. "And look at this handsome boy."

When she approached him, her scent was spicy and intoxicating. Leaning toward him, her long braid swayed between them like a rope. She curled her fingers around Angus' chin and smiled.

"Oh, the things I could teach you."

She pulled away and laughed to her friend, who joined in. Angus sighed inwardly, yes … just an object to be seen and dismissed without an afterthought.

The two, just as easy as they came, left Angus and his companion to paw and handle everything and everyone that

struck their interest. The men following behind the women, who Angus assumed were attendants like Enuk, snuck a glance at his companion who smiled inconspicuously at them. The smile was returned, and Angus thought it had to be a signal or hidden language between servants. He looked back again and saw they had disappeared among the crowd.

Angus' companion turned to him and said. "I want to show you something."

Angus glanced up at the Nubian male, searching his face for a clue of his intentions. Whenever Enuk showed Angus something new, it was one of two things; something really bad, or something really interesting. Enuk chuckled at Angus, smiling again. His white teeth were stark against his ebony skin.

"It will be good," he said.

Angus shrugged but remained suspicious. "Fine."

Enuk spun on his heel, switching direction, and motioned for Angus to follow. The two pushed through the crowd to a more remote and narrow street. The end of the street turned into four more, winding further and deeper into the city until Angus noticed an incline. Looking over his shoulder, Angus noted they were heading uphill. The more they ventured further away from the main street the deeper they went into a hidden part of town. Angus got a bad feeling and was about to ask questions but they stopped in front of a home larger than any he'd seen before. It was white with overgrown foliage vining along the walls, explaining why he'd almost missed it. The outside door had large columns on either side where several men like the ones in the market were standing outside.

There was another man coming outside who stood out from the others. His face was cleanly shaved making him look young and effeminate. When his eyes found Angus and his companion, they came to life.

"Come in!" the man said waving them to the entrance. He was already beside Angus and Enuk. He placed his hand on Angus' shoulder, guiding him toward the door, "And what is your name, young master?"

Angus had never been addressed this way, and when he opened his mouth to speak nothing intelligible came out. He was stuttering like an idiot which infuriated him, making his cheeks flush.

Enuk saw him struggling and gave him a nudge before answering, "Master Angus Wulfe."

"Ahhh! Master Wulfe, please. Please!" the man said. He was bending at the waist with his hand extended toward the door.

He started to sigh and tell Enuk he wanted to leave, but when they got to the door something changed his mind. What he saw beyond that door changed him for the rest of his life.

Out in the open, women and men alike walked around nude. Wine poured freely from fountains. Bodies writhed against bodies, in twos, threes and sometimes more. It was exciting to Angus who'd never even seen a woman's ankles. At fourteen he had seen most of the world but never anything like this. Now, he was seeing all the wonder and splendor a woman hid beneath layers and layers of fabric displayed before him.

Every which way he turned, he was given wine. With his head spinning, Angus felt good for once in his life. All of this debauchery spurned in him something which lay dormant his whole life.

Drunk on wine and excitement, the laughter and merriment turned to horror. Two tanned and voluptuous women lured Angus to another room. Their feathery hair tickled his cheeks as he nuzzled against their bare breasts. He felt foolish and giddy, but he didn't care. Their bodies were soft and sensual. When they got inside the door, Angus paused. Beyond the

threshold was an oasis. Before him, a square pool filled almost the entire room. Alongside of it, an indoor waterfall trickled from the ceiling. There were murals on the wall, and Angus focused on them as they seemed to come alive. Was he drugged? This is impossible, he thought to himself. Each of the murals captured the scenes from beyond the doors behind him. He was drawn closer to them, mesmerized by how lifelike they were. His attention to the murals was disrupted when he heard laughter at the far end of the pool. Turning, he saw a group of men leaning against the poolside. When they saw Angus, they all stopped and smiled. It reminded him of hyenas from the golden lands his father told him about.

"Come in, boy," one of them said.

Angus hesitated. He knew then, he needed to get out. The pit of his gut knotted. Something was wrong. He wished he'd listened to it before being lured inside. When Angus turned to run, the men from the marketplace blocked the door and took hold of him roughly. He tried to fight but the effects of the wine and drug made him easier to handle. Grasping him by the arms, they threw him into the water and went back to the door, guarding it.

The men pulled him in and did unspeakable things. Things his memory would not allow him to recall. He could only remember waking up the next day to his father calling out his name. Angus was lying prone on the grass, his tunic wrapped to his waist. He could never shake the memory of how cold he was, like death. The pain was intense and unbearable. Looking toward his father's voice, he reached out for him. It was the first time he saw fear in his father's eyes. The sight of his son lying half-dead, abused, and discarded must've been quite a shock. It sliced deep into his father's conscience, which until now Angus never knew existed.

When he didn't see Enuk he asked about him, but his father refused to speak on it. It didn't take much for Angus to hypothesize. His father was a proud man, and in his eyes, all of Angus' punishments were for a "better good." To rape and sodomize a boy was unforgivable, even to the Monster. It was an insult to his father's name and honor.

A new servant was brought in to nurse Angus back to health. This time his father chose a woman. She was old but had a motherly and gentle touch. Angus could barely see out of his swollen eyes, but he watched her as she carefully undressed him and cleaned the wounds. He noted her reaction to the red stain on the back of his tunic. She had gasped and covered her mouth while forcing tears to the outer corners of her eyes. It was hours of slow, careful cleaning and wrapping before he could finally sit up to eat. Staring down at the bowl of broth, his stomach growled. He had no desire to eat. He only wanted to starve and die.

***

It was one week later when Angus' father came to his bedside. His father had never been to his room before. Having him appear now and show such concern for him was the same as seeing a stranger in his room. Staring down at Angus, his father attempted to speak but struggled to find words. Angus knew it wasn't pity. He knew the attack on him was as much an attack on his father. This made Angus feel even more weak and pathetic. He was the weak link in the chain. The question now was what would his father do to strengthen it?

"Come with me," his father said.

Angus looked into his eyes, afraid and uncertain, but did not tarry. Grunting, he swung his aching legs over the side of the

bed and stood up on shaky legs wincing a little. His father's head swung away. He could not bear to see what they had done to his son. Angus forced himself to stand up tall and straight, lifting his chin when he was steady. He wanted to cry out to the pain, but instead, he swallowed it and walked to the door. He would no longer allow his father to look down on him. He was no longer a piece of garment to be tossed aside.

Watching the strength it took for his son to walk on his own, his father's demeanor changed. *Yes,* Angus thought to himself, *this was the way to settle the score.* His mind was made up.

"We will set this right," his father said, leveling his eyes on Angus, "now."

Still having no idea what was about to happen, he followed his father. If for nothing else, curiosity of what his father would do to settle the score.

When they arrived outside the old building, Angus' father motioned to the door. Hesitantly, Angus led the way through the door. He noted the wooden door on the floor he knew must be the way to a wine cellar. A shudder ran up Angus' spine. Would his father get rid of him? Subconsciously, Angus took a step back, fighting the instinct to run. His father watched him; his stoic features softened, and his brows pinched above his nose.

"Don't you want to fix this, Angus? To make this right?" his father asked.

"Please, father," Angus begged, "I will not tell anyone, I swear!"

Confusion deepened his father's features even more, making his wrinkle lines more noticeable. His father shook his head, speaking in a softer tone. "No Angus, I will not harm you. Come here, boy."

Closing the space between them, he stood before his father who placed his hands on his son's shoulders. Leaning down, he leveled his gaze at him. "I brought you here for you to make things right," he paused, giving Angus' shoulders a small shake. "For you to face your enemy."

Angus was still confused. The temperature of his body dropped and it felt like ice ran through his veins. It made it hard for him to move. His father turned back around and unlocked the cellar door. The hinges howled in rusted protest. His father led the way, descending the winding, stone steps. Behind them, torch light filled the room from where they hung on the walls. When they reached the bottom, he could see the barrels of wine lined up in neatly placed rows. The center aisle was more open and lead to a dark end. Angus had to force his feet to move. Despite his father's word that he would not be harmed, he still felt like a moth flying into a spider's web.

"Come, Angus," his father urged him again.

The boy was panting but did as he told. When they got to the end, his father lit another torch. The sudden light intruding on the darkness made Angus turn his head for a moment. When his eyes adjusted, he turned to look into the light. His father was standing next to Enuk who was dangling upside down from the chains tethered to the ceiling.

Angus' eyes widened; his heart raced, and he forgot to breathe.

"Look at him," his father ordered.

Angus didn't want to but it was all he could see! No matter where he looked, Enuk was there, filling his sight. The former nursemaid was limp but whimpering. His foot was dangling from his ankle joint. A rat was spinning left and right as it hung from a strand of cartilage, stretching its body so it could

reach his toes. Another one was already there, scratching and tugging on another. They must've been feeding off him for days.

Enuk looked in his direction. Dried tears and snot clung to his face, and his lips were ashen from dehydration. Angus took a harder look and saw the bruises and lacerations along the eunuch's skin. Between his legs, what was left of his mutilated genitals hung in flaps against his pelvis. His father exacted his own vengeance before bringing Angus here. He made sure Enuk was tame enough to be given to his son, who may not have the strength to deliver the rest.

Angus' father leaned down in a slow, fluid movement. When he whispered into his son's ear, he could feel the heat like venom against his earlobe. In his mind, Angus pictured him like a giant serpent coiling its body around his.

"He will do you no harm," he said. "Be sure you deliver him from all of his transgressions until you are satisfied."

His father took hold of his shoulders again and turned his son. There were tools everywhere. Gardening tools, medical tools, tools he'd never seen before. Many of them were crusted with dried blood and rusty, like Enuk's chains. He looked at the Nubian man again and felt all the rage he had pushed down into the well start to crawl up. It was powerful and frightening, and Angus felt possessed by it. It took over all reason until it had total control over his body.

He didn't realize he was moving until he let out a scream. His fingers were wrapped tightly around a pitchfork-like tool, but he was on the outside watching. Angus ran full throttle toward the nursemaid and gave the tool a thrust. The prongs sank into Enuk's skin with ease. Not having much fat on him made it that much easier for each tip to penetrate the thick fascia. He tried to pull back but they were stuck. It triggered Angus awake, and he was once more inside his body.

Enuk's eyes widened, and he released a weak but anguished scream. His entire body shuddered around the forks of the tool. Growling, Angus' eyes narrowed, and he felt the power returning. He took it in slowly, savoring it. When he was in control again, he jerked the prongs back and watched the first trail of blood dribble from the puncture holes. The blood streamed down the handle and over his hands.

Looking up into his enemy's face, all he could see was the countless ways Enuk's hands had touched him, the forceful way he took him, all of the degradation, the violation and finally, the betrayal. Angus let out a primordial howl, and thrust the tool into his belly again. And again. And again.

Each time, the response was the same. Enuk's eyes rolled back, and his mouth opened to shriek in pain. Shuddering and jerking, his ebony colored body spilled blood from every wound until he was standing in a puddle of it. Angus dropped the tool and spit in the tortured man's face. Turning to his father, he discovered he was crying. His chest was heaving, forcing his lungs to suck in large gulps of air. He could feel the heat in his cheeks, and his hands were shaking.

"Are you satisfied, my son?" his father asked him.

Angus looked at his father, at the bleeding man and the pitchfork lying in his blood. Hot tears streamed down his face and he shook his head.

In a dark voice he barely recognized as his own he answered, "No."

His father's posture straightened, seemingly happy with his answer. Nodding his approval, he led Angus back out, closing the door behind them.

CHAPTER 10: BLOODY SUNDAY

Angus awoke from his dream with a start. He had thrown the covers off himself and was covered in a sheen of sweat that made his tunic cling to him. The bedding was soaked. His hair was matted against his forehead, and he clutched the mat in clawed fingers. He didn't realize he was shouting until Marshall burst through the door and shook him.

"Master Wulfe! Wake up! Wake up! It's just a dream!"

Angus' eyes were wild and stretched as wide as they would go. His arms flailed against Marshall while the man tried to hold him. He could feel the rigidity of his muscles which were locked from the lactic acid build up and his heart felt as though it would burst right out of his chest.

Marshall felt Angus begin to find consciousness and start calming down. The doctor looked up at him and recognized him.

"Where am I?" Angus asked.

"You're at home, sir. You're safe. It's alright, you can wake now."

The doctor closed his eyes and fell back against the bed in relief, then let his arm fall over his head. He turned to look out the window and took deep, slow breaths.

"I'm alright now, Marshall. Thank you. Please, go back to sleep."

Marshall frowned and lowered his voice, "It's nearly lunchtime, Master Wulfe."

Angus sprung up out of bed and looked out the window. He had no idea how he slept so late. He quickly began to wash his face in the bowl beside his bed, running the water through his hair. Marshall fetched him a clean cloth to dry off with.

"You didn't mention an appointment today, otherwise I would've woke you sooner."

"It's of no concern. Was my own mistake." Angus reached for the cloth as he spoke.

His fingers walked along the side of the table and over his bed but could not find one. He looked around dripping water onto the floor. Marshall nudged him from the other side with the clean linen. He didn't look well to the merchant. He was constantly in another world where Marshall would have to wait patiently for his return. Angus sensed his colleague's growing suspicion of his faculties. He'd become inquisitive and watchful of his every move.

"I've been overdoing it in the laboratory," Angus offered.

"You need sleep, sir," Marshall replied.

Angus blotted his face and moved to his arms and hands when he turned to Marshall. He tossed the used cloth aside and smirked.

"People are dying, Marshall. Exponentially. Everyone we know has fallen and passed with this plague. I cannot save them unless I find the cure."

Marshall looked down at the floor and went silent. Angus pulled his head through a clean tunic and watched him. His normal, gentler stare hardened, causing him to look grave

"What? What is it?" Angus asked.

"Morrigan. She's ill. I came in to tell you when I found you thrashing."

The doctor's face grew stern, and he rushed to get dressed. "It is my strongest suggestion that next time you come out with the details more quickly."

Marshall felt the anger rolling off Angus' skin, and he kept his eyes on the ground. "Yes, sir. The horses are being

prepared as we speak. I shall gather your things for an immediate departure."

Marshall turned and slipped out of the room. When he was far enough away from the doctor's earshot he cursed under his breath. If it weren't for him Angus would still be sleeping, he would've starved in the cellar, and someone would've discovered it was him all along stalking the young Morrigan. Marshall was smarter than he let on. It was his job to know these things. And soon he'd figure out what was going on in the cellar. As soon as he got his chance, he'd go down there and learn the doctor's dark secret.

The horses were brought to the front, and the doctor flew past him in a rush. Marshall shook his head and followed behind. With their bags fixed into place, Angus gave a kick of his heel and the horse took off into a gallop. They were at the Kingsley home within the hour, where Morrigan's father greeted them. The horses were led away to the stables, and the men were led into the house with a barrage of questions handed out by Angus.

"When did she start showing signs?"

"Around noon yesterday," her father responded.

"Fever?"

"Yes. It's getting worse."

The men kept their interaction brief and to the point until they reached Morrigan's bedroom door. Paul opened the door after a quick knock and announced the doctor had arrived. Morrigan's mother stood up with a breath of relief. She had the worried look any mother would have, and was wrapped in a blanket indicating she slept in the chair next to Morrigan's bed all night.

"Good afternoon, Victoria," Angus said, giving her a courteous bow.

"Hello, Doctor. We're so thankful that you came."

Angus gave her a well-practiced smile and then turned to the vision of his prize. She looked weak and helpless as she lay beneath the pale, ivory covers. He took notice of the pink roses embroidered throughout the fibers. It was perfect. She is my perfect rose.

"Hello, Morrigan," Angus whispered.

He stood at the foot of her bed, his hat held in front of him near his legs. Morrigan was feverish and shimmered with perspiration. Angus wanted to reach out and touch her skin with his fingers and taste the dew from them. But he had to keep his mind level and stay professional.

Hearing the doctor's voice, Morrigan stirred a bit, and her eyes fluttered open. She squinted and turned her head against the offending sunlight piercing in through her matching drapes. She groaned in pain. The doctor's black heart stirred with a semblance of emotion. He moved quickly to her side to block the sun and pressed his hand to hers.

"It will be alright. I'm here to help you."

Morrigan turned her head back in his direction and looked through the slits of her eyes at the doctor's shadowed face. She had no strength but managed to try to pull her hand away. The doctor frowned and released it with reluctance. His features sagged with disappointment. He cleared his throat and turned to address her parents.

"Marshall has a list of items I will need. I will stay here until she is well if that is agreeable?"

"Yes, of course!" Victoria answered.

Paul nodded. He could barely speak as he watched his daughter's deteriorating condition from the doorway.

"There is a room next door," Victoria began. "The tenant ... is no longer here."

Angus knew the person before probably died from the Plague which explains why Morrigan contracted it, but the doctor was confident that with his medicinal drinks they would all be safe. I will save all of you. I'm the only one who can.

Marshall watched from over Paul's shoulder and lowered his eyes again. It felt wrong not speaking up, but he was worried for Morrigan. He did not want to see the girl succumb to the painful death of the illness so many others had contracted. When his eyes rose again, Angus was looking right at him. It sent a chill so far into him, he thought his heart would freeze and cease to beat.

"I'll get your things set up straight away," he said and escaped out of sight to do just that.

When he brought their things into the room, he was met by Robert, Morrigan's adopted brother. He'd grown like a weed since he'd last seen him. The young lad Marshall remembered was now a young man. Facial hair formed a shadow around his square jaw.

"Hello, Marshall," Robert said.

Even his voice had grown deep. Marshall barely recognized him and had to stare for a few moments before responding.

"Heavens, boy, is that you?" Marshall asked.

Robert chuckled and nodded. "It's me, sir. I'll have these set up for you shortly."

He began to unroll the mats for the two wooden-framed beds. His back was strong and his shoulders rounded. His hands showed signs of manual labor which Marshall assumed was from him taking the brunt of the work when death stole their help.

"Aye, lad. That's good." Marshall didn't know what else to say. He turned and pretended to be preoccupied by the setting up of tools and materials.

Angus entered the room and stopped mid-sentence of whatever he was saying and let his eyes take in Robert in awkward silence. The young man turned to face the doctor and nodded at him in greeting.

"Master Wulfe, thank you for coming," he said.

Angus' jaw clenched and his demeanor changed to something darker. He was sizing up the competition. Marshall watched as his nostrils flared and he took in a breath, making his chest appear larger.

"Robert," Angus began, "yes, well the Kingsley family is dear to me. I will do anything to ensure their well-being."

Robert released a sigh and gave a grateful smile. He took a few steps toward Angus and was about to offer his hand.

"That's a relief to hear. You're the best physician–" Robert's sentence was interrupted when Angus turned on him and the offered hand, "—in town."

The doctor removed his overcoat and rolled up his sleeves before turning back to face Robert again.

"Yes, I know. And they deserve only the best. Are you almost through?"

Robert was at a loss for words but quickly recovered when he glanced at Marshall who gave a subtle shake of his head indicating it wasn't worth the bother.

"Yes, sir. I'll be out of your way quickly."

"Good. I'll need privacy. And I'll need you to keep out of Morrigan's room, even to visit," Angus said.

Robert stopped unrolling the mat and looked at the doctor, his eyes narrowed and his lips pursed in anger and confusion. Who was this man giving him orders? He lived here! He could go where he bloody well pleased. Boring a hole into the back of the doctor's head with his glare, the young man gave an annoyed chuckle.

"Excuse me, sir?" Robert asked.

"I don't need you bringing any sickness in from the outside. I think that's a reasonable request."

Robert's shoulders slumped. He couldn't argue with the doctor's logic even if he knew it was a rubbish excuse. He saw how the man looked at Morrigan and knew it made her uncomfortable. Angus stopped what he was doing as if daring him to contradict him, and Robert turned without a word to finish his task. When he was done, he walked to the door and paused.

"Is that all, sir?" he said with a hint of resentment in his voice.

"I believe that's all you can do for me, yes."

Robert's jaw clenched, and he curled his fingers into balled fists but left without another word.

***

That night Morrigan fought off a fever that threatened to burn her alive. She shouted out at hallucinations and cried blood tears. Her mother and another woman on the house staff took turns rotating the cool compresses used to wipe her down. Angus paced his room, frustration mounting at his lack of understanding.

Why can't I cure her?

The doctor sat down and scoured through his journals. He scribbled calculations and formulas on the wall with charcoal. This continued into the following night. By now, Morrigan's screams filled the home. Painful boils covered her torso and legs. The slightest touch made her beg for death. There was an hour of silence when Morrigan was finally allowed a medicinal drink that sedated her.

At approximately four in the morning, it came to him. He rushed to Marshall and shook him awake. His voice was a whisper, but in his excitement the rushed hiss of it filled the room. The half-asleep companion barely made out the words so he looked down at the list and nodded while Angus continued to pull him out of his bed.

"Go, Marshall. Go now!" he urged. "There isn't a lot of time."

Marshall had one shoe on and was hopping to the door. He had no idea if the places he could get the materials from even carried these things let alone if they would open the door this late—or early. On his way to the door, he snatched some fresh bread off the table and set off on his scavenger hunt.

Angus could not be stilled or persuaded to nap while he waited for his list of things. He'd barely eaten anything in three days. Each time a meal was offered, he sent it away and continued to work on his formulas. To the laymen, none of it made sense. It looked like ancient hieroglyphics. Paul stood in the doorway and simply watched, feeling helpless to save his daughter. He hid his grief as best he could, but more than once he'd been caught weeping at her screams in another room.

"Will this work, Angus?" he finally said.

Angus turned and looked at her father then smiled. "Yes. I am positive this will work."

The doctor gestured to his table with the open books. There were drawings and sketches of animals and even human patients. It was frightening to look at for Paul. He ran his finger over a drawing of a toad, then skimmed his fingers over the face of a young woman.

"What does this all mean?" Paul asked.

"I've conducted experiments—"

"On live animals? Humans?" Paul asked.

His voice and eyes showed shock and a tinge of fear. Did he really want to know? He pulled his hand off the picture subconsciously. He needed to hear this would work but the weight of the cost fell upon his moral compass, spinning it. Angus saw the change in his demeanor and pressed his hand over his.

"Modern medicine needs live hosts. Yes, we experiment on animals. The human was already dying, I assure you."

Angus left out the part that she was dying because he was killing her. He lifted the book and flipped the pages.

"I've discovered a way to keep the cells alive. See?" He brought Paul over to a set of jars.

One contained a dead mouse, the other contained one that seemed to be alive but just sat there staring out of the glass. In another was a large squirming snake-like creature.

"By God, what is that?" Paul gasped.

"It's just an eel. Eh, yes, it's rather large. But please, continue watching," Angus went on.

Paul watched as he filled the jar containing the dead mouse with a bit of water. He thought the doctor was going to submerge it but he didn't. Instead, he picked the creature up with a pair of tongs and forced its mouth open. Using a dropper, he forced a concoction into its mouth. The rodent's eyes fluttered and its feet kicked but there wasn't much else.

Angus looked up at Paul expecting a reaction, but Paul was still confused.

"This was a dead mouse. You saw it yourself."

"Yes, but it is still dead," Paul responded.

"Please, indulge me."

Angus lay the rodent down on the table, and then with the tongs he transferred the large angry eel to the next jar. It circled the bottom of it several times before settling. Angus

picked up the mouse again and repeated the process. The dropper pushed the concoction into its mouth, and as the mouse spasmed, he dropped it into the water. The eel thrashed a bit and the jolt from its electricity gave the small animal a kick that restarted its tiny heart.

Angus quickly removed the rodent and placed it in another, empty jar. The mouse lay there for several moments staring at the two men before it jumped to its feet with a sudden burst of energy. Paul shouted and hopped back a step. His voice dropped to a whisper that could barely be heard.

"Impossible."

Angus' voice matched his in tone and level.

"Not anymore."

CHAPTER 11: CRYSALIS

Morrigan lay in bed drenched with misery and sweat. Her fever caused everything inside her to feel like it was on fire. Her eyes were oversensitive to light so to avoid the needling pain it caused throughout her brain, she'd squint only if necessary. Her head felt like it was in a vice and the smallest movements caused her to cry out in torment.

Her mother and Mrs. Frit continued to wipe her down with the cool cloths. No matter how gentle they were, everything felt like sandpaper on her skin. The slightest touch or accidental graze against the black boils resulted in vulgar protests and complaint. She had no strength left to fight back.

"Where's Robbie?" Morrigan screamed.

Her words were childlike in the way she whined, making her sound pained and lost. It was times like this she always searched for Robbie. The two were inseparable from the night she found someone staring into her window until Angus forbade him to see her.

When she told Robert, in confidence, about Angus he believed her. He confessed the doctor gave him an unsettling feeling as well. What he wouldn't tell her was he caught the man staring at her many times before. It was creepy and disturbing to see the doctor's breathing grow heavy from just the sight of her.

"Please! Why isn't he here?"

"He's working, child," Mrs. Frit said.

She tried to pull Morrigan's hair back as she spoke but it was tangled and matted and tugged at her scalp. When the older woman attempted to free her tangled fingers, a thick lock of Morrigan's hair came free. Mrs. Frit held her hand up and covered her mouth to keep the sound of horror from escaping. Across from her, Victoria stopped wiping her daughter down and watched Mrs. Frit's reaction, before seeing the clump of hair in her hand. It was too much, and she had to get out.

"I'll get some fresh water," she said.

Morrigan's mother then gently lifted the bowl of soiled bandages, sniffling. Holding back her tears she gave the older woman a nod and exited. Once in the hall with the door closed behind her, Victoria leaned against the wall and wept.

Morrigan stopped writhing in pain and listened. She could hear her mother. It was as clear as if she stood there beside her still. She knew she was at the threshold of death and grew anxious again. She needed to hear Robert's voice.

"Please, Mrs. Frit. Tell him to come," Morrigan pleaded.

Mrs. Frit kept her eyes on the girl's arm and continued to wipe at the fever, ignoring the girl's pleas. She was under the strictest orders to keep Robert out. Paul and the doctor told her the young man had too much exposure to the livestock and other people convincing them it was too dangerous to Morrigan to allow him in the room.

The older woman stood, trying to tuck the covers around the young woman when Morrigan began to shiver again. The dimpling of her skin, the act of breathing, and even the surrounding air caused her excruciating pain. She was cold, she was burning up, she was tired of being touched, and yet, she still longed for Robert's presence.

She was sick to her stomach every time Angus came near her. She could tell he was gaining some sick pleasure out of "saving" her. The act of being kind to him was killing her.

"Oh by God, please leave me, Master Wulfe!" she cried out.

"Morrigan!" Mrs. Frit said.

The older woman turned to see the doctor standing there then faced Morrigan again, mortified at the girl's lack of manners.

"Morrigan Victoria Kingsley!" she said with a sharp tongue. "I will not have you blasphemin' and bein' rude to th' good doctor who's come t' save yeh."

Angus smiled and shook his head, "It's all well. She's not in her right mind."

Morrigan growled under her breath. She could smell the mugwort. She could smell everything. Her sense of smell was amplified to the point she could smell their blood, the infection in her skin, the food lingering in Mrs. Frit's clothing, and the chemicals used to shine Angus' shoes—beeswax and lemon? Yes, it was lemon. The smell overwhelmed her and her stomach flipped. Rolling onto her side she retched, vomiting black bile on his well-kept, high buckled boots.

Angus lifted a knee, and the substance stretched from toe to floor before it spilled off the top of his boot into a puddle. Mrs. Frit dashed around the bed to wipe the girl's mouth. The liquid kept coming despite the doctor stepping out of the way. He pulled a cloth off the end of the bed and wiped his boot off before setting it in a basket on the floor.

If Morrigan hadn't felt like her insides were being ripped out, she would've laughed. If he persisted on doting on her, she'd let him. Sick, ugly and withering: her eyes dark, her skin like parchment, and her nails so purple they were almost black.

The smell of madness on him was competing with the scent of thick mugwort he was constantly puffing through his pipe. He was always there. In the middle of the night, in the morning, in the late hours of the afternoon—he was there staring at her. Though Morrigan contested his constant presence, her mother and father insisted it was for her own good. He was giving her his utmost attention, and she should be grateful.

***

The Plague began to take its toll on Morrigan's body in the few short days since she'd come down with it. She lost ten pounds, her hair was thin and falling out, and her face had begun to sink. She had to fight for each breath she took. The boils under her arms were hard and painful. Each sac was filled with dark, infected blood that would continuously ooze out and the stench was fetid.

Her mother and Mrs. Frit were exhausted from cleaning and re-bandaging them. Every time they changed her, she'd scream in agony. Morrigan concluded this was just the beginning. Her ending would be when the disease ate away the rest of her. All she could do was beg for God to take her now instead of later.

Her mother struggled to hold back tears but in Morrigan's heart, she knew it'd be better for her mother to cry now than when she rotted from the inside out. Her mother continued to brush her hair and read to her. She changed her bedding and brought her broth that she could not keep down. Everything tasted like blood. It was in her sweat, dotting her forehead and above her lip. Her only relief came when Angus made her his evening cocktail filled with whatever he was drugging her with. After she consumed it she'd go into a deep,

lovely sleep that felt like she was drifting away. If he were poisoning her it would be the only redeeming thing she could find in him. She wanted to die.

I cannot fight any longer. I have nothing … left.

She could hear her mother and Mrs. Frit calling for her frantically from far way. The light from the window was fading, and she began to float away into the cold dark. Against her fever, Morrigan welcomed its cold embrace and gave in. Inside, there was nothing but peace and silence.

***

From the cold depths of peaceful sleep, she floated back to consciousness. The night was drifting in. She could tell by the way the light followed the wall and walked up to the corner where the sun would pass over her house and set on the other side. Her head throbbed, her eyes ached, and she could feel the fire in her veins from the unrelenting fever.

Without the potion Angus made her, sleep was filled with hallucinations and nightmares. Demons scratched at her limbs, tugging at her, and threatening to drag her to the pits of Hell. One time, she'd dreamt she was calling out for her mother and father who were standing near her bed unable to hear her. She tried to get up and run to find Robert, but he was nowhere to be found. Sometimes in her nightmares, she'd wake up to an empty and cold, dark house. She searched for everyone only to find them dead in their beds. Their eyes were vacant and milky white, staring up at her.

Still shaken from the visions, she was relieved when her mother arrived, bringing her the medicinal drink prepared by Angus. Taking it in small, quick sips, she prayed tonight would be her last and she would slip quietly into eternity.

CHAPTER 12: A PROPOSAL

8 Days Later…

Angus stood in the doorway watching Morrigan sleep. After the scare of nearly losing her, she was finally showing signs of improvement. They were small signs, but her fever had broken and the boils were starting to recede. She'd lost almost all her hair and her mother braided and wrapped it in a bonnet. His lovely prize was so fragile, and he wanted nothing more than to offer her more comfort.

Morrigan's father continued to pace and complain it was taking too long. The two gentlemen would debate in the other room about increasing the medicine Angus mixed for her in the evenings. The doctor tried to explain it was not something they could rush; they had to let the herbs do their job.

He watched the slow rise and fall of her chest and how the light rested on her cheek, which was once plump and full of color. It will be that way again, he told himself. He was convinced this was only a temporary illness, and he would save her.

Mrs. Frit came in to do the bed change and lifted the covers from Morrigan's foot. The entire appendage was black and swollen. The doctor's brows furrowed and Mrs. Frit let out a sigh. Dropping her hands, she looked at Angus for what to do. The man walked over to get a better look and examined it. *How?* he wondered. Everything else was getting better. He knew instinctively from the look and smell it was gangrene.

The doctor's eyes darkened, and he paced the room. How could he have missed this? His beautiful flower would now have to be cut at the stem for her to live. She would no longer be perfect!

"What do I do, sir?" Mrs. Frit asked.

Angus knew what he had to do, he just didn't want to. He continued to pace and try to think of something, but Mrs. Frit interrupted his thoughts again.

"Sir! What do I do?" she prodded.

Her voice was firm and laced with anger. When he didn't answer she rushed out of the room to get Morrigan's parents. Alone with Morrigan, Angus went to her side and took her hand in his, gazing down at her face. Her complexion in the light from this angle was yellowing.

"I will not let you die, Morrigan. I will save you, my beautiful flower."

When Paul and Victoria came into the room, Morrigan's mother cried out in surprise to see the girl's foot and hid her face in her husband's chest.

"The infection has tainted her blood. It is best if we remove the foot and allow some of the infected to bleed out," Angus said.

His voice was soft as he tried to offer his best explanation. He opened his arms to encircle them both and led them out of the room to talk further. Paul's eyes were glazed with unshed tears. He was trying to hold himself together, but he walked out so Morrigan didn't have to overhear. Once they were in the hall, the doctor looked toward the front of the house and nodded.

"Perhaps the library?" he said.

The couple followed him, afraid of any other bad news he might have for them. When they were gathered in the library he waited for them to sit before taking the seat across from them. He leaned forward and spoke with his "caring" voice. This was something he had to practice. He usually looked at patients with clinical eyes. The detachment from them being human had

grown over the years. He could cut into a person as easily as he could cut into a holiday ham. This time was different though. This time it was the object of his desire.

"Morrigan has come through a very dire situation. She is getting better. It may not look that way but she has made improvements, and we must keep an optimistic view of this."

Victoria nodded and buried her face in her apron to wipe the tears from her cheeks. Paul looked as though he'd already lost his daughter. He was pale in the face, and his eyes carried heavy bags beneath them from lack of sleep.

Angus looked down at the floor then pointed his gaze at Morrigan's mother. He needed to think of an excuse to get her to leave so he could talk to Paul in private.

"Mrs. Kingsley, could I trouble you to arrange for my dinner? I'll need all my energy to properly care for Morrigan."

Victoria's eyes came to life. She needed the distraction and a minute away so she perked up and forced an almost believable smile.

"Of course, doctor. I think we have some fresh bread, and Mrs. Frit can whip up something for you."

"That would be wonderful, thank you. I appreciate it."

He smiled just enough. It couldn't be too wide or else it wouldn't be appropriate for the graveness of their situation. A soft smile would give the illusion of empathy.

Victoria stood and exited to the kitchen, calling with a soft voice to Mrs. Frit. When the men were alone Angus looked at Paul and allowed a long minute to pass before he began.

"Mr. Kingsley, it is no mystery that I am very fond of Morrigan," he said.

Paul Kingsley came out of his otherworld stare with a blink and met the doctor's gaze. He was confused at first, but the words finally connected and became comprehensible to him.

"What? Oh, yes of course. You've been very kind to her."

Angus stood and took the seat beside him Victoria occupied before. He cleared his throat and straightened his posture while facing the girl's father. Paul was still confused and watched Angus curiously.

"I'm talking about a different fondness, Mr. Kingsley. I care for Morrigan very deeply. I'd like to care for her as more than just a patient."

Paul's features went through a few changes as he sorted through his emotions and processed it all. At first he was angry. His eyes were stern and his jaw was set. Who was this man to come to him so boldly? The more he let the thought sit, though, the more he warmed to it and his jaw softened, and the creases around his eyes followed. He turned then, mirroring Angus before he spoke again.

"Am I correct in assuming you are asking me for my daughter's hand in marriage, Mr. Wulfe?"

His words came out as a slow-moving train, testing each word before allowing them to be spoken. Angus could tell Paul was looking at him with different eyes now. As a father sizing up a prospective suitor for his daughter, and no longer a colleague.

"Yes, sir. I am."

Paul's eyes moved from Angus to the doorway, and the doctor turned to see Victoria standing there. Angus cleared his throat and looked down to the floor. He hadn't expected her back so soon. Gathering himself together he stood and offered her his seat.

"Mrs. Kingsley, please," he motioned to the chair beside Paul. "Sit down."

Victoria tried to hide her approval. She sat down and took her husband's hand in hers and looked between him and Angus.

"Yes?"

"Angus is asking—" Paul started.

"If I may?" Angus broke in. "Mrs. Kingsley, I was telling your husband that I am very fond of Morrigan and have been for some time. I would very much like to care for her as more than a patient. I'd like to care for her as husband."

Victoria could barely contain her excitement. Bless her materialistic heart. She was a good-hearted woman, but she did love her social status and anything that would benefit her.

"Oh! Paul, do you hear that?" she sang out.

Paul still looked unconvinced. He patted Victoria's hand and looked at her with love in his eyes. He wasn't prepared to discuss this with her. Angus could tell he was going through the same thought process he did in trying to get her to leave. Unable to come up with anything that would tear her away from this conversation he shook his head and offered her the truth.

"Victoria, I believe this conversation should be between Mr. Wulfe and I before we make any hasty decisions. I'm her father and I need to be certain of his intentions."

Victoria started to protest, but he raised a finger and with a gentle push, touched her lips with it.

"Please, Victoria. This is a father's duty," he whispered.

His wife sighed then conceded with a nod. She gave her husband's hand a squeeze full of hope that he'd approve, then smiled up at Angus.

"I'll see to your dinner, Mr. Wulfe." She gave them both a final look then left them in the library, closing the door behind her.

Paul watched his wife leave and when the door was shut, he turned to look at the doctor again. Angus stood, fidgeting. He felt awkward not knowing what the proper body language was for such an occasion. The scrutinizing gaze of Morrigan's father

reminded him of the way his own father looked at him after discovering him after … after what happened.

Paul finally broke the silence, motioning to the seat across from him. "Do you think this is an appropriate time to ask this of me, Mr. Wulfe?"

Angus noted how formal everything became and adjusted. "I don't think there's a time more appropriate than now, Mr. Kingsley."

Paul's brows rose in surprise to his response. "Why is that?"

"Morrigan is very sick. She will get better, but if she and I were betrothed I could devote more time to her, justifiably. Otherwise, in this time of tragedy, I could be called away. To be frank, Mr. Kingsley, there's no telling if I could come back in time to finish her care."

Angus had practiced this explanation over and over in his head for days. He anticipated Morrigan's father asking him this. He even thought about waiting for that reason, but he couldn't hold out any longer. He knew just how to get his prize. A father's love.

"Once I'm in contact with a patient who has positive signs of the Plague, I'm supposed to be quarantined." He paused for effect. "For thirty days or more." Angus let the words hang there in the air between them. He wanted Paul to work them through, counter them in his mind, search for ways around it. Angus knew he wouldn't be able to.

"I see," Paul said at last.

Angus leaned forward and whispered, keeping his eyes trained on the other man's, driving home the point. "I have a cure, Mr. Kingsley. When people find out I have the cure, they will flock to me. I'm obligated to treat them. If I treat them, there will be little left."

By the look in Paul's eyes, he got the point and hammered the nail into the proverbial coffin.

"I—I would like time to think about this," Paul stammered out.

Angus nodded with enthusiasm. "Yes, of course, Mr. Kingsley. Just understand time is of the essence."

The doctor stood and bowed, "I must get back to Morrigan. Hopefully, I will have your answer soon."

Paul nodded. "Yes. Yes, of course. Thank you, Angus."

And with that, they were back on a first name basis. With his heart racing in both joy and the thrill of the win, Angus exited the library, passing the beaming Mrs. Kingsley on his way to Morrigan's room.

Victoria offered a bow of her head and rushed past him into the library where her husband waited for her.

Since the doctor now had the negotiation of marriage in his corner, there was nothing to hold back. He could effectively keep the young Robert from interfering, and he had free range to treat Morrigan of her affliction. He compiled a list of things he'd need to turn the Kingley cellar into his laboratory, and sent Marshall to fetch the remainder of his things from his own home.

Marshall stared down at the list to conceal his shock at the unlikely engagement, and his fear for young Morrigan. He was convinced something was not right with the physician, but up until now he only needed to worry for himself.

"Marshall," the doctor snapped.

"Hm? Yes, I'm listening," Marshall responded.

"You look miles away."

Marshall tapped the list against his palm then faked a convincing smile, "Just making a mental inventory so we don't forget anything."

"Good. How long before you can have this all back here?"

Marshall tried to think of a way he could stall, but he was being put on the spot. Someone with Angus' intelligence would only make any excuse suspicious.

"I shall have it all to you by sundown tomorrow. I'll have my horse readied then make my departure."

Angus nodded and started to collect some of his things to carry downstairs. "Do not tarry. Safe travels, then, yeah?"

Marshall feigned another smile and headed out to the stables. His heart raced as if he'd been chased by a man-eating lion. He had to think of something, and it had to be fast. Tucking the list into his satchel, he waited for his horse and went through every possibility in his head.

By the time Marshall's horse was prepared he was still trying to formulate a scheme and coming up with nothing. Staring at the large, black eye of his mount he could see his own worried reflection peering back at him. He pinched the bridge of his nose between his forefinger and thumb then let out a sigh. He still had the duration of the trip to come up with a plan. Pushing up on the stirrup, he hefted himself onto the horse's back and gave its flanks a dig of his boot heel sending them both on their way.

***

Victoria and Morrigan were alone in the girl's bedchambers no more than ten minutes before the hallway was filled with the mournful cry only a girl clinging to life could make. With what little strength Morrigan had in her body, she flung her arm out and knocked over a bowl of soup.

Her mother just delivered what she thought to be happy news to her daughter. Victoria stood there, bewildered at Morrigan's reaction.

"Morrigan! What has gotten into you?" she cried.

The woman went down to her knees to mop up the mess and shook her head. "This doctor has been more than generous to you! He is a respectable man and you should be both grateful and earnest in accepting his proposal."

Morrigan turned her head and sobbed silently despite how it made her head drum with more pain. She lay there wishing the sickness would come in the night to sweep her away. Her mother cleaned the mess on the floor and chastised her while Morrigan's thoughts drifted to Robert.

Does he know? She thought to herself. *Does he even care?*

Morrigan knew she felt a reciprocated fondness from Robert. The two had grown so close, and now she was betrothed to the man she feared the most.

"Morrigan! Are you even listening to me? He has a cure, love." Her mother's voice lowered to a softer tone. "You can be right as rain soon if you'll just be a good girl and show him some kindness."

When Morrigan wouldn't look at her, Victoria's jaw tightened and she gave her daughter a disappointed shake of her head. She couldn't understand why her daughter was being this way. She was always a stubborn girl, but this was going too far.

"You will not make your father, or this family, look bad. You will do your duty and behave like a young lady," she lectured. "Not a spoiled princess!"

Morrigan took in a deep, ragged breath. Her lungs burned and felt heavy with pressure, as if she were under water trying to breath. The air came into the soft, irritated tissue slowly

before she exhaled. She was back in the better place she created in her mind. Her mother's voice drifted to a distant cloud in her imaginary sky until the birds and the sound of a babbling brook rushed through her. It was here she would remain until the nightmare ended, she decided. She would either wake up and this would all be over, or she would sink into the icy depths of Death's grey waters.

In the middle of Victoria's lecture the door opened and Angus entered.

"Hello, Victoria," he said watching her. "How is my Morrigan doing?"

"Hello, Angus," Victoria said.

Her voice changed with a sudden shift. It was now light and cheerful. Morrigan still lie there in silence but she could hear her mother fidget with the bowl and wooden spoon that was tossed to the floor.

"Oh, she's doing well! Much better than before. In fact, I am sure she cannot wait to begin planning for her big day!" Victoria chimed with over enthusiasm.

Angus stood in quiet observation, even allowing a single brow to rise. "Is that so?"

Victoria swept her gaze back and forth between the doctor and Morrigan before wiping her hand on the smock she wore.

"I was just sharing the exciting news with her," she explained. "I should go and get cleaned up now," she added.

"Indeed," Angus began before he stepped to the side, still holding the door. "I wish for Morrigan to rest, Victoria. Even news of a new engagement can be too much excitement for her in her condition."

Victoria smiled, but Angus could see it was to mask her nervousness. The power he felt from making her feel so small

growled to life within him. It infused him with a rush of adrenaline that made him revel in euphoria.

"As you wish, doctor."

Morrigan's mother picked up her things and rushed out wearing the hot sting of embarrassment on her cheeks. When she was over the threshold, Angus pushed the door shut and made his way toward Morrigan. He took slow deliberate steps, watching and measuring her breathing. She was awake. He could tell by the way her eyes jumped beneath her eyelids at the creaks of the floorboards beneath his feet.

"Hello, Morrigan," Angus said with a soft voice.

The tone was almost unrecognizable to him. Never, since he could remember, did he care for anyone like he cared for the fragile girl he looked down at. It was a strange feeling for him. He wasn't sure if it was his own feelings or if it belonged to someone else. Angus looked over the girl's dainty hand lying against the sheet. It was pale and small, and he desired to hold it.

So long had he obsessed over her from a distance that he never realized what being so close to her would stir inside of him. Angus felt nothing for most of his life remotely close to kindness and … love … as he felt in that moment. The juxtaposition of emotions threatened to tear him apart right where he stood.

"You are so beautiful, my love," he whispered.

He took another step closer and pulled her hand into his. Her fingers were cold. Like a worried nursemaid, he pulled the blankets up to her chin and leaned closer to tuck her in. It was then he noticed the tear filling the corner of her eye grow and slide down the side of her face to the pillow beneath her head.

She is repulsed by me.

The monster was furious and rattled at the cages of his mind. He had to control it. He had to force it back down into the cellar where it belonged before it unleashed its wrath upon the beautiful Morrigan.

I will not let you harm her!

The monster growled and shook the cages louder, filling his mind with a painful cacophony of sound.

She will learn to love us!

When the beast continued, Angus thrashed himself on the sides of his temple with the heel of his palm several times until pain won over. The beast slithered back into its dark hold. When he opened his eyes, Morrigan was staring at him in terror. Angus bolted upright, his posture now rigid and straight. Morrigan said nothing, but she didn't have to. Her expression said it all.

Fighting back the panic the doctor spoke in a hushed, soothing tone. "Everything will be just fine. I'm going to take care of you."

He gave her hand a squeeze. "I can fix you, Morrigan."

Angus went to the table where he began mixing together powders and herbs.

Morrigan didn't dare scream or utter a sound. All she could do was stare at the horrific tools all laid out to the side. Each blade's razor sharp smile glistened against the dim light coming in. Is that a … saw?

When Angus faced her again he saw the reaction to the instruments. Her eyes grew double their size, and her lip trembled. Her fingers were kneading at the bed, and he could see by the rise and fall of her chest she was finding the act of breathing harder than before.

"Oh, no dear! Please don't let those frighten you. I will not—" He paused and sat beside her on the bed. "I would never hurt you."

Morrigan recoiled by instinct when he got close. Angus' heart, which was normally cold as iron, clanged within his chest like a mission bell. He held her medicinal drink in his hands and stared into the liquid.

"Morrigan, I know your mother upset you earlier with the news of our engagement, but I assure you there will be no more talk of that while you are recovering." His voice was quiet and gentle.

Morrigan's body seemed to release some its rigidity in relief. Her eyes darted to the tools, and then to the drink in is hand.

"The tools are frightening you. I will have them removed, presently."

Angus handed her the drink, careful not to make too sudden a move. The young woman looked at the cup with uncertainty then looked back up at Angus' eyes. Her brows furrowed. She'd never seen him so close before without wanting to crawl out of her skin. For certain she'd never seen him so doting and warm. He still held the cup outward in offering. He was not trying to be forceful or make her drink it like her nurse or her mother. He was giving her a choice to accept it.

She didn't have enough strength to reach for the cup with both hands, but Angus took the gesture as a huge victory. He extended his hands toward her until they met, and then he helped her bring it to her lips. The taste was bitter and strong, making it hard to keep from coughing it out. With a fast hand, Angus brought his handkerchief to her mouth and dabbed the liquid before it could soil her chin or clothing.

Morrigan watched him as he hand-fed her, realizing she might be able to get out of this! All she had to do was get well enough and regain her strength. If she tricked herself into believing she was warming up to Angus, he'd let down his

guard. Despite the sickness it caused to her stomach, she offered a small smile and leaned forward for more of the drink.

"Thank you," she said, clearing her sore throat.

The words came out as a raspy croak, and the pain made her wince.

Angus lowered the cup. He was either in disbelief or shock at her sudden change in demeanor.

"You're welcome, Morrigan."

He continued to assist her with the medicine and the two spoke quietly for an hour until Morrigan's eyes grew heavy. Angus stood and smiled down at her.

"I should leave you to sleep."

When he turned, Morrigan's hand reached out for his wrist.

"Will you read to me? I … don't want to be alone yet."

The doctor was caught off guard by her request, and his eyes softened from their normal stern, set appearance to betray his vulnerability.

Eyes are the window to the soul, Morrigan reminded herself, even if it is a dark and hidden cavern.

What normally revolted her, was now her power. It would take time, but she was strong-willed. Still holding onto Angus' wrist, she closed her eyes and smiled before whispering in a sleepy tone, "Read to me."

CHAPTER 13: BAD MEDICINE

The sun was beginning to fall below the horizon when Angus finished administering the medicine to Morrigan. He conducted another examination of her condition. She was breathing better and in a sound sleep. Angus sat down on the side of her bed and brushed the tip of his pinky over the back of her hand. She was far away somewhere in a deep, unconscious state. He watched her eyes tick back and forth behind her lids until they began to slow down and fall into a steady, dream-state rhythm. This was good. She'd be able to get some much needed rest.

Recalling the night's event, Angus was confident he made a breakthrough with Morrigan. She seemed more open to him and dare he say, even accepting. If he could win her heart it would be worth everything he's gone through to get to this point. She would finally be his, in the truest sense.

Angus took care not to wake the girl with a slow retraction of his touch. He stood and walked to the door, avoiding the creaky boards as much as possible. When he looked over his shoulder, he could see she was still sound asleep. He whispered goodnight to her and left. There was still one more problem he had to contend with.

The nurse sleeping in a chair outside Morrigan's room opened her eyes as soon as Angus emerged. Standing, she tugged her shawl snug across her shoulders. In this section of the house, the fireplace's warmth did not reach where she was. Angus thought to himself the woman should learn to layer better if she was going to keep from dying of a freeze.

When the worrisome nurse approached him, Angus lifted a hand to stop her.

"She will sleep through the night," he whispered.

The nurse smiled and nodded.

"You should catch up on sleep, too. She will need to be cleaned and redressed as soon as she wakes."

"Are you leaving, sir?" the nurse asked.

"No. I will be in the cellar putting together my laboratory. I am not to be disturbed for any reason."

The firmness in his voice sent another kind of chill through the woman, and she tugged again at the thin material of her shawl.

"Aye, sir. I will see to it then."

Angus had no desire to assert an awkward silence on the nurse. Now that he'd made headway with Morrigan the taste for anything less made his stomach tighten.

"Good evening, then," he said and disappeared down the hall like a spider in the dark.

Angus could feel the woman's eyes watching him until he was out of sight. When he was sure he wouldn't be noticed, he slipped out and went to fetch his horse. With a snap of the reigns he and the mount raced toward his home.

***

Marshall was at their home giving directions to several of the men who were carrying Angus' belongings to the carriage. Box after box of glass vials and medical equipment tinkled against one another like chimes in the wind. He was lucky to find the few men he did; the entire village was near death. He secured the cloth around his face and held an additional layer from his hand against his nose and mouth as a precaution.

"Be careful, or I'll take the damages out of your earnings," Marshall barked.

As the men began fastening the boxes and locking them in, Marshall walked to the front door. "Finish what you're doing then take an hour to eat and rest. We'll be heading out afterwards."

The men all nodded and kept their heads down, continuing with the task.

Marshall walked into the house and did a final check to be sure nothing was left behind when he came to the kitchen. The large wooden door to the cellar looked even more ominous now that the house was empty. He stood staring at it in the half-lit room. The flames of the candles cast their dancing shadows over it, and the memories laced with doubts came flooding back.

He remembered once again the uneasy feeling he'd get walking past the cellar and how peculiar Angus acted around it. He recalled the strange noises that reminded him of a tortured cat. Marshall had tried to listen at the door but couldn't make anything out for certain. Angus spent days and weeks in there alone—or so he thought. When the Plague became worse, Angus would lock himself away for the mandatory one month's quarantine. That's when his behavior grew more worrisome. He did not display the same symptoms of the others who had come out of lengthy isolations. With Angus, he seemed to enjoy it quite a bit.

There were rumors some of the healers suffered from small bouts of madness. Angus never seemed bothered at all. In fact, he seemed to crave the isolation even more. Something in the lair at the bottom of the stairs seemed to call to him.

Marshall's mind swam with all kinds of theories while he stood in the dark, empty house. Curiosity was getting the better of him. He gave the kitchen a once over and discovered a meat tenderizer on the preparation table. He went over to it and

wrapped his fingers around the handle then turned back to the cellar door.

"You do know what they say about curiosity?"

Marshall could barely complete his sudden breath of surprise when a rope lassoed his neck and cut short his oxygen. His eyes widened, and the mallet fell to the floor so his fingers could grasp at the fibers tightening around his windpipe. Angus came around to the front of him. He was staring deep into his eyes, and Marshall could see the emptiness behind them.

The two men struggled. Marshall's oxygen was cut off, putting him at a huge disadvantage in the fight for his life. Angus' large hands tightened their grip causing immense pressure to bear down on his victim. Marshall was losing consciousness. His eyes bulged from their sockets. He had to do something or this was the end of his story. Before his life could be snuffed out, he jerked back and dragged Angus with him to interrupt his balance. Once he built up enough momentum he tried to kick out one of Angus' legs but the good doctor was too agile and strong. Picking Marshall up by his neck, Angus slammed the other man against the wall with a deep growl.

"Your life is slipping away, Marshall. How much longer can you hold on?" he hissed.

Marshall's feet kicked and dug into the floor with frantic desperation. He could taste blood in his mouth. Just as the light was about to go out behind his eyes Angus released him and sent a fist crashing against the side of his temple. Marshall went down like a rag doll.

It seemed like hours before he woke, but in truth he had no concept of how much time had passed. For all he knew it had been mere minutes. Marshall attempted to move his head to get a bearing on where he was, but the instant he turned his head he was overwrought with nausea. His brain throbbed with a tiny

blacksmith pounding to get out of his skull. The man lay there completely still until the wave of sickness passed over him. He closed his eyes trying focus on his breathing and the fluttering of his heart against his ribcage.

"I will fix you something for your headache." Angus' voice came from someplace to his right.

Marshall's heart thumped a few extra times in reaction to Angus' voice. Stay calm, lad, he said to himself.

Marshall took a long, slow breath through his nose then let it out in a five count before repeating.

"Very good," Angus said in a cheerful tone. "I'm glad you picked up something during your time with me."

The chiding from his former partner did nothing to help Marshall calm down. The physician's next words were chosen carefully. He knew how to get to Marshall and could pluck from the air all the right elements to concoct the perfect mixture of desperation and fear. He preyed on the man's weaknesses with surgical precision.

"I thought to kill you off several times. Each time I came close, I stayed my hand when I recalled those few redeeming qualities that became convenient. You can thank yourself for being such a loyal companion. That is, if you make it out of this alive."

Marshall could hear the preparation of one of the doctor's infamous medicinal drinks. Trying not to be too obvious, he made an attempt to move but as he suspected, he was tethered.

"Come now, old friend," Angus called over his shoulder. "You really didn't think I'd be that careless."

"One could hope," Marshall responded through gritted teeth and strained larynx.

"Yes, there's that, I suppose. But where has hope gotten any of us?"

Angus moved to Marshall's side and held a spoon to his mouth. Marshall did not accept. With a sigh, the doctor lowered the cup.

"I've already told you. I haven't decided to kill you, yet. You may still have a chance to save yourself. In order to accept the negotiation, you must be of clear mind. We wouldn't want another tiff between acquaintances, would we?"

Angus lifted the spoon in offering again. Marshall didn't have time to decide. Opening his eyes, he peered up at the blurry shape that was the doctor.

"That's a good lad," Angus said.

Bringing the spoon to Marshall's mouth, he allowed the foul-smelling concoction to pour past his lips a few drops at a time.

"I am admittedly disappointed, though," Angus began again. "I thought we had a solid understanding of boundaries."

Marshall forced the liquid past his tongue and tried not to spit it back up. It burned his bruised and raw throat when he swallowed.

"Gently, now. You'll be healing for some time from that nasty wound."

Angus dunked the spoon again and brought another dose to his new patient's mouth.

"It's hard to look the other way when there is no trust," Marshall finally croaked out.

His voice was barely recognizable even to himself. It was hoarse and scratched as it strained through the swelling in his neck. He had to clear his throat a few times before taking another sip from the spoon.

"We had a professional relationship, Marshall. We were never friends."

Friends. Looking back, Marshall could see a clearer picture of their "relationship." He always thought Angus was cold and distant but Marshall thought it was just his personality, and he tried not to judge him for it.

Because …

Because he thought they were friends. Odd friends, yes. But "friends" nonetheless.

It dawned on him through another mouthful of vile herbs, and who knew what else was in the gritty tea, Angus had no friends.

"I thought we were," Marshall swallowed. "So I'm sure you can understand my injury when I discovered you were holding back from me."

The spoon lowered again out of Marshall's reach. For this he was thankful. Another spoonful right now and he might have vomited.

"Holding back what?"

Marshall released an inward breath of relief. Yes, keep talking!

"I don't know. Treasure? Money?" he gave pause. "Women?"

Angus let out a laugh and set the bowl down. He leaned forward, pressing his weight against his knees.

"You thought I wasn't sharing my toys!"

Marshall shrugged and tried to look as sheepish as possible, and guilty of envy.

"I figured you had your eyes on Morrigan, so why shouldn't I get to share in the others. You already had the most magnificent of all the beauties."

Angus set the medicine on the table and pretended to sort through the items that lay strewn across the top. He did not trust the merchant any more. Not that he did before but he did enjoy having the loyalty and service of the man. It was a convenience for him. The doctor contemplated whether it was worth it to keep him around or if it was best to get rid of him and start over. Loyalty was a strong, desired trait in any of the few relationships Angus had. If he could not trust the other person, he had no use for them.

"I'm not confident I can trust you any longer, Marshall," Angus said, voicing his concern.

To nail his point home, he made sure the other man could see him caress the edge of one of the dull blades he'd placed among the tools intended for Marshall's demise.

"Angus," Marshall said in his sincerest tone, "I never meant to break your trust in me. I've been your friend—"

Marshall paused. Angus didn't consider them friends. He had to choose another word.

"—acquaintance. I've been a reliable and faithful acquaintance for years. An honest associate in all our dealings. Does that not earn me a solitary pass for my unintentional transgression toward you?"

The fact Angus was still listening to him and not separating his limbs from their host gave Marshall a small bit of hope. Perhaps he could make it through this alive.

"Please, Angus, sir. Allow me to prove once more I am still that man."

The doctor turned and regarded the man. Marshall never felt more stripped of all defenses as he did now. The doctor's eyes felt like they not only penetrated the darkness but through his soul. Marshall had never been a godly man, but in those quiet, deciding moments he prayed for Angus' mercy.

"You seek my forgiveness then?" Angus finally responded.

"Yes. Yes, please. I will do whatever you ask."

Angus smiled. A gesture made more sinister with the animated shadows of candlelight dueling with the darkness on his features. It made Marshall's heart leap into his throat.

"Then let's discuss penance."

The doctor was already moving forward as he spoke and Marshall's bowels watered. He could not imagine in his worst moment what horrors the doctor could conceive of to atone for his fall from grace.

But he knew he was about to find out.

Watching the mad doctor approach, Marshall could see the short, curved blade glistening in the candle light. Angus brought one of the candlesticks over and displayed the sharp edge.

"Are you a man of your word, Marshall?"

Marshall's jaw chattered despite his efforts to maintain a level of calm.

"Y—Yes, sir. I am."

"That is good," Angus purred out in a slow drawl.

The doctor passed the blade over the tiny flame of the candle, heating it up.

"I demand recompense for what you've done," Angus announced.

Marshall's eyes opened so wide they ached. He watched the other man move along the table he was strapped to and stand by his ankles. The doctor observed his helpless prey like a hungry wolf, true to his surname. Marshall tried not to whimper or let out a cry, but it filled his throat regardless of his effort. Each movement Angus made was slow and deliberate so Marshall could follow along without missing anything. The

doctor then extended his arm way back facing the tip of the blade toward the ceiling.

"Are you going to give it to me?" Angus asked.

Marshall's prayers turned into screams of silent fear within his thoughts. He willed his muscles to obey and give a convincing performance. If he was lucky, Angus would give him a few cuts and be done. The longer the blade hovered above them both, the more his panic grew until finally Angus brought his blade down in a swift arc slicing through Marshall's britches. The material fell away, exposing the man to the cool air around them.

The merchant let out a cry of anticipation and terror. He felt the precision of the blade skate along his outer thigh barely nicking him. The momentum of the blade's direction caused Marshall's pant leg to flap away from his skin.

Angus stood in silence for a moment. He wanted Marshall to process everything he did. When Marshall stopped screaming he was panting. With his hands still tethered he jerked down at the rope wanting to protect his groin. His eyes were wide and wild as he thrashed about. When he calmed down Marshall realized there was very little pain. He let out a groan, and his head fall back to the table with a heavy thud.

Angus remained quiet and patient. He waited for the mental process to take its toll. Marshall began to sob then laugh until he became hysterical. When Angus' patient was adequately distracted, the doctor gripped the other man's testicles. Marshall's laughter came to an immediate silence. Staring up into the abyss of Angus' eyes, he watched as the doctor lifted his arm high above his head and brought the scalpel down, carrying with it the sting and tear of his scrotum. Shock held his scream a prisoner.

The skin of Marshall's scrotum split open and with a firm squeeze of Angus' fingers, the meat within the sac was extracted to the chorus of Marshall's released screams and violent retching. Vomit flew from his lips like a fount while the doctor continued his vice-like grip, ensuring the man didn't bleed out. A few splashes of spittle stained the apron he wore but he was never bothered by it. He seemed to have all the time in the world.

In the meantime, Marshall flopped and twitched on the table in his own excrement and bile.

The doctor finally lifted the bulbous prize to show Marshall and watched victoriously as the man choked on his sobs. Marshall flailed against his binds and tried to reach out for Angus, but it was no use. Marshall strained his neck, trying to pull his body off the table's surface; the chords on either side of his throat were stretched to their limit, and his abdomen burning in pain before his head fell back.

The exertion of all his strength induced a wave of fatigue. He had no fight left within him. Docile as a lamb, he continued to cry in utter silence until he slipped into the oblivion of unconsciousness. Angus let the testicle drop inside a small bowl at his side with a wet plop. Then began the tedious task of stitching the man up. Angus used several rags from his tool table to mop up all the blood between each suture. When Marshall came to again Angus smiled at him.

"There, see? It was not so painful, was it?" Angus asked in a soft whisper.

Marshall's jaw was clenched so tight he thought he'd break all his teeth.

Speaking through gritted teeth he hissed out, "You're fucking mad!"

The pain washed over Marshall immediately causing his head to fall back yet another time.

Angus nodded and shrugged non-committedly, "This could be true, but you should remain still so I can continue to stitch you up correctly. You don't want to pop these, believe me."

Angus then peered at him and smiled from between Marshall's legs. The abusive hands which had just inflicted damage were now healing and correcting with the gentlest touch. He wrapped the stitch thread around the other, then pulled back and repeated the motion. It took him nearly an hour to finish. The doctor finally took a few steps back and admired his handy work.

"Quit blubbering, Marshall. You'll be fine," Angus said. "You're such a woman. Oh! Maybe I cut the wrong one. Perhaps we should take the other one as well?"

Angus pretended to move toward Marshall once more, but the man flinched. Still in his binds, he was unable to go far. The doctor chuckled.

"We have an understanding, yes?" he asked when Marshall went quiet.

Marshall could only nod.

"Good. Because if I feel I cannot trust you again, or you give me reason to be cross with you?" He held up the scalpel again. "I'll take more than your left nut. Are we abundantly clear?"

Marshall nodded again.

"Perfect!" Angus declared.

The scalpel dropped onto the metal tray with a loud clank. Marshall recoiled, drawing in another satisfied grin from the doctor, who was now washing his hands in a bowl of water.

There were tiny droplets of blood spattered along the sleeves of his shirt that made Marshall sick to his stomach.

Angus stared at his craftsmanship before he began to apply more rags as a compress. He mopped up the blood then poured cold, clean water over Marshall's lower extremities. The merchant yelped and shivered from both the cold and the shock. The doctor paid him no attention and continued to bathe him. When he was done, he removed the tattered clothing and replaced them with clean, fresh ones.

CHAPTER 14: WHAT HAVE I BECOME

In the morning, Marshall awoke with a terrible headache and pain in his groin from his unfortunate surgical procedure. He was lying beneath a heavy wool blanket, still shivering from cold. His mouth was as dry as the desert. When he tried to look around his head began to swim until he felt thick saliva pooling in his mouth. He rolled over just as Angus came into the room with food. Even though Marshall was starving, the smell made him ill and his stomach churned, pushing the bile past his throat and onto the floor at Angus' feet.

"Good morning, Marshall. How are we today?"

Marshall debated whether to answer at all, but at this point he knew he was at Angus' disposal. Keeping him talking was the best option. He looked around the dark, windowless room. Angus made sure there was no way for him to escape. Even though any attempt by him would be fatal. He'd die before he got too far with his wound. As if to remind him, the stinging between his legs caused an involuntary flexion of his muscles into a fetal position.

"Is it morning? I can't tell. There are no windows."

Angus chuckled with a soft shake of his shoulders.

"It is. Though, just barely."

Pouring water into a cup and setting it down, he moved toward Marshall's side. "I'm going to untether you now. If you do anything foolish I will kill you."

Marshall nodded. His desire for talking left with the reminder of the danger he was in.

The doctor cut the ropes then turned, allowing his back to face Marshall, adding further insult to injury. He was completely unafraid of the merchant.

"My head is swimming. I do not think I can eat or drink," Marshall explained.

Angus turned with cup in hand, "Oh yes. That's the laudanum. I had to make sure you slept deep enough throughout the night."

Extending his hand, Angus offered the drink to Marshall. "I took the liberty of preparing you a medicinal drink to counteract it."

Marshall was wary but accepted the drink, bringing it to his lips. If it were poison he no longer cared. He was practically a Eunuch, now. After several deep swallows, the drink was gone and he handed the doctor his cup.

"Eat. We will head back in quarter of an hour." Angus' voice was sharp. It was not a request.

Marshall had no idea how he'd be expected to make the trip in his current condition but he knew he didn't have a choice.

***

The ride back to Morrigan's home was long and arduous. Marshall felt every bump in the uneven surface of the dirt path. The swaying and rocking of the carriage behind them pulled at his stitches, and he could feel the wound growing red and inflamed. If he was lucky, he'd get an infection and die quickly. He'd prefer that option over a life of servitude to the monster riding beside him.

Angus noticed Marhsall's grimacing and quiet grunts. The doctor laughed on the inside but kept a stoic façade while steering the carriage and horses. Every few miles or so, he'd see Marshall found a position that offered some relief, and he'd give a pull on one of the reigns to throw the wagon off again. The old

wooden wheels bounced over the edges of another uneven path in cruel fashion.

What felt like days, was in truth, half as long. When they arrived, Marshall had never been so happy to see the Kingsleys' home before. Angus rolled slowly in and pulled on the reigns. The horses came to a stop, and Marshall's agitation overcame him.

"Please, Angus! This has gone on long enough. You've wo—"

"Shut up," Angus snapped.

Marshall was about to protest, but Angus dismounted and took off in a run toward the house. The merchant sat there in momentary confusion before he climbed down with care. Angus was already near the house when his pace quickened to a full on sprint.

Marshall shook his head. "Aye, that's not going to happen. My runnin' days be over."

There was no speed to Marshall's pace as he followed. He was pretty sure the snails in the piles of leaves were beating him. What could he do anyway in his condition? Still, he leaned down and picked up a thick branch, just in case. He hobbled along, stripping the smaller branches away as he went. Angus was at the house, yelling for Paul and Victoria. When no one responded, the doctor burst through the front door.

Marshall stopped where he was, "What is he going on about?"

He didn't see anything awry so he continued forward about a hundred paces when the stench hit him like an invisible wall. It was as if Death was hung up to dry. Marshall blanched and covered his nose and mouth with the crook of his arm, but the scent had invaded his nasal cavity. Putrid air like a diseased,

festering wound wrought with infection passed through his sleeve, and Marshall gagged until he had to spit.

When he gathered his composure, Marshall hobbled a little more quickly toward the Kingsley home. As soon as he reached the doorway, he could hear the doctor's anguished howls.

Despite the immense pain, Marshall walked down the hallway toward Morrigan's bed chamber. The smell thickened, growing more intolerable the closer he got. A few times he had to stop and force back the gag reflex threatening to empty his stomach.

Marshall stumbled into Morrigan's doorway and almost fell to his knees. With only the door to cling to he saw a site of horrors in front of him. Morrigan's mother, father, and her attending nursemaid were all splayed across the floor with bite marks all over them and chunks of flesh missing. The softer portions of their abdomen were dug into as if by giant rats with red ribbon trails along the skin of their arms.

When Marshall looked into the face of Victoria his entire body was chilled to the bone. Her eyes were missing completely, and her mouth looked gnawed upon.

"By God, what …?" Marshall could form no other words or thoughts.

Angus stood, peering around him, "I cannot find Morrigan."

The merchant was still fixated on the half-eaten woman's face on the floor in front of him. The doctor strode past him and began checking in every room, and every closet. Marshall could hear him on the other side of the house calling out to her.

"Morrigan! Morrigan! It's safe, please come out!"

Marshall stumbled out of the bedroom to find Angus. He was caught between two monsters; the one who mutilated him, and the one who massacred Morrigan's entire family.

The two men scoured the house top to bottom and then stood before the cellar door. Angus stared at it in disbelief. Marshall watched him, then he too stared at the door.

"Angus?" Marshall's voice called out.

"Please," Angus said, mostly to himself. "Dear God, please. No …"

Angus looked afraid, which in turn terrified Marshall.

"What is it, Angus?" Marshall asked, the pitch of his voice rising.

The doctor stepped to the door that hung by a hinge. Angus let his head drop. The merchant watched on in silence.

"It was a simple task," Angus whispered. "Keep the door locked, and do not go in."

Marshall took a step back. Anything that would make Angus this unsettled was bad news. He had no idea what to expect coming out or going in.

Angus pushed aside the broken door with as little sound as he could. The air rushing out at them bathed them in a scent so rancid Marshall swayed and grabbed for the wall. Angus' knees buckled, and he purged the content of his stomach. When he was able to stand again, the two men were assaulted by an army of flies. There were so many it was hard to see. Marshall batted at them, but it was no use. Several flew up into his nostrils making it hard to breathe.

When the swarm dwindled, Angus went down the stairs first, followed by Marshall. The doctor's measured steps led the way into the blackness of the cellar. The only sound they could hear was the howl of the wind against the windows and throughout the hallway. Both of them were nearly all the way to

the bottom when Angus came to an abrupt stop. Marshall's heart galloped in his chest, and the sound of blood rushing against his eardrums began to drown out the wind.

Angus did not speak. Instead he motioned for Marshall to turn his attention toward the farthest wall. There, a shadow that was clearly of a female form lingered, swaying to and fro in a strange kind of dance.

Marshall's instincts told him this was all wrong. They told him they should run and board up whatever, or whomever, was standing there and throw away the key. Every fiber of his being was on high alert, yet he was frozen still. Feet like lead were sealed firmly on the stair. His spine seemed to grow roots that planted him where he was. Even his voice betrayed him, crawling to the back of his mind and down into the pits of his bowels.

Angus took another step down and waited.

The shadow stopped and turned around. A figure began to emerge from the corner where a single candle was lit. She was nude and filthy. Marshall felt shameful even looking at her, so he turned his head to keep from staring at her while keeping her in his peripherals. She was weeping. Marshall could hear the sound as it bounced off the stone walls and echoed in their direction.

It was Angus who broke the silence once her face came into the half-light.

"Morrigan?" He asked with a strange timidity to his tone.

The weeping stopped, and the girl let out a sob. Angus took another step toward her making Marshall want to reach out and pull him back. He continued to watch while keeping his hand vice-locked on the large branch he'd been holding since he came in.

"Please …" the girl whispered. "Help … me."

Angus rushed to her just as Morrigan collapsed. She fell, unconscious, into his arms.

CHAPTER 15: BEAUTIFUL MONSTER

2 Days Prior

Paul was lying awake in bed when he heard a rustling outside his door. The hour was late. Everyone was in their bed asleep, by now but he had been wide awake for hours staring at the window. Ever since the night Morrigan saw a man outside her window Paul found it difficult to rest. Most nights he sat up after Victoria fell asleep, rifle in hand, listening for intruders or staring out across the property. This night, the sound came from right outside his door, and Paul moved slowly toward it.

He could make out an argument ensuing in hushed whispers, but he couldn't make out the words from his position behind the door. Tucking the rifle under his armpit, he reached out for the doorknob and paused. He hesitated, listening closer to hear what was being said or who the voices belonged to, but they were so low it was impossible.

Though he used his rifle many times before and was a fine hunter, Paul never had to use it in self-defense before. With the safety of his family at stake, his palms began to sweat, and his saliva grew thick on his tongue. He took several deep breaths to steel his nerves and then, with a fast twist of the knob, he threw the door open aiming the rifle at the faces of Robert and the stable boy who stood beside him. His blood turned to ice when his mind processed their faces.

Paul took his aim away and whispered angrily, "I could've killed you both! What are you doing?"

The stable boy's face turned ghost white, and Robert tossed his hands over his head. When Paul dropped the barrel, Robert leaned over and breathed a sigh of relief, holding his hand over his heart.

"Apologies, sir. Little John and I came to tell you that Angus has left," Robert whispered back.

Paul pushed his way into the small, now crowded, hallway before glancing over his shoulder at his wife who was still sleeping. In order to not raise alarm, he closed the door with care as to not disturb her. Once the door was secure he turned back to the two and prodded them for more information.

"Left *where*? What happened?"

The stable boy's color was beginning to come back, his features were pink again but he was still fidgeting and jittery. "Sir, I was only doing as instructed. I've done nothin' wrong! The horse belonged to the doctor, I swear it!"

"Shh! Lower your voice, boy," Paul chastised. "Where did the doctor go?"

"He did'nae say, sir. He woke me with a slap to me ear and told me to ready his horse. I just did as he ordered."

Robert's jaw clenched, and he broke in, "Mr. Kingsley, Morrigan has been …" He paused trying to find the appropriate words. "She's been up and behaving strangely."

Paul tried to take in everything. The update about Morrigan caused him to push past Robert and the boy where he made a beeline to his daughter's room. The nursemaid was already there drenching the girl in cold water from rags. When she saw Paul enter, she explained right away in a nervous rambling of words that all seemed to mash together which he could barely understand.

"I came in to check on her, and she was red as a beet, sir. I touched her cheek, and she felt like she was on fire. She's got blisters along her lips and arms."

"Daddy … Please," Morrigan wailed. "Make it stop! I'm burning!" Robert stepped into the room then backed up against the wall in shock. Morrigan resembled a skeleton with thin,

stretched skin. There was no muscle or fat padding the layers as it lay against her bones. The blisters on her arms and around her mouth were dark red, some as large as an egg. The stable boy took off running at the very sight of her. He'd seen the outcome of those afflicted with this disease and no doubt lost some of his own family to it.

Paul walked to the bed and leaned in to brush Morrigan's hair away from her face. The gentle gesture caused a clump to fall out between his fingers. Looking up, the nurse stared back at him, both knowing that was a bad sign.

"The doctor left to his cellar hours ago," she continued in a hushed voice. "He said not to disturb him. She's not had any medicine since then."

"Not to be disturbed?" Paul's voice rose in anger. "Well he's gone completely from the house!"

"Beggin' pardon, sir?" the nurse said, still trying to keep Morrigan still.

"He's left us!" Paul shouted.

Morrigan cried out at the shouting and began to kick her legs in pain. More enraged now that the situation had progressed, and the doctor would leave her in such a way, he stormed out of the room. Robert followed close behind. He had no idea what help he could be to Paul, but this was his family and he'd stand by them.

The noise had finally disturbed the sleeping Victoria, who snuck down the hall holding her flickering candle in one hand and clutching her blanket around her shoulders with the other.

"Paul, what is it? What's happening?"

"The *Doctor* is nowhere to be found. Left here hours ago!" He bellowed.

He didn't stop to explain further and continued past his dumbfounded wife with Robert trailing. She fell into step behind them.

"What are you going to do, Paul?" she asked.

"I'm going down to see if he's left any medicine. Morrigan's burning up in there!"

Torn between her husband and her daughter, Victoria finally decided she was no use behind the men, and she went down the hallway to be with Morrigan.

Paul pulled at the cellar door, which seemed like it had been locked from the inside. No matter how hard he tugged at it, it wouldn't budge.

"There's another way," Robert offered. "Follow me."

The two men ran outside, and Robert showed him a hidden entrance.

"In case of invasions, it's a quick way to get out. Morrigan and I used to sneak in and snatch fresh rolls from the kitchen together." Robert's voice trailed off at the end.

"She's not gone, yet, Robert," Paul said.

The young man stared up at her father and nodded. "Let's go then." The two climbed down through the entrance and waited for their eyes to adjust to the dimness of the cellar. Robert lit one of the candles he found and held it out before them. There was no one there. Boxes of Angus' stuff lined the walls and glass jars were stacked on the table. Small leather pouches of herbs were neatly lined up with a small, handwritten label that said, *Morrigan*.

"Here," Robert announced holding one up.

Paul looked over the glass jars filled with a strange smelling liquid.

"What did he mix them with? These?" Her father held up the jar and took a whiff.

The scent was pungent, and he had to pull it away from his nose quickly.

"I don't know. Maybe there's a clue somewhere in all this mess," Robert replied.

The two set about searching the scattered papers and books there and on the shelves around them. Paul came across a large one that looked worn and used. When he opened the first page, he read aloud the text written in Angus' own hand.

"From life to ash, a phoenix will rise again. So shall the beautiful rose, Morrigan Kingsley."

Paul flipped past the first couple pages. The words were in another language he didn't understand. Symbols floated across the page, formulas and numbers, and drawings of the human anatomy. His head spun just looking at them.

"I don't understand any of this," Paul growled in frustration.

Robert took the book from him and flipped through the pages. With the same frustrated growl he used his one hand to pinch the bridge of his nose.

"Let's take it up with everything else. Maybe the nurse or Mrs. Kingsley watched him prepare her dosages," Robert said with a sigh.

Paul's eyes were heavy with sadness but he nodded and began to collect the jars with care. Following Robert to his daughter's room, he set the jars down and met the concerned gaze of his wife. Morrigan was curled up in a fetal position, holding her stomach and groaning in a fitful sleep. Victoria rose and went to him with a sad smile.

"You are doing everything you can, love," she consoled.

"It's not enough," Paul said. His voice cracked, and he forced back tears. "The Doctor is gone. What else can we do?"

Victoria pulled her husband into her arms where, finally, the tears could fall against his wife's neck. He'd never felt so hopeless in his entire life. Robert stepped out to get more of the jars, and as he was about to step in, he saw Paul's undoing. Out of respect, he turned and placed the jars on the closest table and went back down to the cellar. It was there he let out his own grief. Once the tears began he could not stop them. His whole body trembled with hopelessness. The young man lost everyone he loved and now he was about to lose Morrigan, too. His sobs grew louder as he poured it all out. When he could no longer hold himself up, he crumbled to his knees and leaned forward until his head found the cold floor.

Time was of no consequence anymore to anyone in the household. Days and nights ran into one another like oil paints on canvas since the arrival of the Plague. Robert, too, was not immune. He lost track of how long he had been lying there, half asleep, half awake, and jumped when Paul touched his shoulder. *Was it minutes? Hours? Did it even matter anymore?* He was still trying to come out of his sleep when Paul pulled him up from the murky world of dreamlessness.

"Robert. Wake up, son. Come, now."

"Huh?" Robert shook his head. "Sorry, yes. I'm coming."

The young man was still a little wobbly as he stood. He tried to steady himself by putting his hand against the stone wall. The stone shifted out of place causing Robert to stumble. Paul reached for his arm to steady him. Upon closer inspection, he noticed the hole was deliberately dug out.

This makes no sense, he thought to himself.

Paul released Robert's arm and leaned forward, peering into the hold. *Something is in there. The stone was placed there as a ruse.* Inside the hole a book had been neatly placed within.

Robert was still dusting off as Paul pulled the rolled leather book out. Aware of Paul's discovery, Robert came closer to observe.

"Could it be the Doctor's?" Robert asked.

"We're about to find out."

They cleared the table and untied the leather binder, rolling it out flat before them. Within the pages were formulas and more detailed pictures of the cure that Angus began showing him days before. Paul flipped through the pages and began to laugh.

"This is it!" he said tapping his finger on the paper. "These are the formulas for Morrigan's medicine!"

Robert let out a relieved laugh. "Are you sure?"

"Almost entirely positive. Come quickly!" Paul said as he rushed back up the stairs.

Victoria stood when the men came back and entered the room together. The change in their demeanor gave her hope. They were smiling, and life had come back into her husband's eyes.

"Is the Doctor back?" she asked. "Has he returned?"

"No," Robert said. Victoria's hope, along with her features, fell and Robert cut in quickly. "But we've found his cure! It was hidden in the cellar behind a stone."

"What do you mean?" she asked.

"Look," Paul took the book from Robert and opened the pages to explain what Angus told him the night he asked to marry Morrigan.

Robert listened, too, as Paul recounted the night the physician approached him. Using the fear of losing their daughter, Angus had made his proposition. *The doctor was blackmailing Morrigan's father with the promise of a cure.* His

blood boiled with rage, and he balled his fists discreetly at his sides.

"We don't need the Doctor," Robert interjected, "We've got everything here. We will cure her ourselves."

Paul and Victoria exchanged glances.

"He is right," Paul said to her.

Victoria looked over at Morrigan who was still lying in pain on the bed, then nodded. "Yes, let's do it. We have to at least try."

Paul could feel his heart racing as he turned to Robert.

"Go fetch the nurse, please. Tell her we need her help."

Robert ran to call the nurse, leaving Paul with Angus' memoirs to decipher the recipes and formulas written on the pages. Though he was fairly good at science these notes were more advanced than his understanding. Running his hand through his hair, he paced the floor and muttered the doctor's notes aloud. Anxiety was creeping back in, bringing doubt with it. With little to no sleep he would not be able to put all this together to save his daughter's life.

And then he remembered! Angus had a stack of reference books lying in the cellar. He recalled watching him stack them neatly in place as if recreating his workspace from home.

Paul waited for Robert to return with the nurse. He left her with new instructions for Morrigan's care then led Robert back down into the tossed about cellar.

"Robert, would you be so kind and assist me with the Doctor's reference books? Between the both of us, we will need to put all of this together."

Robert moved closer and looked down at the book lying open on the desk.

"I know some of this."

Paul blinked in surprise and stepped aside, allowing the young man more space to read.

"Yes, I think I understand most of this. There are some things we'll have to look up, but I'm sure we can do this."

It was the sweetest words Paul heard all night. For the next few hours the two of them worked diligently to recreate and mix up the recipe for Morrigan's medicine. To be safe, they repeated the process three more times. It was imperative the results were consistent and when they were, Paul and Robert were satisfied they had succeeded.

Victoria did what she could to help. Besides taking care of Morrigan, she brought the men their tea and food to help keep up their strength. As she set the tray down, Paul grabbed her hand and looked up at her through tired, glazed eyes.

"I pray God has guided our hands," he whispered.

"Aye, love. You and I both," she said, giving his hand a squeeze. "Only God has the grace to save her, if it is His will," she added, knowing if it didn't work, her husband would blame himself.

For a few moments, all they could do was stare at the jars of medicine. The liquid was thick and milky white with a pungent smell that reminded Victoria of rue. Robert rubbed the back of his neck where all the tension settled along with the strain of hovering above the books for long hours.

"We've got nothing else," Robert said. "We have to try this."

He stood and took one of the jars. His face marked by renewed determination, he brought the concoction to Morrigan's bedside. Victoria and her husband were too afraid and nervous to move. They stood and watched their daughter's chest rise and fall with labored breath. The nurse, seeing their trepidation, took

the jar from Robert's shaky hand and motioned for them to take a seat.

"I'll give it t'her, lad. It's alright," she reassured him. "Aye, sit."

Robert didn't release the jar at first. He froze, staring down at Morrigan's dwindling body, her sunken features, and the blood-filled buboes. There was no turning back. No other option.

Morrigan's nurse cradled the girl's head gently in her arm and tilted her head back. She pressed the jar against Morrigan's sore, infested lips with care allowing the medicine to pour into her mouth.

At first, there was no reaction from Morrigan. Some of the medicine started to pour out from the corners of her mouth. When the nurse was about to pull the jar away, Morrigan's lips parted and she began to swallow. After a few gulps of the medicine Morrigan choked and coughed. Drops of the precious drink spewed from her mouth before the nurse lifted her head higher and handed the drink to Robert.

The woman cleaned off Morrigan's mouth with a rag and cooed softly into her ear. "It's all right, child. You're gonn'ae be jus' fine."

Morrigan's eyes rolled around as she tried to focus on everything around her. She could feel her heart rate speed up then slow down again. Her throat was on fire, and it fed the flames down into her belly. She couldn't speak as her mind pulled the heat upward. Every nerve began rapid firing. She could smell the blood of the nurse holding her, and the soft cadence of her heart. Morrigan began to pant in response to her metabolic system's sudden increase.

The nurse and Robert stared down at her. From their point of view, it looked like she was having a fever induced

nightmare. Robert, her sweet Robert, had finally come to her side. She could smell him, too. She reached out for him and he sat beside her, taking her hand into his.

"I'm here, Morrigan. Don't worry. I'm right here."

Morrigan responded with a tight squeeze of his hand. Robert smiled and looked up at Paul and Victoria who had rushed over to see their daughter.

"We did it!" Paul cried out with relief. "We really did it!"

Victoria threw her arms around Paul and held him in a tearful hug. She tried her hardest to be strong, but it was difficult watching her own child dance a fine line between life and death. No matter how much tension there was among them, she loved her daughter with all that she was.

The nurse gently laid Morrigan's head on the pillow and turned to them all. "I think we've earned some sleep. I will make sure she has her regular doses. Why don'ya all get cleaned up and take a bite b'fore ya's go to sleep?"

Paul let out a long exhale and pulled Victoria into him more tightly. "I think that's a good idea."

Morrigan's parents leaned in and kissed their daughter, one after the other, then headed out to their room on the far west corner of the house. Robert lingered beside Morrigan's bed until the nurse gently coaxed him, "Come lad. She'll be fine. You must reserve your energy."

Robert eventually conceded. He brought Morrigan's hand to his lips and kissed the only spot not afflicted by the buboes.

"All right. I'll leave her in your hands. Only if you promise to call me if she takes a turn for the worse."

The nurse smiled and nodded, shooing him out of the room. According to the instructions given to her by Robert and

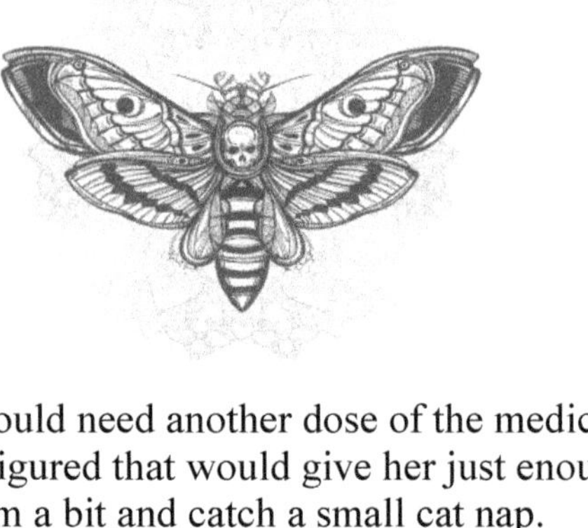

Paul, Morrigan would need another dose of the medicine in two more hours. She figured that would give her just enough time to straighten the room a bit and catch a small cat nap.

Throughout the night, the nurse continued delivering the medicine like clockwork. By the third dose she was shocked to see the turnaround of Morrigan's condition. Color was coming back to her cheeks, and she began to acquire an appetite. Robert was clear she must take at least four doses before she could eat any food to test for tolerability. The nurse tried to explain that to Morrigan even though it broke her heart to deny the withering girl.

In between the delivery time of the medicine Morrigan had maddening dreams of ghostly fingers without bodies curled around anything they could get hold of. Teeth appeared out of darkness and gnashed, enamel clicking against enamel. Everything was dark and red, like a sea of writhing people with no faces.

Each time she had the dream, her stomach pangs grew more intense until it woke her, forcing her to curl up between cries of pain. When her nurse would come running, all Morrigan could hear was the racing of the woman's heart. The smell of human flesh made Morrigan's hunger grow, but she didn't know why. The room was warm and dark around her. She could still make out shadows and movement. Inanimate objects were shades of dark grey but things that were alive, like her nurse or her plants, gave off a warm amber glow around their silhouette.

Sounds had become amplified beyond normal and irritated her entire body. Even the linens made a loud rustling noise with her movements. What she couldn't smell or hear, she could *feel*. The shift of the air made the hair on her arms rise up, detecting in which direction it moved. Morrigan's nostrils would flair and hone in on the scent of flesh.

A slow opening of her eyelids allowed shadow and light to filter in. She could not rush opening her eyes, the light was too painful. She had to take baby steps and relearn how to process everything. Spotting the nurse across the room by her scent, Morrigan jut her chin toward her, taking in deep breaths.

Blood. Yes. Blood.

She sniffed the air more deeply, pulling it into her lungs until they filled to capacity. It made her mouth salivate. *Menses.* The nurse was having her cycle. *Why is the blood giving me hunger pangs?* Morrigan thought to herself. *And why can't I speak?*

Morrigan tried again to call out to the nurse, but her lips were paralyzed. All that came out were moans and grunts. The nurse stirred in her sleep. Frantic to be heard, Morrigan tried to yell until her moans grew louder. The middle-aged woman stood stiff and slow, trying to stretch out her stubborn joints.

"I'm comin', girl," she called out with sleep still in her voice.

Shuffling across the room with the fourth jar, she held it up to catch the small glow of the candlelight. She noticed some of it had begun to settle at the bottom so she swished it around, and made a face at the smell.

"After this dose, you'll able t'eat somethin' hearty," the nurse reminded her. "Won't y'be happy, then?"

The pains in Morrigan's stomach were so horrible her mind began to break down to a primal act of need. *I'm so hungry!* Became the only thought that consumed her. Her mouth began to act on its own agenda, opening and closing against her will. Her jaw stretched, ripping at the corners of her mouth and threatening to dislocate the bones to unhinge like a serpent. Another loud, lugubrious moan pushed out from her belly to her throat. The sound of it stopped the nurse who was only a step

away. Her warm, glowing shadow filled Morrigan's sight and her brain shut down to fulfill her one, dire need.

To *feed*.

"Morrigan?" the nurse breathed out.

When she heard nothing, not even breathing coming from the girl, the nurse panicked and moved to her with a sense of urgency. She lowered her head, tilting her ear toward the girl's mouth to detect any breath from between her lips. When she was close enough Morrigan sat upright and the nurse fell to the floor. The jar of medicine rolled from her hand and shattered against the wall. The poor, frightened nurse rolled to her side and reached for the chair to help her stand. When she got to her feet she glanced over at Morrigan. The candle's meager light washed over her features. The girl's lips were pulled back exposing her teeth and gums. Both the top and bottom teeth bit down making a horrible clacking noise, followed by the grinding of the enamel.

"Mother Mary n' Joseph!" the nurse exclaimed, bringing her hand to her mouth.

Turning, she stumbled over the chair as she scrambled to get away. Morrigan could not fight the hunger any longer. Though she was weak, she managed to slide out of bed. Her legs wobbled when she bore them weight, barely holding her upright, but that did not deter her. She grabbed the overturned chair and used her whole body to fling it at the nurse who tripped over it somewhere in the dark.

Morrigan's stomach growled and churned. *Eat. Must ... eat.* She was so desperate to stop the pangs in her stomach. The need to feed became a siren in her thoughts, drowning out everything else. Her muscles gave out under her, and she fell to the floor, contorting in pain. She could hear the nurse crying a

few feet away. The woman was huddled in a corner crippled in fear, whimpering softly.

Pushing up onto her palms, Morrigan began to drag her body toward the nurse. The smell of her fear and her tears filled the room with pheromones. It was driving Morrigan mad. The closer she got to the nurse, the brighter the glow around her became. Morrigan was no longer herself but a half-crazed, half-starved animal in pursuit of a feast. Her mouth watered until it drooled along the floor into a trail that fell from her chin to the floor.

When her blackened fingertips touched the nurse's foot, the woman let out a scream and tried to pull away, but it was too late. Morrigan began to crawl on top of her in a frenzy, pinning her to the floor. The nurse tried to fight her off, but Morrigan lunged at her with her teeth, biting any body part she could find like a wild animal.

The nurse let out a scream as Morrigan's teeth clamped down on her forearm. The pressure of the bite combined with the breaking of skin, and the pull of muscle from the bone caused the nurse's scream to rise up like a banshee. Paul and Victoria were ripped out of their sleep and to their feet. Paul grabbed his rifle instinctively, and Victoria huddled behind him. For a moment the two remained silent, too stunned to act. They both listened, creeping toward the door together. Another shriek rang through the hallway propelling them out of their room and into a sprint to Morrigan's room.

"Morrigan?" Paul shouted, aiming his gun in front of him.

"Nurse!?" Victoria cried out.

"Help me! Oh my God, she's ki—" the nurse gurgled then coughed.

Skidding to a halt at Morrigan's doorway, Paul's eyes widened and Victoria screamed. Morrigan was leaning over the nurse, her fingers squeezing at the wet, slippery lengths of her intestines. Blood oozed from their daughter's mouth to her chin. Long strings of masticated muscle hung in strands from between her teeth. The entire front of her gown was soaked in crimson. The nurse's blood covered the floor and was making its way to the door where Morrigan's parents stood.

"Morrigan!" Her father yelled, backing up.

Victoria was in hysterics, clutching her husband's arm as he pushed her back into the hall. She'd lost all sense of reason and darted toward her daughter to try and help her. Paul had to catch her and keep her away. His wife's foot slid in the pool of blood, and he lost his grip on her. Before he could reach her, Morrigan pounced again and landed on her mother's back.

"No, Morrigan! Stop!" Paul screamed.

Morrigan snapped her head up and growled at her father. Consumed by hunger, Morrigan's mind was completely absorbed with the need for more. Victoria tried to slither through the blood and get away from her daughter, but Morrigan took a grip of her hair. With a rough tug of Victoria's thick, black hair, Morrigan pulled back, stretching the woman's neck. Her mother screamed again, and Paul watched in horror as Morrigan ripped half of her scalp free. Her father let out an unearthly cry and ran toward the two women in an attempt to save his wife and detain his daughter. He wrapped his arms around Morrigan, but she threw her head back, smashing his nose. Paul's vision filled with stars, and he fell back unconscious in the pool of Victoria's blood.

Robert had fallen asleep in the cellar going over the doctor's books. The screaming upstairs barely reached down past the heavy door and stone walls. In his dreams, they were far

away. A distant cry from somewhere in his unconscious state. It wasn't until the thumping and fighting began that he woke with a start. Drunk on exhaustion, he rubbed his eyes and looked toward the ceiling.

"What wa—" His question was cut off by another scream. Paul's scream. Then more banging and thumping.

Robert ran toward the stairs then froze when he heard the wild shriek that came from Morrigan's room upstairs next to the doorway. The sound was monstrous, and his heart stopped before it kicked back to life, racing so fast he felt it might explode. He forced his left foot to lift, but before placing it on the next stair he looked down and saw the blood. Small streams began to creep down the steps toward him like tendrils from above.

"I must be dreaming. Please wake up, Robert," he whispered to himself aloud.

The dark crimson liquid looked black in the darkness of the stairwell causing Robert to back up. He missed the bottom stair and fell back, hitting his arm and head on the hard floor. When he tried to push himself up pain shot from his elbow to his shoulder, and he let out a scream. His arm was broken. Robert bit down on his lip and pulled his useless limb against his stomach. Using his good hand, he pushed himself up to his feet. The banging against the cellar door caused a panic to rise up within him. He had no idea what happened upstairs but his gut was telling him he needed to stay down here.

Crouching low, Robert began to sneak back toward the table when he heard the banging turn to scratching at the door. From where he stood, he craned his neck to peer up while avoiding the blood with his feet. The scratching stopped, then started up again, furiously. Whatever, or *whomever*, it was, was trying to get in.

"Go away!" Robert shouted, "I—I'm armed!"

The scratching ceased.

Robert's breaths came as quick as his heart was beating. The silence was like a cold bubble around him. He couldn't even hear his own breathing. Robert's body trembled in fear, and he could barely hold himself up on his own wobbling legs.

"Breathe, Robert. Get a hold of yourself."

The scent of his fear rose up past the dense, wooden door. It seeped through the cracks and intoxicated Morrigan. She was already in a frenzy from her feeding, and now she needed to get down to the source of the pheromone kneading at the back of her brain. Being unable to get through the door drove her to another level of madness. She howled at the top of her lungs and slammed her fists and legs against the wood. Solid oak cracked and groaned under the blows. The metal hinges bounced and threatened to give. Down at the bottom of the stairs Robert broke down. He had no idea what happened to Paul and Victoria, or to Morrigan for that matter.

"Stop!" Robert shouted. "Just please stop!"

The young man covered one ear with a hand while cradling his broken arm and rocking back and forth. The pounding and screaming only got louder. Morrigan was throwing her entire body at the door now. Robert watched the hinges and knew they would break down. He had to do something. Then he remembered! The door!

He stood up, threw the boxes and chairs out of his way and raced to the rear, hidden door he showed Paul the previous day. Just as he reached it, the door behind leading up from the cellar crashed in. Wood pieces splintered everywhere, and the bulk of what was left of the door hung from its hinges. Morrigan didn't even stop. She tore down the stairs pausing at the bottom, seeking out the source of her desire. Robert hid in the shadows

and along the back wall. The young woman he fell so in love with was now transformed into a hideous beast. Her eyes were as black and glassy as a spider's. Her lips were pulled back exposing her teeth making them appear even larger.

And her skin … *Oh God, her skin*! He thought.

Robert closed his eyes to the vision that would forever be etched into his mind. He could smell the festering wounds across the cellar from her. He had to go. He could not save her like he thought he could. While Morrigan screamed and threw things out of her way looking for Robert, he rose to stand. He'd have to move quickly and get out of the cellar before she could reach him. Once outside, he could seal the door and run to safety. Wherever that was anymore.

When Robert pressed his hand on the door, the latch squeaked with old age. He grimaced and held his breath. Morrigan's head rose up immediately from where she was hunched over. Robert could see her nostrils flare to sniff the air until her eyes landed right on him. Morrigan's mouth opened and stretched. The right side of her jaw made a loud cracking noise and pushed itself upward, unhinging from the joint, before dropping. The left side had a harder time unlocking, causing Morrigan's face to distort and her jaw to click when bone rubbed against bone.

Unable to move, he was struck dumb by shock. He watched helplessly as her hands reached forward in his direction. Then she lunged!

"No!" Robert shouted before springing into action.

He jumped through the hidden door and spun, slamming the heavy lock in place. He knew it would only be a matter of minutes until she broke through so he fled as fast as he could into the trees and toward the lake.

He needed to find help, if there was anyone left. He needed to make it to the only possible relative of his who might still be alive. If he was not dead, his ship might still be in port.

CHAPTER 16: HOME IS WHERE THE HEART IS

When Morrigan collapsed, Angus caught her in his arms and fell to his knees with her. Staring down at her in fear and shock, he knew what she had done to those inside of the house, but his mind was unable to process it yet. He rose, holding her limp body in his arms and tried to will himself to stand.

How is this possible? He asked himself.

His confusion was interrupted by Marshall calling out to him. The physician blinked a few times and turned to look at the other man who was waving him away from the girl, but Angus could not bear to abandon her. What she was on the outside mirrored who he was on the inside. To him, she was finally perfect in every way. His equal. His soulmate. His bride. He was struck with a deeper sense of infatuation and devotion to her.

Managing to swallow and regain his faculties, Angus snapped at the man hovering on the stairs. "Shut up, Marshall! Go get me a blanket."

Marshall's jaw fell open. *Is this man serious?*

"Sir, I must protest!" Marshall cried out.

"Do as I say, Marshall, or I will finish what I started with you!"

Marshall spun on a heel and hobbled up the stairs. When he reached the top, he continued to Morrigan's room and almost fell over the devoured bodies and coagulated fluid on the floor. He found the closest blanket he could put his hands on and fled from the room. The merchant would find time later to question his own sanity. For now, he returned to the doctor. Angus wrapped Morrigan up and lifted her and maneuvered past the boxes and overturned chairs.

"We need to get her to my home," Angus ordered. "Quickly! Ready the horses."

Marshall limped along as fast as he could ahead of them until he reached their steeds, where he began pulling items off the buggy. Angus came up fast behind him and set the young woman inside before climbing in himself.

"Let's go. There's no time to waste," he ordered.

Marshall nodded to the doctor and climbed painfully to his seat where he navigated them back to where he'd just endured his own private Hell.

Dawn had barely come up over the horizon when they reached the front door. Servants ran out half-dressed and blurry-eyed. They had been hired to keep up the doctor's home while he was away and hadn't expected a quick return. They were met with shouts and orders from the doctor who ran past them and into his house.

Marshall was exhausted and slid from his mount in excruciating pain. When his boots hit the dirt the shock of hard surface to heel caused him to buckle. One of the workers shot a hand out to steady him, saving him from a rude meeting with the ground.

The merchant muttered his thanks and dragged himself into the house. He heard Angus shouting at the help from down in the cellar. The door was left open. He had to laugh, but the action made his groin sting in renewed agony. Marshall went to his room and lie awake for several more hours before he passed out from exhaustion.

Below him in the cellar, Angus directed the hired help. "Fill the basin with water and light the logs beneath. I need it hot, fast."

He looked like a conductor and a dancer all at once. One arm cradled Morrigan who hung limp at his side. Each turn

Angus made caused her hair to swoop and her arms to swing out. His other hand pointed everyone where to go.

Once he had given them all a task, Angus pushed everything off the table in the center of the room with one pass of his free hand. He then lifted Morrigan and placed her on its surface with care like a fine piece of china. He brushed her hair from her face where it had hung like strands of wet yarn on a doll's head.

"Morrigan, we're home, love. It's going to be fine. Stay strong."

The doctor squeezed her hand and kissed it before setting it gently at her side. "I'm going to undress you, Morrigan. I need to place you into the bath and return your temperature to normal. Please forgive me."

He surprised himself at the apology for having to put her in an indecent, exposed position. The combination of her being in imminent danger, and the manifestation of her monstrosity caused a stir within him. It was as if he'd truly, for the first time, understood what it was to both desire and love someone, simultaneously.

Until now, he'd only known possessiveness. This feeling was—dare he even think it—gentle and tender. But how does one nurture something such as this?

He felt the sudden thrill she could at any moment wake again to kill him. The rush it caused him made him erect. A shiver ran through him, and he took in a deep breath. He had to control himself. She needed his help to survive this. Without him, she would die.

"Sir, the water is warm," a servant said from behind him.

Angus waved him off without a word. The man disappeared, and the doctor lifted Morrigan to the tub where he lowered her into the water. Positioning her head against the side

he cupped the water and let it pour over her hair to remove the thick clots of blood from her dark strands. The water turned pink. Morrigan's eyes fluttered after a few moments in the warmth, and she gazed around.

"Where am I?" she asked.

Her voice was different. Dark and sultry, unlike before.

"You're home, Morrigan," Angus answered.

Morrigan looked around, taking in everything. "I do not recognize this place."

Angus followed her gaze before letting his eyes fall onto hers again. He noted a change in her demeanor from the innocent girl he was familiar with. Her lips were more sultry and her eyes, once wide and bright, were now smoldering as they held his gaze without wanting to look away. Something had changed.

"This is my home," he said. "*Our* home now."

With a slow rise, Morrigan sat upright. She didn't seem to mind that she was naked and exposed to Angus, and the doctor could not help but drink in her form. The water trickled down her torso to her firm thighs rushing to reunite with the warmth of the bath water. Lowering her chin, she gazed down at him and caught him off guard. Never before had he felt the desire to avert his eyes from a woman.

"Does it please you?" she asked.

"I'm sorry?" he asked in confusion.

"Does my body please you, Doctor?" she asked turning to show herself fully to him.

Angus was drowning in rapture. His eyes locked onto her breasts. Her firm nipples stood out against the cold and the remaining drops of water clung to her waif-like figure. The candlelight reflected off each drop making them appear like gems adorning her in a sensual, ornamental way. He had to take in a breath.

The doctor's mouth went dry, and his jaw hung open in salacious hunger. He wanted to *taste* her. To run his lips along her damp skin and feel her against his tongue. He was drifting into the fantasy ever deeper until his teeth snapped shut. He then took in another deep breath and closed his eyes, steeling himself from her guiles.

"Yes. In every way imaginable," he whispered gruffly.

Morrigan sank into the water until she was kneeling in front of the doctor. She could smell his need and sense the way he trembled. Before now, she was only a girl. That had all somehow changed. Presently, she was a woman who was overwrought with an insatiable desire. One she had no idea of how to sate.

She gazed into the doctor's eyes, and drew in a shaky breath, feeling her body being drawn to him. She leaned forward and pressed her parted lips to his, allowing her tongue to pass over his teeth and fill his mouth. Angus released a moan full of longing. He pulled her tongue into his mouth further and suckled it. Whatever reservations and inhibitions he once harbored, he was no longer in possession of them. She was fiery and delicious on his tongue, and her body melted against him like confection.

He grabbed her by the hips and pulled her against him harder until her breasts were pressed firmly to his chest. They rose together, and Morrigan's strong legs wrapped around his waist. Angus could feel the heat between her thighs teasing at him through his trousers. The bulge within his codpiece grew hard and pressed against the girl's pelvic mound.

When Morrigan broke their kiss, she released a lustful whimper and tilted her head back. She was consumed with the flames of her own hunger. The more they touched and caressed, the more Angus' body pulsed. His blood was rushing in his veins to fill the stiffened flesh between his thighs, forcing it against

her. She could smell his sex as droplets of cum pooled against the swollen tip of his cock.

Until then, she had never known the touch of a man. Innocent to the ways of such intimacy, she had no way to express the feeling she had burning inside of her. Nothing else to compare it to, to know such feelings were darker and more sinister than normal sexual longing.

The girl pulled his shirt aside and brought her lips to Angus' shoulder to taste his skin. He let out a moan and lifted his hand to cup the underside of her ass. He was forever lost in her starting from that moment. Content to swim in the depth of her groans of pleasure, he'd already long forgotten the look of disdain she once cast upon him. Morrigan's entire body began to writhe against him. He wanted her so badly he trembled.

Entwined in one another's embrace, Morrigan could no longer keep her craving at bay. Pulling back her lips, she bit down on Angus' shoulder until she drew blood, but instead of reacting in fear, the doctor cried out in ecstasy. She could feel his fingers curl in and bite at her skin. The taste of his blood washed over her like a drug, and Morrigan slid her tongue over the wound, lapping and suckling at it for more.

Once again, Angus responded with a deep, guttural moan. The clothing between them grew warmer and a spot of moisture began to form where his codpiece had been stretched to its limits.

"Morrigan, please," he begged. "Let me have you."

Without waiting for an answer, he gripped her hair pulling her away from his bleeding shoulder. Morrigan responded by hissing and fighting him, which only served to arouse the doctor more. He returned the growl and slammed her onto the floor, covering her with his full weight. Morrigan's eyes were filled with crimson as she stared up at him. Her body

writing beneath him made him lose what little control he had left. With one swipe of his hand, he unleashed the hard flesh raging to be freed and pushed the head inside of her.

Morrigan cried out with an animalistic screech and arched her back. Her fingers clawed at his back as he pumped deeper into her, forcing himself past her hymen. The screeches softened to a mixture of pain and pleasure, and Angus continued to thrust his hips into hers, claiming her virginity. It didn't take long before the two were thrashing and squirming against one another exerting all their unspent lust through every proclivity they could imagine.

Though their hunger originated from very different places, Angus matched her brutality head on; every gnashing of teeth, every claw of hand, until they cried out in release. They lay there, a tangled mess, covered in sweat and blood on the floor, where Morrigan fell into a deep sleep.

Angus watched her as she slept. Tracing the curvature of her body with his fingertip, he followed the path of her ribs down to her thigh. Teeth marks between her spread legs where he'd tasted her swollen lips were fresh and bright against her otherwise unmarred skin. He smiled wide. He'd marked her; claimed her like the beast he was, and she returned it with fervor. He loved the way she looked right now as if she were still the innocent girl in the marketplace and he the caretaker of her secret enchantments.

When Angus' fingers passed over Morrigan's knee his eyes caught sight of her foot again. The flesh had grown even darker, and the smell reached his sensitive nose, whisking away his blissful denial of her state of health. It made his chest hurt to know he'd have to take the appendage away. He rolled onto his back and stared at the wall. The painted scenes of debauchery were still there staring back at him. He was about to smile in

fondness when the idea came to him. The doctor rolled onto his side and sat up.

"Yes," he said aloud to himself. "Yes, precisely!"

He snapped his fingers at the thought and rose to his feet. He'd need to fix Morrigan another concoction before he could begin so he pulled his trousers on and slid his arms into his shirt. He didn't bother tying anything before he ascended the stairs.

When he opened the door, Marshall was sitting in his usual spot at the table. The broken companion looked an absolute mess. By now, Angus was sure his wound was festering with infection.

"Get my horse prepared," Angus said.

He passed Marshall and went for the bread laid out on the counter, probably from Marshall's unfinished breakfast. No doubt the man had grown nauseous and unable to keep much down.

"Doctor," Marshall said in a weak, tired voice. "I am in no condition …"

The doctor cut in between mouthfuls of food. "I wasn't aware you became a doctor, yourself, in the night."

Marshall lowered his head and fumbled with his cap in his hands. "I am not."

"Then leave the decisions to me about what you're capable of, and what you are not."

Angus turned to face Marshall. "I will need my horse so that I can tend to your wound as well as Morrigan's illness."

Marshall's eyes rose up and glanced toward the door leading down to the cellar where Morrigan lay asleep. "It sounded as if you already *tended* to her."

Angus slammed his palm against the tabletop and rushed at Marshall. He leaned down, invading the comfortable distance

between them both, and bared his teeth as he spoke. "Do not speak of my bride-to-be with your filthy words, again!"

Marshall tried to look away, but Angus pressed his forehead to his, forcing their eyes to meet, "I will give you no more warnings, Marshall. It would be a wise choice on your behalf to mind your tongue, lest it suffer a similar fate as your cock."

In emphasis, Angus' knee shoved between Marshall's legs and pressed against the torn stitches. Marshall crumpled at the bolt of pain and tried to swallow the cry back into his throat from where it arose but failed. The doctor smiled with satisfaction and crouched down to give the merchant's cheek a hard slap.

"That's my *girl*," Angus whispered cruelly. "Now go fetch my horse."

Shoving another piece of bread into his mouth, Angus walked to his room to change and prepare for his errands.

CHAPTER 17: SUFFER WELL

Marshall made his way to the stable to prepare Angus' horse. Along the way, he thought about how distraught he was by the events that had taken place in a short span of time. His country had fallen to the Plague, and where he once felt it would be to his benefit, he now began to see the error of those beliefs. The curse of hindsight was upon him with overwhelming clarity. He should have taken his wealth and fled. Instead, he remained content with his modest fortune, and he allowed his greed to lead him into the spider's parlor.

Angus Wulfe was aptly named for his true nature, a nocturnal predator. Marshall could feel the darkness surrounding the doctor like a cancer, and it was closing in to steal him, too. He was ashamed of what he'd become. All of the horrible things that happened to him were the result of turning a blind eye, and he would endure the suffering without complaint.

Standing beside the horse, Marshall threw the reins over its neck then wrapped it around the horn of the saddle. He was lost in his thoughts when he heard rustling behind him. Thinking nothing of it, he began to walk the animal out and stumbled across the stable boy writhing with sickness. He was curled up, lying in a pile of his own waste in the hay.

"Boy!" Marshall called out from where he stood, "What's happened?"

Marshall already knew the answer. The Plague had reached this boy. It was on their own doorstep. *It had to have been Morrigan!* he thought.

Marshall moved quickly, leading Angus' horse to the side entrance. "Doctor!" he called out, "Please come, it's urgent!"

Angus made his way out with a casual stroll as if he were being called to dinner. The agitated merchant dropped the reins of the horse and limped toward him.

"The stable hand is dying in the birthing den. He will bring the Plague to all the livestock as well as the staff if we do not contain this."

Angus was tugging a glove on, paying it more attention than the sick boy. When he had it fitted properly on his hand he glanced up. "Alright, then. I will contain it."

Marshall looked at him, confused. "What? How?"

"I have the cure," Angus explained. "Or did you think I had contrived a story to gain consent to marry Morrigan?"

Angus watched Marshall, challenging him to confess his suspicion.

"I had my concerns," Marshall said.

"Of course you did," Angus sneered. "You're nothing more than a titmouse."

Marshall looked down at his shoes, cursing beneath his breath.

"Wait here," Angus said with disgust.

Angus walked to the stable and into the stall where the horses were kept when they were about to deliver. There in the large pile of hay, just as Marshall had said, lay the young boy. He was sweating blood from his pores and had a distant stare as if seeing something beyond.

"Where is your family, boy?"

The boy, who was barely conscious, pointed toward the neighboring field where an old weathered hut stood. There were faint signs of smoke drifting out of the smoke holes in the decrepit, thatch roof.

Angus pulled out his small rag and placed it over his mouth before he knelt to the ground and reached out for the

boy's chin. Turning his head side to side, a quick examination revealed swelling and a lump the size of an egg on the right side.

"You're lucky Marshall found you, lad. *I'll* be lucky if I can save you."

The doctor stood and tucked the rag into his pocket. "I trust you'll be here when I return?"

Angus did not wait for the boy to respond. Not that he could, anyway. He went back to where Marshall stood, holding the reins of the horse.

"I'll be back in a few hours. Keep the side doors open."

Stepping onto the small stairs next to the horse's leg, he used it to heft himself onto the animal's back and pushed his foot into the stirrup. Angus adjusted his weight in the saddle then gave the horse's flank a kick with the heel of his boot.

When the doctor was out of view, Marshall went back into the house to search for Morrigan. The staff bustled about, cleaning and doing chores as if it were a normal day. It felt like he was living in a nightmare he could not wake from. When he got to the cellar door, he stood there, contemplating.

What are you going to do Marshall? He asked himself.

He was broken in both strength and will. Angus had seen to it he was demasculinized and compliant. Without Angus, his wound would grow, fester, and weep until he succumbed to infection.

Even so, it was a better fate than those suffering from the Plague were experiencing.

Before he knew it, his hand reached for the door and turned the knob. He was careful when he opened the door, to make as little noise as he could. Peering down into the dark stairwell, Marshall listened. There was no sound coming from below. Anxiety crept along his spine like ice melting against his fevered skin. Whatever was down there, he reminded himself,

was no longer Morrigan. What they brought back with them was a monster that killed and *devoured* her whole family.

Marshall's heart pounded against his ribcage. The fear that Morrigan's hands would reach out and snatch him filled his mind until he could hardly contain himself. He swallowed the lump forming at his throat and edged his foot closer to the threshold leading down. The ringing and pounding in his ears was deafening.

What exactly will you do once you're down there? he thought. *I have to see her*!
He had to know if behind her eyes there was any humanity left, or if she was truly an abomination.

Marshall lowered his foot down to the next step. Nothing. Only the cacophony of sounds from his own breathing and fluttering heart. He could hear the soft murmuring of the staff conversing behind him and the shuffling of feet as they tended to their busy work, but Marshall's attention remained fixed on the abysmal darkness forming a pit at the foot of the stairs.

He took another step and waited. Still nothing. *Should I call out for her?* he wondered. If he could find his voice behind the dry heat in the back of his throat that might have been an option. The world thinned around him as he panted, a feeble attempt to bring more oxygen to his brain.

Finally, his legs began to work, and he took the steps one by one at an excruciating pace. He wished he could stop shaking. *Damnit!* He cursed himself. *Why didn't I bring a candle?*

He stopped just a few steps from the bottom and turned giving another trepidatious look over his shoulder. The light from the doorway seemed as far away as the moon from where he stood. Marshall argued with himself whether to run back up to

the safety of his room or to continue his way into the pitch black below. He could board up the cellar, run far from here, and die from his recent castration before the Plague ever got ahold of him.

Using what moisture he had left in his mouth, he passed his tongue over his parched lips but there was no relief. Reason found its way back into his racing thoughts. How long would he last, and how far would he get before Angus found him? The doctor would drag him back, amputate his legs, and keep him chained like a dog in the fields if he tried to run.

Deciding to conquer the last couple of steps, Marshall saw movement in his peripheral. The muscles of his back stiffened and he scanned the black, cold space. *Did I imagine it?* Blinking a few times, he attempted to adjust his eyes to the unlit room. Still, nothing. He took a couple of quick, short breaths to fill his lungs and steel his nerves. Throwing fear behind him he pushed himself forward to make his final descent.

When he reached the floor he found a moment of respite. He smiled in short-lived triumph before sensing someone pass by the door above, slamming it shut.

"No! Wait!" he cried out.

Stumbling over himself, he tried to run back up the stairs, but missed the first step and fell backwards. A bolt of pain flashed behind his eyes, and he was tossed into unconsciousness.

Marshall was struggling to break free from the deep recesses of his mind when he started coming to. He was dreaming of being on the ships and making deals with importers. The smell of the water, crisp and pungent, blowing across the wind, filled his lungs. The rot of fish and other foods that hadn't survived the long journey, the rodents, and the men who had been to sea for months, maybe years, stung his nostrils.

Large barrels rolled across the arch of the ship's floor which was splintered from exposure despite being swabbed daily. He was home again, among his element. The sound of the flapping mast brought his attention upward to the grey-blue skies of London.

"Marshall!" the watchman in the bird's nest called out.

Marshall waved and smiled.

"Marshall!" another voice shouted.

He tried to look around and find the owner of the voice when one of the hounds came running toward him. With its ears perked high and its tail swishing back and forth, Marshall crouched and laughed. The mutt licked at his face, and he gave it an excited scratch behind its ears. The dog began to whine and search at Marshall's hand for food.

"Sorry little guy. Nothing for you, today," he said and pat its head.

The persistent hound leapt up knocking Marshall over with its solid weight and momentum. The playful assault of licks and sniffs became more aggressive all at once. He tried to fight the hound off, but its demeanor changed without warning to a ravenous beast desperate for food. When Marshall could not provide any, the hound began to tear at his fingers and pull at any soft flesh it could find.

"Marshall!" came the voice again.

This time it pulled him away from the overcast sky back into the darkness of the cellar. Marshall shook his head to try and wake himself. The pain where he hit his head was fresh, and the gash stung. He tried to sit up when the sudden realization came to him of where he was. He felt another pain. This time it was teeth on his fingers. It was no longer a dream, it was real! He turned his eyes to his hand and tried to pull it back but Morrigan was gnawing on his fingertips. He watched in horror as she sank

her teeth into the stubby tips and tore back, rending flesh from bone.

Marshall let out a scream and tried to fend Morrigan off, but she growled and locked onto his arm with a vice-like grip.

Once more the voice called out his name, and he frantically turned his head, screaming for help. At the top of the stairs was Robert.

"Quickly!" He yelled, then tossed a large piece of wood down to him.

The piece of wood toppled down the stairs then bounced to the left of Marshall's reach. Morrigan, was distracted and pulled her attention away from her "snack" to hiss like a possessed cat at him. Marshall used the advantage and rolled away toward the weapon, using it to strike the girl on the side of the head. Her neck made a popping noise that sounded like bones snapping, and her face was thrown to the side.

The man was rooted in place by fear until he heard the rabid growl coming from behind the curtain of hair covering her face.

"Now, Marshall! Hurry!" Robert shouted.

Marshall sprung forward and hitched. His head was throbbing and the walls spun around him. He moved as quickly as he could, stumbling up the stairs through agonizing pain. Morrigan skittered behind him, and he cried out while reaching for Robert with his mangled hand. He felt Morrigan's breath on the back of his neck and squeezed his eyes shut but was pulled to safety at the last second. He opened his eyes to see Robert's hand around his, yanking him from harm's way and shutting the door behind them. The two collapsed outside of the door with their backs against it. Behind it, Morrigan screamed and pounded in fury.

"How did you get here?" Marshall wheezed.

"No time. We must go!" Robert said as he stood.

The younger man tried to help the merchant to his feet when he heard the arrival of the doctor at the side entrance, near the stable. Marshall became panicked, but Robert gripped his arm.

"You cannot let on that I'm here," he whispered. "We cannot run, yet. Look at me, Marshall! Pay attention."

Marshall was trembling, but he looked at Robert and listened.

"Tell the truth when he asks. You fell. You woke up to Morrigan doing this to you," Robert continued, then held up Marshall's bloody hand.

When he did, Marshall could see the missing fingers and he began shivering and losing consciousness. He was going into shock. Robert gave him a shake.

"Do not try to run. He will kill you and me, both. Wait for me tonight when everyone is asleep, next to the stable. Do you hear me?"

Marshall nodded.

"Good. We *will* escape and I will come for you. Do you trust me?"

Marshall nodded again.

"Go, now! Lest he grow suspicious." With those words, Robert ran to the other exit and snuck out unseen.

Marshall stumbled to the large double doors on the side of the doctor's home that opened into the courtyard between the house and the stables. When he emerged the staff was already unloading Angus' satchels. The doctor dismounted and looked over at Marshall.

"What did you do, man? What happened?" he demanded.

While Marshall stammered through the account, Angus slapped him against his temple causing bells of pain to ring in his ears.

"I said to leave her be," Angus seethed. "I cannot keep you alive if you will not listen."

The staff paused, afraid the doctor would turn his wrath on them, then scattered like flies, leaving them alone.

Marshall tried to form words, but the blood loss became too much, causing him to sway. Angus snarled and pulled his scarf from around his neck. While he was tying it around Marshall's hand, he continued to belittle and chastise him. The world was spinning again. He had no idea how much more he could endure before his sanity broke or he followed Death to wherever he led him. Within moments, darkness embraced him and he was out, once again.

When the morning light began to filter in, Marshall's room went from black to charcoal. He tried to move his head to look around, but there was a sharp throb. It started behind his eyes and penetrated deep within his skull. It felt like he'd been beaten for hours. Every muscle was on fire. Each movement he made caused him pain. Marshall let out a small groan and closed his eyes.

"Ah," said Angus. "The Merchant survives another round with the claws of Death."

Marshall hadn't realized there was anyone there with him. His eyes fluttered, and he lay there in silence, staring upward.

"That's fine if you wish not to speak," Angus continued. "Perhaps now my words will find home between your ears."

The physician stood from the chair and walked to the edge of Marshall's bed so the man could see him.

"This is a game that is out of your league, old friend," he began. "I will do what I can to keep you alive but remember this … it is a privilege, not a right."

Angus was casual about pulling out his pipe and using the candle to light up a small piece of wood he called a "light-inch stick." Bringing it up, the tiny flame illuminated the surgeon's face manipulating shadow and light, tricking the eye. *Were his lips and eyes disfigured?* Marshall tried to focus on Angus' face, but his vision was blurred. When the other man blew the flame out, grey and white plumes of smoke seemed to curl into spiraling horns. After a double take, Marshall still could not decide whether it was the fever or if his eyes were true. He swore looking at Angus, he could see the devil himself.

Angus extinguished the flame and pulled at his pipe. The insufferable scent of mixed, dry herb filled the room. When the physician blew the smoke out it carried the pungent stench toward Marshall.

"If you wish to die I can also make arrangements to accommodate you. Though, I doubt you will be satisfied with those circumstances, either." Angus took his seat again before continuing. "I appeal to your common sense, Marshall. Let us be friends again so that there is no more grief between us."

The corners of Marshall's eyes moistened and filled with drops of thick, red tears. He knew that despite anything coming from Angus' mouth, he truly had no choice of his own. After a few moments of silence, Marshall acquiesced with a slight nod of his head.

"Good man!" Angus proclaimed in triumph. "I shall see to your tea."

When Angus left him a woman he'd not seen before came in.

"Who are you?" Marshall struggled to ask.

The girl looked to be sixteen or seventeen. Close to Morrigan's age. She also had the same height and weight, Marshall noticed. She said nothing in return, but her eyes spoke volumes.

Whoever she was, she was scared and was a prisoner like him.

It then dawned on him that he missed the window of opportunity to meet with Robert. Panic swept through him as he tried to sit up. When he got halfway there, the muscles in his stomach cramped with such intensity it rent a scream from him.

The girl ran to his side and pleaded with him through quiet grunts to lie back down. Marshall was angry. Angry he stayed when the Plague took over their land, angry he sold his soul to the Devil for material things, and angry he was too much of a coward to end his own life to be free of it all. Whether he lived or died should not be the sole decision of Angus.

The girl beside him continued to tug at his arm and motioning to the bed.

"Girl, please!" he coughed out, but the girl was becoming frantic.

Marshall's coughing ripped through his tender lungs and chest in a violent manner. He was sure that at any second pieces of flesh would dislodge. He was almost correct. From between his lips, spittle laced with blood stained his hand and the sleeve of his bed gown.

"EEh!" The girl pleaded, "Ahhn! Ahn!"

When Marshall was able to catch his breath, he turned to look at the girl who continued to tug his arm and pat the bed. "Ahhn. Peeh!" she said over and over.

The merchant finally saw the girl could not formulate words because her tongue was completely missing!

"Did he do this to you?" Marshall whispered, his eyes trained on the door. "The Surgeon … Did he cut you?"

The girl turned pale and brought her hands to her lap. Her eyes dropped in an instant to stare at the floor.

"Tell me!" he hissed.

The girl nodded.

Marshall fell back against the bed and wept. He was in Hell and had no idea where the gates that led out could be. He was trying to process it all when the girl tucked him in. Angus had seen to it she kept her vow of silence in a most heinous way.

After Marshall was cleaned up, the girl picked up the soiled blankets and turned to meet the watchful eye of her captor, Angus. His eyes wandered over her but not in a lecherous way. More so in the same way a butcher sizes up a prized sow. Then, carrying his eyes toward Marshall he said, "I see you've met Analyn."

The girl's spine stiffened when she heard her name. She shook behind the basket in her hands.

"Analyn will be assisting us,' Angus continued. "While you are recovering, I will bring more help. If you have need of anything ring for a member of the staff."

The surgeon walked over to Marshall and placed a warm mug down on the table next to a small crystal bell. A plume of steam rose up from the dark brew against the cold air around it as Angus made quick work in examining his patient then called over his shoulder. "There are more items to be laundered in the cellar. See to it that you fetch those as well."

Analyn ran out of the room as soon as she could. She could not bear to be near him for any length of time.

"What did you do to her?" Marshall asked when she was gone.

"The same thing I did to you, my friend. I clipped her wings."

Marshall turned his head away from Angus and the surgeon smiled. Lifting the edge of the blanket up over the merchant's chest, he gave it a pat.

"One big happy family," he said in a cheerful voice. "You'll see. Now finish up your remedy."

Angus handed him the mug, and Marshall accepted it. He was determined to get well so he could stop this evil. He didn't know how yet; that would take time. For now, time was what he had, if he played along.

A few minutes after he'd finished his medicine, Marshall could feel his eyes grow heavy and his body floating with detachment. Whatever Angus put into the concoction was potent. The grayness of the room danced with shadowy movement causing his eyes to bounce under half-closed lids. He wouldn't have to worry about it much longer because his mind would soon be cast into dreams filled with colors more vivid than he'd ever seen before. Dreams filled with confusion, and laced with the drug he'd been given, lasted two days before releasing him from their strange lands.

When he awoke, he had to admit he'd never felt more rested. The aches in his body were still there but were nowhere as uncomfortable as they were previously. Marshall's mouth felt dry like sandpaper. He remembered the bell at the side of his bed, and rolled over to fetch it. It took a moment while he got used to moving again. The crystal let out a loud, fairy-like jingle when he gave it a shake. He had no sense of time of day when he looked around the room. He observed the windows were now boarded up from the inside.

Was there a storm? He wondered.

There was a tapping on the floor coming from down the hall and heading in his direction. Marshall tried to make out what was causing it but could not place it at once. Everything was still foggy in his brain. Analyn then appeared in the doorway. She was carrying a tray, distracting the merchant from his thoughts. He offered a smile but noticed as she made her way to his bed the tapping noise came from *her*. He leaned over toward the side of his bed and looked down at the hem of her skirt, only to shudder in horror. One of Analyn's legs was gone, and in its place was a wooden peg!

"My God!" He croaked.

Analyn's eyes filled with tears and shame. She set the mug of fresh water down on the table with a shaky hand and turned to make a hasty exit. Marshall could not help himself. He grabbed her arm to stop her.

"I *will* get you out of here," he said with a quiet voice.

Analyn met his gaze for only an instant. Her dead eyes showed a hint of life before giving him a silent nod of her head. She could tell Marshall was earnest and meant what he said. Their locked gaze was broken when Analyn heard footsteps coming up from the cellar stairs. She disappeared before Angus caught her lingering too long and got suspicious.

"Look at you,' The surgeon said as he entered, "Nearly right as rain."

Marshall feigned a smile of gratitude. "Nearly."

"You've been through worse, old man," the other man said, and sat on the edge of his bed.

Marshall lifted his cup to take a sip of water to wet his tongue then asked, "What happened to the girl?"

Angus' smile lost some of its brilliance. "An accident. One beyond repair."

The coolness of Angus' eyes told Marshall what he already knew; it was not to be discussed further. If he was to convince Angus he was on his side, he'd have to tread with care.

"I only ask out of curiosity," Marshall winked. "I rather fancy a woman who is silent and obedient, as you know."

Angus studied him.

Marshall pushed on to another subject, "When can I get out of this wretched bed? I've slept enough."

Angus chuckled, and gave the merchant's leg a tap. "See? Almost right as rain. Come, test your land legs. Are you able to stand?"

Breathing an inward sigh of relief, Marshall sat up and swung his legs off the edge of the bed. "Here goes nothing," he said, then placed a bit of weight down.

His legs felt like jelly at first but with a little time he was standing on his own. He took a couple of short steps to get his joints loosened. All the while he was under Angus' scrutiny.

CHAPTER 18: TORTURE IS IN THE MIND

It had been several days since Marshall was able to get up and walk around. Though each day he became stronger, the medicine Angus gave him still made him sleep for more hours than usual. He woke up the next day as if there were rocks in his head. Lifting it up was almost impossible. He grew restless and was anxious to get his strength back.

He decided to roll over and ring the bell for service. Perhaps Analyn would bring him something to eat so he could regain his much-needed energy. Reaching for it, he gave the bell a light shake, trying not to make a ruckus. In the silence of the house, it pierced the darkness with its jingle. Marshall cringed a little at how loud it seemed.

After a few moments when Analyn did not appear, the merchant ran out of patience and got up to help himself. As he swung his legs out of the bed he heard a faint scream. Resting his feet on the cold floor, he paused and listened. He thought he heard it again, but it was so far away he couldn't be positive. Pushing his feet into his shoes, Marshall pulled the blanket around his shoulders and walked to the door. Just as he was about to open it, the cry came again. This time it was louder.

The man was still groggy, and when he crept out of his room, the world seemed to weigh upon his right side. He tried to walk straight but ended up leaning and bumping into the walls. Marshall finally made it to the cellar door when the screams grew loud and clear.

He was torn.

Did he race down there and give away his hand? Or did he push aside all morality and continue his charade?

Sweat poured from his brow as he weighed the options before him.

It would do him no good to go down into the cellar as he was. He had no balance, no weapon, and if he charged into the Devil's Den now the only result would be his death. Angus would easily overpower him and continue on with whatever atrocities he was carrying out. Marshall had to keep his wits about him.

Leaning against the door, he took in slow, deep breaths and tried to calm himself. The sound of footsteps making their way upstairs from the cellar caused Marshall to advance toward the pantry where he pretended to have reason for being in the kitchen.

When the door swung open, Marshall was slamming crates and pushing things around. "Where are the fresh eggs?"

The surgeon emerged from behind the door and paused, glancing around.

"Marshall what are you doing out of bed this late?"

Marshall stopped and turned to face the surgeon. "You could've told me we were this hard up for help, sir. No fresh eggs or bread to be found? You know how I love my midnight meals."

Angus looked around the kitchen and down the hall where Marshall's bedroom was. "Reliable help is hard to find. Even more difficult is finding trustworthy staff."

The physician leveled his gaze at Marshall who raised his brows in a questioning way.

"Since when do you not trust me with the *hens*, Angus? Am I a wolf now?" Marshall asked.

The merchant turned and threw the kettle arm over the fire with a pot full of water. He did everything he could to appear busy and normal so Angus would not become suspicious of him being up and walking around.

"I trust you, old friend," Angus said in a cold, distant way.

"While that's refreshing to know, I'm still wondering what I shall eat besides week-old stew."

Pretending to be disconcerted at the present lack of their resources seemed to be working because Angus' demeanor changed. His shoulders were more relaxed, as were his features.

"I pray you'll endure one more evening of stew, and then tomorrow you'll accompany me to the market," The physician announced.

Damnit, Marshall cursed to himself. He was hoping to get away to the market alone, at least so he could purchase a weapon of some sort. Marshall wondered how much was even left of the town. If there *was* anyone left alive, he couldn't rally help if Angus was going to hover like a hawk.

"It's about time you offer to ride with me to the market!" Marshall quickly threw out. "All these years I go and face the crowds and search for your crazy ingredients. Now they'll see! They'll see I'm not crazy!"

The merchant ranted as he walked around Angus, grabbing some vegetables to toss into the water. Angus wasn't completely convinced, but he turned back to the door and called over his shoulder before disappearing again. "Get some rest. You don't want to overdo it and make yourself ill again."

When the cellar door closed, Marshall collapsed against the tabletop with his weight. He was almost healed but still very sore, especially in his groin. Easing his way into a chair, he pulled the bowl of potatoes near and began to clean the dirt off of them. Twenty minutes or so passed and his head began to bob. He couldn't fight the sleepiness that came over him. He leaned his head against the wall and fell back asleep.

It wasn't a long nap he could tell. In fact, it felt like he'd just fallen asleep. The sound of the cellar door opening roused him. It was still dark everywhere in the house.

The candle, an inner voice said. *Yes! The candle!*

Why hadn't he thought of that before? Looking at the candle beside him he could gauge he'd only been asleep for about fifteen minutes. When he'd come in and lit it, it was still new. Looking at it now, it had just begun melting away at the tip.

He was so focused on the candle he didn't see the shadow moving across the wall. It inched closer with its owner until it went no further. The merchant turned at the sound of a chain falling to the floor.

The sight before him made Marshall jump from the chair, knocking it into the kettle, which spilled over.

"My God!" he screamed. "What has happened to you!"

The girl, Analyn, was shackled by a collar around her throat. Fingers were missing from one hand, and her clothes were tattered. Her missing leg confirmed, the girl wobbled on the peg of wood that appeared to be jammed into the blood stump of her thigh.

"Oh God, Analyn," he whispered to her. "I should've helped you. I'm so sorry."

Analyn was tugging at the chain, reaching for Marshall in desperation. Marshall knew he was being tested. He knew Angus had let her walk upstairs on purpose. The merchant's face was filled with pain as he stood upright again. *She's already dead, Marshall,* he tried to convince himself. He walked over to her and wrapped his arm around her shoulders. She was so cold.

Analyn began to cry in silence, seeking his arms for solace, but Marshall was walking her back down the stairwell. The girl, realizing this, flew into hysterics. She tried to run, again, but Marshall grabbed hold of the chain.

"Please, girl. Please!" he said as he fought with her.

He was reeling her in like a large fish on the choppy seas. He would give her some lead of the chain then pull back. Every

time she made it up two or three steps, he'd pull her back down one. She was wearing herself out little by little. The more she clawed at the stairs and the stone wall, the more her nails peeled back and her fingers bled. Marshall was killing his humanity with every jerk of the chain. He was torturing this girl. The one he promised to save. The one he convinced to trust him. Marshall gave a final grunt and tugged with all of his remaining strength until the girl bounced down the stairs and landed with a loud crack of her skull.

Did I kill her? Part of him hoped he had.

Releasing the chain, Marshall crawled to the girl's side. Analyn was alive. Barely.

The girl had given up and was staring at the cellar door; her hope just out of reach.

"I'm sorry," Marshall whispered so Angus could not hear. Analyn ignored him as fresh tears spilled from her eyes.

He stood once more and grabbed the girl's wrist then turned pulling her behind him to the back room. When Marshall got to the door, it was already partially open. He extended his arm and gave a soft push, peering inside. The surgeon stood in the candlelight. The flame of the fire in front of him danced in the reflection of his eyes, making him appear all the more demonic. He could not possibly be human, Marshall thought to himself.

He had to convince himself of this in order to process the abhorrent things this man of flesh and bone had done.

"Very good, Marshall," Angus said. "Place her back on the table."

The surgeon remained where he was but motioned with his hand to the bloody table in front of him. The leather straps where the arms and legs went were frayed and worn. Marshall could tell Analyn had been down here fighting for her life.

It was the stench that got to Marshall. The stench was like warm, spoiled pork left in the sun for days. It filled his nostrils, clinging to the inside hairs so he could not shake it, even by breathing through his mouth. He struggled to keep the bile from rising past his tongue and focused on unwrapping the chain from around his arm.

"I don't have all day. Please move quickly," Angus prodded.

Marshall could not contain the sickness any longer. He doubled over and spilled what little contents he had in his stomach. When he thought he was done another wave overcame him, forcing him into a dry heave, strangling him. He inhaled, taking in another huge gulp of the rancid air. When Angus' patience ran out he grabbed a bucket of water from the floor and dumped it over Marshall's head.

"Place her on the table," he repeated, throwing the empty bucket at him. "And go get more fresh water."

Marshall ran from the cellar, grateful for the chance to leave. When he got to the top of the stairs he stopped at the loud whack from behind. It sounded like a cleaver meeting a wood block. Analyn's gurgling cry followed. Marshall took off running again and kept running until he fell into the mud, sobbing.

The lake was only a few feet away from him, but he could not will himself to move. Burying himself in the soil he screamed, using the earth to muffle the sound, then leaned his head back and stared at the sky.

"Why, God, have you brought such a vile creature to us?" he asked with a croak. "He is an abomination worse than Lucifer himself. Even the devils weep before him."

There was no answer from the heavens, only the ominous sound of thunder in the distance.

CHAPTER 19: THE WATCHERS

It had been several months since Marshall had seen Morrigan. He tried to convince himself she was dead. The reality was that she was, in some form, down in the cellar with Angus. Things were unnervingly quiet except late at night when Angus began construction again. Marshall's anxiety grew stronger, weighing on his chest at the thought. *What if Angus was scheming to capture another girl?*

He sat, gnawing like a rat on the edge of his piece of loaf, lost in the thought. Angus had insisted on a daily routine as a way of getting back to normal. All around them the villagers fell like birds from their perch, cold and dead, as the Plague saw fit to pluck them. Inside homes, the fire was warm and inviting. Outside, bodies lay strewn about in various stages of decomposition, waiting for someone to carry them away.

Marshall stood from the table and cleaned his place, then began his inventory of the pantry. He sighed to himself, realizing he could no longer put off going out to fetch supplies. It was getting harder to find them, resources were dwindling with the population. He'd have to scavenge among the ships and the abandoned homes. Most of the vendors were dead, and the ones still alive, hid from illness and thieves.

"M'lord," he called toward the cellar. "I'm on my way out."

He listened for a response but heard nothing. "I'll return as soon as I can."

The walk to find supplies was dangerous. A man would kill another man for the tattered shirt off his back. Angus

allowed Marshall to arm himself when he made these trips. Not out of kindness, but to protect his "property." The merchant's fingers crept down along the blade under his cloak to reassure himself. The cold blade pressed against his belly brought him both comfort and distress to feel it there. If times were normal and he was found armed with no escort, they would assume him to be up to no good.

"Who cares anymore?" he said aloud. "Everyone is dead."

The silence around him was disturbed by a snapping of a twig in the line of trees beside him. Instinct and muscle memory put his hand around the hilt of his weapon. The merchant may be getting older but his eyes were still keen and well-trained. He scanned the trees looking for the source of the noise.

"Probably just a hungry stray," he said to convince himself.

Marshall continued on, but the hairs on the back of his neck rose in warning. Something was out there, watching him.

A man with Marshall's experience knew trusting your gut was paramount to survival. He picked up the pace and kept his ears open to the surroundings. Another cracking of twigs, like the snapping of bone, came from the trees that sounded him. This time it was closer.

Suddenly, and without hesitation, Marshall sprinted forward. He wanted to outrun whatever was following him. It was what *they,* or *it,* wanted—he fell for the trap. No matter where he ran, the snapping of twigs and rustling of underbrush came from every direction. To the left of him. To the right of him. In front of him. Behind him. Fear and panic filled him like a rabbit running from the wolf, and he lost all sense of good judgment. He could see no other path before him and cut left in

another direction, into the tall grass fields, and away from the trees.

"Stay away from me!" he shouted. "I have nothing!" Up ahead he saw several areas of smoke rising and ran in their direction. It was most probable there were other villagers burning bodies. He hoped seeing there were others around, possible witnesses, would dissuade whatever was chasing him from harming him.

"Help me!" Marshall called out and waved his arms.

He pushed his frail body as far as he could. When he got closer to the clearing of trees, he noticed the sun was being swallowed by an incoming storm.

"Help!" He screamed louder. "Please! Someone help me!"

Marshall's lungs burned within his chest, but he pressed on. The first drops of rain fell hard and angry against his cheeks like tiny needles. He knew the dirt beneath his feet would turn to mud soon and slow him down. He had to push harder to reach the others!

The sky darkened and grew dense with the promise of a good downpour, coupled with thunder and lightning. Marshall could barely see in front of him with the tall grass and insects being stirred up. He looked behind him to see how close they were. He could *hear* them and the loud crunching of their feet on the leaves against the earth, but could see nothing. It was pure adrenaline pushing him onward. Looking ahead of him again, he saw light from under the smoke and felt a sense of relief. *A bonfire! To burn their dead,* he thought.

Marshall's relief began to wane quickly when it dawned on him he didn't smell bodies burning—he smelled incense! He put the brakes on by digging his heels into the ground and slid, almost falling. The tall grass opened up, and his eyes grew large.

Standing before him were figures dressed in masks, holding lanterns. The masks had long beaks, and the smell of herbs permeated through the tips billowing eerily around them. Their glass eyes shimmered with the reflection of the amber glow from their lanterns. The feathers around their neck glistened with beaded rain drops, and the large, rubber gloves they wore on their hands made the figures appear all the more inhuman like monstrous bird creatures.

A shot of lightning stretched across the sky, illuminating these "things" in front of him. He took notice of the tattered, black cloaks made from scrap leather. It all added to the illusion that these weren't humans at all, but otherworldly spirits or wraiths come to exact their judgment. Out of fear and awe Marshall found he could no longer move. He'd long forgotten what was chasing him.

From behind, three more figures joined nine who were standing before him. He was wolf-packed. Chased and herded right into their hands.

"What do you want?" Marshall managed when he could speak.

The first figure came forward. Each step was slow and measured. Its boots had risers underneath—giant soles which added inches to their overall height. The incense from within the long, curved beak rolled forward and reached out like mist, encircling him, and leaving him feeling hazy.

"We are watching," the figure said, his voice filling Marshall's skull buzzing like a thousand angry bees.

When he tried to respond, he couldn't. Something was in the incense, and it was making him feel incapacitated. Marshall watched as the figures surrounded him, two more circled him several times searching for … *for what* ... weapons or anything of value, perhaps? He wasn't sure about anything anymore as his

mind spun from the hallucinogenic effects of the incense. The rules of *this* world defied laws of nature and reason.

"Take him," the first one warbled.

Marshall wanted to ask where to, but he was still paralyzed and his vision was growing blurry. He could hear them shuffling around him, but he could no longer make out distinct shapes. One thing was for certain, Marshall was learning his place in the new world's food chain.

CHAPTER 20: TRANSCEND

When Marshall hadn't returned in a timely manner, Angus grew furious and began his angry pacing. He had other things to worry about than his missing whipping boy. He paced a few more steps then went back to stand in front of Morrigan.

"I'm sorry, my beloved. I know you are hungry," he said with a tenderness reserved for her alone. "I will make Marshall pay *dearly* for causing you discomfort."

Angus lit the candle beside him and examined Morrigan, again. She was corpse white with shades of blue circles around her eyes and mouth. Around her teeth, her lips were thin, and she recoiled in pain from the light which broke through the dark. One of her eyes was a ghostly white, now.

"There, there, Precious," Angus soothed. "How about a small snack?"

He placed the candle down to lift a metal trapping cage. Inside, a large rat was clawing to get out, sensing the impending danger. Morrigan smelled the rodent and swung her head. Her stomach churned painfully, and she lurched forward, snapping her jaws at the cage. The rat squealed, terrified of becoming a meal. The high-pitch noise taunted Morrigan, who pulled at the chains around her neck. The shackles around her ankles kept her restrained from attacking both the meal … and Angus.

With a smile, he placed the cage back on the floor and slid it over to his captive bride-to-be. What was once a beautiful, carefree young woman was now a monster to behold even in the dim light. Morrigan had only one thought in her scrambled mind. *Hunger.* It burned at the base of her skull and twisted her stomach into unbearable pain until she lunged at the cage again

and fought to open it. Her fingers were clumsily pulling and banging on the wire, driven by the hunger of her dying body.

"Morrigan," Angus said and tapped a stick on the ground. "Focus, dear."

Morrigan hissed and slammed the cage down, once.

"You must learn to control your urges. I *know* you're still in there. You must fight for control or else I cannot take the chains off, and you will not get your snack."

Morrigan opened her mouth wide and let out a low, guttural growl. The sound was primal, ticking and hitching from her dry throat. It reminded him of the sound an insect would make.

Angus was unmoved by the sight of her. All he could see was the woman she once was. The one he desired above all else. No matter how broken or horrific she looked, he was content to cherish her. Watching her now, he sat back in his chair and lit his pipe, giving it a few pulls. Once the fragrant smoke filled the room, he lifted a book from a pile on the floor and began to read.

Morrigan glared at him with pure hatred before turning her attention back to the cage she still held in her hands. She tried to control the hunger and the pain. What was barely left of *her* fought against the urges but her teeth chattered up and down making a sound like a rattlesnake's tail. Gripping the cage tight, the rat dove at her fingers. Its teeth dug into one, gnashing and gnawing in a futile attack.

She brought the cage to her eyes to get a closer look. With the light shining, everything looked as though she was gazing out at the world through a jar of honey. She *could* smell the rat. Its heady, musky scent rising up with its fear. She could smell bodies a mile away and every heartbeat within that same distance. Whatever Angus fed her changed her, and when one part of her brain shut down, another compensated. Her sense of

touch became dull, but her sense of smell grew stronger. She could not taste what she ate, but she could hear the fluttering of its heart as she ripped into its flesh.

When Angus saw she was focusing, he placed a shade over the light to give her relief from the intensity of the flame. As the light around her dimmed further, the outline of the rat in her sights grew brighter. She could see the shape of it by its body heat. Her mind was beginning to process everything, associating which smell belonged to which shape. The background noise of the hunger revved in response to the sound of the rat's battering heart and the slow steady drum of Angus' as well. With urgent fingers, she worked at the cage until finally, the latch unhooked!

Angus lowered his book and peered into the shadows at Morrigan, who was staring back at him. She had a deep gaze of triumph and control as she held up the writhing animal. He offered a smile at her and nodded.

"Very good, flower," he said.

Morrigan responded with another growl, this one was more sultry than menacing.

When Angus went back to his reading, Morrigan tore into her prize.

***

When Marshall awoke, he was in a strange place.

He was getting used to that. He moved cautiously. A mental note of his body's movements told him he had all his parts. Or at least what was left of them. He hoped he was correct in that assumption.

The window beside his bed told him it was probably early morning, unless another day of storms were upon them. In which case, it would make time of day hard to guess.

     The door opened and a man stepped in with a tray, "Oh my. Good morning'!" he said, bringing the tray to Marshall's bed. "Ye gave us a fright, lad."

     Marshall remained silent and confused.

     "Well we heard bangin' a' th' door in th' wee hours. When we opened 'em there ye were. Justa' lyin' there starin' at th' sky. Th' rain was pourin' on ye an' ye were nearly froze t'death."

     The man sat beside Marshall and smiled. He wore the typical frock of a local friar.

     "St. Agnus?" Marshall guessed, aloud.

     "Aye," the friar said, his smile brightening.

     "But don't ye be worryin' about all tha' now. Get ye somethin' in ye t' get ye strength back. When ye are feelin' better we can sort it out."

     The friar stood and turned back before he got to the door. "Oh, m' manners. Forgive me. I'm Alexander."

     "Marshall."

     "Good t'meet ye, then," he responded. He gave a wave and left.

     Once he was gone, Marshall stared at the door. "I've fallen into a rabbit hole. Nothing will ever be normal again."

     He had to come up with a plan of what to do next. He didn't know if Alexander and this place was another sick adventure, but either way, Angus would come looking for him. St. Agnus was ten miles further than St. Michael's which would be Angus' first stop. If he was lucky, he would have time to finish his meal, collect his things, and have it figured out where to run.

***

When Morrigan finished her snack she sat down on the cushion Angus provided for her. She knew this routine by heart. Eat. Clean. Mate.

Angus went to Morrigan with the water bucket and set it on the floor. He tapped his stick and Morrigan emerged from the shadows. Bits of fur and blood were still stuck on her lips and chin. Her hands were a mess, and so was her dress. The needling in her brain to feed was duller, and because of this, she was tamer. Still, Angus approached with caution. He held clean clothes and fresh linen.

"Will you please turn around, my dear?" he requested.

There was a small twitch of Morrigan's brow. She was working it all out. He could see it on her face, she was milling ideas and thoughts around behind her glass-like eyes.

She turned to face the other direction, placing her back to him.

"Thank you, Morrigan. I'm going to proceed like last time. I will remove your soiled clothing first, and then wash you."

Morrigan lowered her chin to one shoulder in a gesture that almost seemed demure, and lifted her eyes to watch him. However delicate her body seemed, her eyes reminded him she was still a predator. *Yes,* he thought, *she's still in there. She's changed, but she's still in there.*

Setting the bucket down, Angus removed the soiled clothing from her shoulders pressing his lips to her skin in a gentle way. Her cadaver-like body was cold against his touch. He brought his arms around her and slid his hands upward along her ribcage. Pressing his palms just under her breasts he could feel her heart beat. It was slow and almost non-existent.

I'm already dead, she thought.

Angus' lips trailed up along her jawline, and she opened her jaws slowly, baring her teeth. He had to control his heart rate. If it climbed too high she would go into feeding mode. To calm them both, he hummed a quiet waltz from a distant memory, and allowed his hands to lower her dress to the floor. Morrigan's head twitched at an angle, watching it. Her movements were always stiff unless she had been fed well.

Kneeling down to the bucket that was steaming against the cool cellar air, Angus lifted the soapy cloth. He pressed it against Morrigan's leg and worked his way up in small circular motions. He took in slow and steady breaths to keep his desire at bay. It was like courting a black widow. At any moment she could turn on him and devour him and his foolish, weak heart.

He pressed on, testing his luck. Raising his hand over the curve of her firm, round arse, Angus pressed his lips to her lower back. Morrigan's skin rippled. The boils she once had when she was infected had disappeared. Now all that remained were the tracks of sutures. It was a strange sensation to be attracted and aroused by them. He had replaced parts of her body that had decayed or been destroyed by infection with new ones and the difference of texture from one limb to the next exhilarated him. Yes, she was pieced together, but each piece was sewn in place with great care and love. Each time another piece began to show signs of imperfection he'd hunt for days for the right material in which to replace it.

Morrigan stirred in his embrace. She had not been fed as much as usual, but it was imperative he adhere to a strict schedule. It was the only way to condition and train her. Everything came down to timing and ritual.

Angus continued to clean Morrigan, revering her body in the process. When he was finished, he wrapped her in clean linen which had been warmed by the fireplace.

"Are you ready, Morrigan?" he asked, holding his hand out to her.

Morrigan's head ticked downward to his hand, and she gazed at it for a count of five beats of his heart before her eyes flicked up at his. It was her language. Her acknowledgement that she understood him. She lifted her arm and placed her hand in his. Angus closed his fingers around hers before unlatching the chain from the wall. He was discreet in the way he held it. He didn't want to cause her disrespect by holding it like a leash, but he had to be prudent. Once she was secured, he led her to the bed chambers.

Inside *their* room, Angus brushed Morrigan's hair from her face. When it was free from tangles he smiled at her, motioning with his free hand toward the bed. It was ornate and custom designed just for them by his own hand. The headboard was constructed in such a way it could withstand the weight of her being restrained. Above it was another set of straps and beams. Across the Asian silk dressing the bed was an elaborate, silver horse bit he had commissioned years before the Plague ever hit their village. He used it for his *other* escapades to debase them. For Morrigan the bit would be used to keep him safe from his *Femme Fatale*.

Angus picked up the bell at his bedside, giving it a shake. The chime summoned two women. Both wore silk wraps to cover where eyes once were, and their mouths had been sewn shut. It had taken some months of practice and training to get the two prepared, but Angus had finally done it. Standing beside Morrigan, each of them took one of her hands in theirs, leading her to the bed where her chain was reattached. One of the girls fastened the bit around Morrigan's head, and both girls returned to the edge of the bed beside Angus.

"You may undress me now," Angus said with quiet command.

The girls removed Angus' clothing with the reverence they were trained to display. He stood with unabashed pride, in the nude while allowing the cool air to rush over him. He moved closer to the bed and watched as Morrigan crawled toward him, her robe sliding off her like a snake's discarded scales. When the heat of his skin was close, she pressed her face against his chest and sniffed at his skin but grew agitated. What she sought was not there.

Morrigan lunged forward and was halted in her attempt to attack Angus by the chains. She knew this game. And she wanted her prize.

"Easy, beloved. It's coming," he cooed to her.

The girls beside him trembled in anticipation. They, too, knew this sadistic game, and they weren't as eager to play.

Angus fixed his eyes on Morrigan and reached out for one of the girls. His fingers tangling in her hair, he drew her to him, inches away from Morrigan. The girl whimpered behind her sealed lips, and her heart drummed like a hummingbird, causing a spike in adrenaline.

Reaching up with his other hand, Angus pulled on a wheel which shortened the lead on Morrigan's chain. She growled and fought against it, but it did not yield. While Morrigan thrashed about, Angus was clearing a spot on the bed where he pinned one of the girls who fought against him. She felt the closeness of Morrigan, and tried to still herself so as to not attract her attention. She knew from watching him before losing her vision, Angus used their fear to rile up the monster. It worked well; it was how the girl had lost her eyes.

The memory of Morrigan devouring one of her eyes as she was forced to watch with the other was still fresh in her

mind. It was obvious to both girls, torture wasn't purely a physical game to Angus. It was also mental.

The surgeon wasn't content with causing anguish through external punishment alone. He desired the destruction of who they were, piece by piece, until he owned the body, mind, and spirit. He could smell the small success he'd made with this one already as he strapped her to the bed.

"Remember, pet," he began, "hold still. If you move or spill anything I will let her dine on another piece of your flesh."

The girl immediately acquiesced, going rigid. Struggling against primal instinct, she fought to control her breathing by pulling deep breaths through her nose. Morrigan was watching and pacing inside her invisible cage like a lioness.

"Girl Two," Angus called out, "bring the box."

The other girl flinched when summoned but moved without hesitation to comply. She barely fumbled as she maneuvered her way around the bed to his side table. Pulling the small, rectangular item out, she turned and presented it to him.

"Ah, thank you," Angus said, taking it from her. "You did very well this time."

The girl's head lowered, showing thankfulness for his praise. He had promised to open her mouth and allow her to eat if she did well this time. Her counterpart, Girl One, had been deprived for so long she ate part of her own tongue.

"Take your position, Girl Two," Angus directed.

The second girl did as she was told and moved to the platform used for her display at the side of the bed. Once she was sure she was in the correct location, she went down into a kneel.

Angus opened the box and took out a small jar. Holding it up to the light of the fireplace, he watched as the leeches swam over one another. He took up his silver tweezers from the box

and plucked them out one by one before attaching them to various spots on his body.

The small, black creatures began to suckle at once, fattening their bodies to nearly twice their original size. Replacing the jar and tweezers, Angus removed the scalpel and spoke to the first girl, trembling against the silks.

"Hold still, Girl One, and maybe you will live to eat tonight."

The girl's chest rose and fell to the rhythm of her panicked breathing, and Morrigan jerked at her chains in heightened frenzy. Angus watched her with love and pride while lifting his hand in the air, calling her to attention. Like a trained beast, her eyes snapped to attention on it, and Angus swiped his blade down, lashing at Girl One's outstretched arms with three deep but unfatal cuts. Each laceration bled out into the silk, and the girl screamed behind her sewn mouth, stretching the sutures until a few popped through the flesh.

Morrigan was in a frenzy, thrashing at her chains. Angus fell into a whirlwind rush of sexual arousal. He replaced the scalpel and closed the box setting it out of reach before crawling on the bed to claim Morrigan. There, the two fought against one another until Angus overpowered her. Once he had her pinned he pushed himself inside of her with a victorious grunt. Morrigan raged, grinding her teeth on the bit in her mouth. He asserted his position over her by forcing her head into the blankets until she submitted. To "reward" her, Angus would pull off the leeches, fat with his blood, and feed them to her until she was docile, and he could have his way with her.

When he was spent, he rolled off her and untied Girl One. She was as white as the silks once were before she bled into them.

"Girl Two, take her away," he ordered, still breathless from his tryst.

Perspiration glistened on his skin, and he took in a deep breath imagining he could breathe the flames in straight from the fireplace. He felt powerful and sated. For the moment. It would not last long when he remembered Marshall had escaped, defying him. It was time for Angus to devise a plan for retrieving his titmouse.

"Fetch the others to draw my bath," he added to Girl Two who was dragging the other girl out.

CHAPTER 21: THE WULFE AND THE CROWE

Angus sat in the bath contemplating his next move. It was inconvenient not having Marshall around to care for the upstairs while he tended to Morrigan and the ladies. The ones who were not a good match for harvested parts were subdued and trained to serve him and his bride.

Indeed, Angus had taken advantage of the devastation around him. In his eyes, it was survival of the fittest. And he was both fit and intelligent enough to sit on the throne of the new world. Soon he'd unveil his bride and sell the cure, hoping to gain enough funds to overthrow the monarchy. Perhaps, depending on how wiped out the rest of the world was, he could even expand his reign. He'd scarcely kept up with any of the news from abroad since taking on his new role.

Angus pulled the smoke from his pipe, released the smoke he held within his lungs and then looked down into the water. The girl between his legs was beginning to thrash, so he gripped her hair harder and pulled her up to catch a breath. The surgeon almost forgot he was holding her under water while she bathed him.

The girl came up gasping for air, taking several large gulps into her lungs. Her body was shaking with fear, and her hands clawed at whatever they could find as she searched for the edge of the pool in blind desperation. Angus rolled his eyes, letting her slip and slide her way to the edge of the bath. Once there, she huddled in the corner and curled into her knees.

Angus waited for her breathing to slow down. "Fetch my clothes, girl."

"Y—Yes, m'lord," she whimpered.

Luckily for her she was beautiful with her brown skin and exotic looking features. The girl was tall and athletic. Her

eyes were the shape of almonds and glistened in the dark like a fawn peering out at the world. She would not be a match for Morrigan's reconstruction. *What a shame*, he thought to himself. *She is a lovely specimen.*

Standing up, Angus climbed the marble stairs and stood waiting for the girl to dress him.

"Get put together and dressed. We are going to find my assistant."

The girl faced Angus in confusion. She had no reason to believe she'd ever feel the light of day again.

"Are you dumb, child!" he shouted at her, annoyed. "Go! Now!"

His voice bellowed off the walls and caused her to flinch before she ran to obey.

"Oh Marshall,' he growled, "why must you make me *chase* you?"

Angus turned to stare at the murals on the wall he'd painted when he first began remodeling his home. The beautiful Morrigan stared back at him from every scene of torture and sexual fantasy displayed before his eyes.

"You will be whole once more, my sweet Morrigan. I saved you from this plague, and I shall cure you of death. Soon, we will wed."

He pressed his fingers to the wall and caressed the shape of her body. Risking infection by going into the bad air of the city made him irritable, but he would not allow Marshall to abandon his post.

"Ungrateful welp," he hissed between gritted teeth.

Curling his fingers inward, Angus clenched his jaw. The rage was rising in him again. He needed to control it before going out in public. Emotion was a weakness he would not allow

others to see. When he was able to settle himself down again, he caught his breath and stalked out of his bath chambers.

He had a good idea where the merchant would hide. Someplace he never would have set foot in before, but these were desperate times for Marshall. Pulling his riding cloak around him he went to ready the horses. In the distance, the church bells filled the air causing the edges of Angus' mouth to curl into a knowing smile.

***

Marshall finished his meal and got up to dress. He continued to watch outside the window for any signs of Angus' arrival. He had to get away while he had the advantage of gaining distance, even if he still had no idea where he was headed. Marshall and Angus were well travelled and spent many days talking of their favorite, remote getaways. No doubt, Angus made a mental library of each of them.

Perhaps Marshall was being paranoid, but he wanted to take no chance on it. He needed to be as far away as possible. As he was fastening his belt, he heard the approaching sound of voices. It didn't matter if they were whispering, the acoustics of the stone walls allowed sounds to echo throughout. He couldn't make out what they were saying, but Marshall could distinguish three separate voices.

Facing the door, Marshall hesitated when the knock came before answering. "Yes. Please, come in."

Better to get goodbyes out of the way than to disappear and make a suspicious departure.

"Oh! Master Marshall, how ambitious of ye t'be up and dressed already," Alexander said.

The friar stood beside two other gentlemen. One was the rector, and the other was dressed in the attire of a physician. Marshall's heart sank.

"This be Father Thomas, and this be Mister Crowe. Mister Crowe has taken over th' infirmary for our humble residence."

Mister Crowe gave a nod and stepped forward, allowing his eyes to travel over Marshall. His bushy brows rose, and he grabbed one of Marshall's hands, tugging it toward himself for observation. It was obvious he had no regard for personal space or boundaries.

"It's extraordinary," he said in a quiet tone. "You have no signs of the Black Death, yet you've been out in the bad air."

The man then helped himself to Marshall's other hand, turning it over in his own.

"I give thanks to God for that," Marshall said, pulling his hand back.

"Hmm, yes," Mister Crowe replied.

"Mister Marshall," Alexander broke in, "Friar Thomas said that if ye show no signs of th' illness ye may stay a few days t'recover properly."

Mister Crowe had taken a few steps back. Something about the way he moved seemed familiar to Marshall.

"I could not impose. You have an infirmary to tend to. I imagine your hands are full."

"Tis no imposition, Mister Marshall," Alexander chirped happily. "Most of th' patients have gone."

"Gone?" Marshall asked.

"Aye," Alexander smiled. "Mister Crowe has given them med'cine, and they have made a full recovery."

Marshall's eyes narrowed in doubt. "What sort of medicine is it, may I inquire?"

Alexander turned to Mister Crowe for him to answer.

"It's all quite complicated for the laymen—"

"I'm not a layman, Mister Crowe," Marshall cut in with a sharp tongue.

"I didn't mean to imply you were. Forgive me," Mister Crowe said with a careful measure of words.

"Then how do you explain this cure?" Marshall pressed.

"As you say. God's grace," Mister Crowe smiled, "And a mixture of precise science, a knowledge of botany, and a mentor well-versed in medicine."

Marshall's brow grew damp with perspiration, and the blood drained from his head to his feet.

Alexander looked between them as they spoke before noticing Marshall's pallor.

"Mayhap you should sit down, Mister Marshall," he suggested, guiding the man to sit on the edge of his bed.

"I just need a moment. I'm fine, thank you," Marshall said, catching his breath.

The silent Friar Thomas stood observing. He didn't seem moved to action in any of it. Something was decidedly off about all this. Marshall's head swam, and he felt as if he might float away.

"Do you feel feverish, Mister Marshall?" Mister Crowe asked, watching him.

"No," Marshall said with a frown. "I feel a lightness of head."

Mister Crowe looked around to everyone, "I think we might be overwhelming him. Let's depart and allow him to rest."

Mister Crowe stood at the door and held it for everyone. When Alexander took a step forward, Marshall grabbed his arm.

"Please stay," Marshall began. He saw the abrupt pause everyone took at his peculiarity, and recovered. "I've had an eventful evening; a little conversation would help to soothe me."

Alexander's face lit up at an opportunity to be useful. "Aye, Mister Marshall, t'would be a pleasure."

Mister Crowe objected with a sour look at the young man. "Don't you have some work left to do?"

It was obvious he looked down on Alexander, reminding Marshall of how he'd been treated by Angus.

The silent Friar put his hand out and shook his head, motioning for Mister Crowe to exit. Mister Crowe's eyes crinkled at the corners, and he stiffened before exiting.

Once they were alone, Alexander brought a chair closer to Marshall's bed. "What should we discuss, Mister Marshall? I'm afraid I ain't much educated, but I be learnin' wit' th' other friars."

Marshall pulled his gaze away from the door and looked at Alexander. The young man was eager to please. Marshall wasn't sure if Angus taking his man-jewel made him softer, or if he genuinely liked the lad. He decided, it was a little bit of both. And because he understood Alexander's need to please, he'd have to be content with the "loyal dog" syndrome. Something Marshall was quite familiar with.

"Alexander, I need to confide in someone I can trust. But I have no one left in the world, and I don't know who can help me."

Alexander's eyes changed from mirthful and bright to sad and tearful. "Mister Marshall have ye lost yer family t'th' Black Death?"

"Something like that," Marshall answered. "You see, you and I are actually a lot more alike than you think."

"Oh, sir. Thank ye kindly but I'm just a lowly friar come from th' gutter, unwanted." Alexander looked down, embarrassed but still kept a friendly smile.

"And I, too, was once discarded trash washed ashore until a man found me," Marshall recounted. "I was a street rat, nothing more. And a man helped me gain respect."

Alexander's chin lifted and hope shone in his eyes. "Aye, Mister Crowe has given me his word tha' he will help me t'read an' t'write."

Marshall looked down at his hands. He had to work fast, but he couldn't make a false move and risk Alexander running back to his mentor.

"How long has he been promising to teach you?" Marshall asked with a cautious tone.

Alexander shifted to conceal his nervousness. "It be quite a while, sir. But Mister Crowe be a very busy man."

"Of course he is!" Marshall played along before adding, "Though I'm sure he's given you materials to practice with?"

Alexander looked confused but intrigued. "Materials, sir?"

Marshall had him hooked on the line. *Careful now,* he thought, *I must reel him in gentle-like.*

"Yes, you know, ink and quill to practice letters? It's all standard. I'm sure he's given you these things."

Tension grew in Alexander's face. Mister Crowe had been leading the young man on, probably with no intentions of ever teaching him to read nor to write.

"Is that what ye started with Mister Marshall?" Alexander asked.

"Oh, yes. Plenty of practice to keep my hours content."

The young man grew agitated in the realization that he'd been duped. Marshall watched it process through the expressions

on the lad's face and his body language. He didn't want it to
fester, only linger and nag at him.

"But, as I was saying earlier. I've no one, now."
Marshall let out a sigh, and gazed out toward the window. He
was trying to gauge the time but made it appear he was drifting
in a state of reverie.

"My mentor, who I thought was my *friend*, turned out to
be quite a deceitful man," Marshall continued. "He—He even
lashed out and harmed me, in unspeakable physical ways." He
waited and allowed the words to hang between them, adding a
bit of drama to go along with the story. He watched Alexander
getting pulled in further while hanging on his words.

Marshall turned to face the younger man with tears he
contrived filling his eyes. A small lift of his mouth into a half-
smile, and Alexander was hooked and pulled into his "boat."

"My God, sir. Is that how ye ended up here?" Alexander
asked.

"In a roundabout way"

Marshall spent the next hour going over the events
which led up to now in a well-manicured, edited version. He was
a merchant, after all. He could still weave a tale and fill it with
drama and swindle sympathies for characters in his stories like
old days. By his last word, Alexander was leaning forward in his
chair, jaw hanging slack.

"And this is why I need someone I can trust," Marshall
ended.

"Mister Marshall, tha' is a tale t'end all tales!"
Alexander said in breathless response.

He stood and paced the floor to sort his thoughts.
Marshall waited. He could not appear to be swaying the young
man, or else Alexander's guilt would come rushing to the

surface, dragging him back under. No, Alexander had to believe he was trading his loyalty to do some greater good.

"Mister Marshall," he said when the decision was made in his mind. "I have seen things here tha' make me believe tha' what ye say be true."

Marshall played along, feigning disbelief. He tempered it back enough to not frighten Alexander into thinking he did not believe the young man's testimony.

"My God, Alexander, here too? How have you managed to bear it?"

The young friar looked both relieved and ashamed, "It has been a burden, sir, I do confess."

"Have you no one to help you share this burden?" Marshall asked.

"I dare not, sir! Unless I be wantin' my hide used as a seat cushion!"

Marshall released a deep breath. "Maybe we could help each other, then?"

Alexander was in deep consideration of the idea, and Marshall could see the line he worked so hard to reel in was starting to give resistance. He had to think fast.

"But sir, what could *we* do? Where would we go?" Alexander said, looking doubtful.

Marshall leaned in. This would be his only shot, "The man that hurt me is a physician, and I think he has ties to your Mr. Crowe. If that be the case, I think it is too dangerous for us to stay here for much longer."

Alexander looked frightened and anxious, but Marshall continued. "I have an idea, though. We have many hours of light left, it seems. There are plenty of homes further out. If we were to leave now, we could continue outward, and be safe;but we'd have to keep moving."

Alexander was taking it all in. He looked to the window to see the light in the sky, then back down to his hands. He was still sorting it all out.

"I think I be wantin' to leave, too, sir. There be too much death an' things tha don't seem natural. But," he stopped and looked up at Marshall, "I'll be wantin' to take another."

Marshall's brows rose, "Who? I thought you said you had no one to share these burdens with."

"Aye sir, I did say that," Alexander went on. "But what I meant t'say was tha' we don't be speakin' on it. We know things because we been seein' it an' we hear it. We jus' don't be talkin' about it."

Marshall could see he was going nowhere without this friend the young friar had made so he nodded. "Yes of course. Then we must bring them, too."

Alexander smiled and came back to life. "I be knowin' a way out that no one will see us leavin' from. I'll go fetch some bread an' cheese from th' kitchen an' alert Josef. When I come for ye again, it'll be safe t'leave."

Marshall felt a bit of uncertainty and quickly asked, "When? How long?"

"Don't ye be worryin' Mister Marshall. The afternoon prayers be startin' in half of an hour, or so. When they go in, Mr. Crowe goes to th' patients. I'll come then."

Marshall nodded and offered his hand. "Thank you, Alexander. My new friend, thank you."

CHAPTER 22: ESCAPE

The bells rang out announcing the afternoon prayer time. All of the friars began filing in from various chambers in slow, swaying marches. The monastic chants floated down every hallway until they touched the door where Marshall stood waiting for Alexander.

The sound brought back memories of his childhood, of the friars who would walk through the village carrying the music of heaven to the poor, the downtrodden, and the discarded. The memory was vivid, the smells of poverty dragging him back to the days he wished to forget. Even still, there was a feel of nostalgia. No matter how hopeless the world felt, Marshall was driven by a desire to change his stars.

The door in front of him rattled, jarring him out of his daydreams, and Alexander stood there like a ray of light behind a dark cloud. He kept his word!

"Mister Marshall, we must go *now!*" he whispered in a rushed voice.

Marshall didn't hesitate; he sprinted forward and followed Alexander before asking questions.

"What's happened?" Marshall asked when they cleared the first hallway.

"I heard Mr. Crowe speakin' t' Father Thomas," Alexander said before ducking and pulling Marshall with him. Two of his fellow priests headed down toward the chapel. When they passed, Alexander turned to explain. "He sent word fer ye mentor, Mr. Angus Wulfe."

Marshall felt like he'd been crushed under a large stone. The name of the man he was running from made his spine turn to liquid, and his legs seemed to buckle.

"Mister Marshall, we must be leavin'," Alexander said with concern in his tone. "Are ye able t'make th' journey?"

"I have no choice, my friend," Marshall said, steadying himself.

The friar nodded and led the way down to the kitchen which appeared to be abandoned.

The chanting continued from a distance. Every papal body had been called to prayer, and according to Alexander, Mr. Crowe would be tending to the patients in the infirmary, set up down in the cellars.

The two men tiptoed cautiously between shadows that separated the light that filtered in from the tall, thin windows and the fires burning from the hearth.

"Josef," Alexander whispered out. "Where are ye?"

When there was no response, he called out again. "Josef! Josef where are ye, ye stewed prune?"

In the corner near the doorway from the main hall they heard a sound and paused in silence. Both men sensed danger and began to back up slowly. As they did, a shadowed figure slowly came forward who Alexander immediately recognized. It was Mr. Crowe.

"Run," he said, and shoved Marshall toward the exit they were to escape from.

Marshall moved to follow the friar and was blocked by another figure, this time sending the merchant backpedaling in fear. Angus stepped through the doorway and toward them both, as Mr. Crowe came up from behind, corralling them like sheep to the slaughter.

"Mister Wulfe," Mr. Crowe said, nodding his head in greeting. "I'm glad you were able to make it."

Angus kept his eyes on Marshall and responded, "I wouldn't have missed the invitation, Mister Crowe. It is worth every penny to see the looks on their faces."

Angus turned toward Mr. Crowe before he left. "Do not kill them. I want them alive. Break every bone in their body, if you must, but make sure they are alive when you deliver them to me."

The physician threw a purse toward the other man who caught it and gestured to the men behind him.

"Yes, sir," Mr. Crowe said, smiling at the weight of the purse. "It will be a pleasure."

Several large, burly men came out of the shadows, and the fight ensued. Marshall found courage from his fear and snatched a knife from the block. He spun and slashed at the first man, catching his throat. The man's eyes widened in surprise before he threw his hands up to clutch at the gaping wound. Crimson passed through his fingers, and down his arms while the color drained from his face.

It was an unexpected move that stunned the others for the second needed for Alexander to react. The friar cried out and ran toward the second thug, knocking him into the wall. One of the shelves fell, sending the heavy pots rolling onto his head. One of them hit Alexander. He saw stars and wobbled to regain his balance.

Mr. Crowe used his walking stick to thrash the third man into action, who had watched the fray without much clue to his part in it from the sidelines.

"Get in there, and bring them to me, you waste of air!"

Marshall could see the man was chosen for his size and lack of intelligence beyond taking direct orders. He changed hands with the knife used to take out the first man, and circled left in order to keep Mr. Crowe in his peripheral.

Alexander stood, having shaken the cobwebs out, and joined Marshall in front of the giant. The giant lunged after them, and the fray began again. The oversized man began to toss them around like ragdolls while the other tried to jump on him from behind. Any bystander witnessing might have thought it was a comedy skit. Alexander and Marshall were starting to lose stamina when, out of sheer frustration, Alexander slammed a large clay pot over the giant's head, knocking him out.

Panting and trying to catch his breath, both men turned to face Mr. Crowe. He shook his head at the worthless crew and then looked back at Alexander and Marshall.

"I guess if you want something accomplished, you must complete the task yourself."

Mr. Crowe lifted the walking stick in is hand and pulled at the bottom revealing it's secret. A small, rapier-like blade hissed as it was pulled from its sheath. Both Alexander and Marshall sighed and allowed their shoulders to slump. They were exhausted, and the prospect of contending with Mr. Crowe's blade made them take steps back in second thought.

Mr. Crowe bridged the distance by walking toward them, aiming the tip at their chests. "I underestimated how much trouble you two are. It makes no matter now. How sad it is to say, you will bo—"

Mr. Crowe stopped speaking mid-word. It all happened so fast the two men were stunned. Mr. Crowe's eyes widened and a look of shock transformed into pain. He opened his mouth to speak, but instead of words, blood spilled out. The thick stream poured down his chin where it clung to long lines of spittle before staining his shirt. His chest pushed forward before it popped with the sick sound that Marshall could only compare to the sound of crab shells being cracked. It made both men jump with a start.

When Mr. Crowe fell, a man was standing behind him with a fire poke. It angled downward as Mr. Crowe slumped to the floor with its end still embedded in his back.

"Robert?" Marshall said with confusion.

"Josef!" Alexander shouted.

All three exchanged looks.

"Josef is the name I made for myself when I ran and hid here."

Alexander looked confused for a half second before realizing that Marshall and Jos—Robert—knew one another.

"Robert, then," he said smiling, still happy to see him. "We should leave."

The three made it outside without further incident and escaped to cold wind coming off the water. Once outside, they looked around, each one having their own ideas of where to go.

Robert turned to them and pointed north toward town "we should stick together. My uncle has a merchant ship. Marshall knows of it and …" Robert paused to control his emotions.

The other two looked down knowing he lost his whole family.

"Anyway, it's been looked after by some people. If we can make it there, we will have help."

Marshall, being a naturally distrusting soul, especially since his latest ordeal, spoke.

"Why have you waited to go, then? Why didn't you go there when you ran that day?"

Robert sighed. There wasn't much time for this but he understood the skepticism. "My uncle's assistant needed me to stay here and lay low. He said a man came looking for me. So under his advisement I remained here, hidden among the monks.

From time to time I would sneak out and send them supplies, from that we stockpiled."

Marshall and Alexander listened without a word.

"I was planning on making my escape when I saw you brought in. Alexander told me what you two had discussed when you recovered, so I postponed my escape so we could all leave together. Marshall was moved by Robert's sacrifice. No one had ever done anything like that for him. At least not without wanting something in return.

Alexander was processing all of it. He looked around and assessed the world from where they stood. His eyes squinted in deep thought. He looked to the north where his original intention would have led him. Thinking better of it, he grimaced and turned toward the west where the ships were kept. He put his hands on his hips and looked up at the sky. Marshall didn't know if he was praying or just working out the problem in his head.

Robert waited as patiently as he could, but every second that passed made him more uncomfortable.

"Alexander, we must stick together," he reminded him. "They will not stop hunting us. There is only strength in numbers."

Alexander nodded. He knew what he said was true but it was all too much, too soon. One moment he was safe, life was simple, and he had a roof over his head. The next he was being hunted like a rabbit in winter.

"Ya. You're right. What be th' plan, then?"

Robert looked out toward the west and pointed toward the ships. "There is a ship docked and loaded with provisions. My uncle's assistant and his colleagues are waiting for us. We have until sundown tomorrow to reach them, and we will travel to a safe destination and find help."

Marshall took in a deep breath. His lungs filled with the air outside, and he let it out in one slow exhale. A small chill ran down his spine as he thought about those he'd encountered before waking up in the abbey. It all seemed like a distant dream or memory from another life. No matter what though, he knew he wouldn't stand a chance alone.

"I think we have a sound plan, Alexander. I'm in."

Alexander conceded. After all, he had nothing waiting for him if he traveled toward the north, and he wasn't keen on losing the company he'd acquired. Even if it meant he'd have to fight to survive.

"I'm guessin' we be travelin' together, then," he said, motioning to Robert to lead the way. "Aftah' you.'

The men looked around to make sure the coast was clear then ran across the field toward the ship.

Somewhere beyond the trees they were being watched.

CHAPTER 23: DON'T KILL THE MESSENGER

As the sun crossed the sky, Angus began to pace. He should've heard something by now. He cursed himself under his breath for not staying to ensure the task he'd given Mr. Crowe had been carried out. Under normal circumstances he would've, but he was on his way to collect more cages for his "guests." The fact his plans were ruined, by all appearances, made the doctor flush with anger.

The two men who accompanied him shifted with restless anxiety. Angus' reputation for violence preceded him, and they were well aware of his tendency to unleash his displeasure on those around him. For now, the doctor wore a groove in the stones beneath his feet, growling and muttering to himself. Both men took a step back and gave him a wider berth, which he didn't seem to notice, or care. He ground his teeth and watched the road leading to them until he heard the clopping of hooves approach.

The doctor left his position and stalked toward the gate with purpose, "Open it!"

The two men left their post and ran to either side, pushing open the large wooden doors. A thin, older man galloped in. He wore a scarf over his face and an oversized cloak that accentuated his lack of size. He looked to be half starved and barely hanging onto life.

Angus lifted his chin and stared expectantly for word of his delivery. The thin man dismounted and approached the doctor, hunched over like an abused rat.

"Where are they?" Angus bellowed.

The other man flinched, "They have escaped, my m'lord."

Angus' eyes widened and bulged. His face filled with a deep crimson, and he let out a scream so loud it caused the birds to scatter from their perch in a nearby tree.

The doctor flew at the thin man who let out a whimper and fell into a pathetic crouch on the ground. Angus reared back and landed a boot to his ribs. The poor fellow yelped before the breath was stolen from his lungs. Leaving him stunned and wounded. Angus climbed up onto the other man's horse.

"Find them or take their place!" He barked to the others.

Without waiting another moment for them to scramble to their horses, the doctor was already galloping off to track his prey.

The men traveled back to the church grounds and spread out. For hours they weaved in and out of the trees that lined the abbey until one of the men, a short, stocky figure with deep set eyes, raised his hand and let out a whistle. He'd found something. To the untrained eye, it was nothing, but to this man, who was a hunter by trade, it was a sign they were finally on a hot trail.

Angus rode up alongside the hunter before hopping down. The hunter was kneeling next to a fresh track in the mud with a branch in his hand. One of the twigs was bent, and he pointed it out to the doctor.

"How far?" Angus asked.

The hunter flashed two fingers, twice. *Twenty miles.*

Angus stood and smiled with satisfaction before mounting the horse again, "We'll reach them before sundown."

The hunter and the other man re-saddled and followed their master into the trees. With calculated steps, the hunter then took the lead and kept a trained eye on the land with its surrounding foliage. The others followed close behind and were careful not to disturb anything that would lead them to the three

men they were tracking. When the man in the front stopped, they all stopped and remained silent. Angus nudged his horse, bringing it to the side of the hunter and looked around.

"What is it?"

The hunter tugged on his earlobe, signing for Angus to listen.

They were close to town where there weren't many people left alive, but there were noises coming from that direction. The doctor narrowed his eyes, listening and trying to discern what was happening. It sounded like screams. In the sky to the west before them, large stacks of smoke were rising to the tops of the tree line. Angus turned and waved to the man behind them.

"Scout ahead."

The man nodded, turning his horse to find the road toward town. Angus and the hunter backtracked, setting up a temporary camp to wait for his report.

Whatever was happening, it sounded chaotic, and the doctor wasn't going to take any risks by heading into the village. If there were more sick and dying, he'd be detained and his plans would fall apart while Morrigan was being held back at his home. Keeping her alive and fed would be harder if he was not available to care for her. Tying the reigns around a tree trunk, he sat down on a nearby rock and read from a small journal. Keeping track of how long he was gone, Angus began to grow anxious again. It'd been a full day. He's never left her alone for longer than that.

In her advanced stage, Morrigan's hunger had grown. The lacerations on his back and shoulders were deeper and more painful from the bruising of her teeth breaking through the skin to the muscle. He struggled for a way to sustain her hunger. Finding fresh resources to keep her fed were growing slim.

CHAPTER 24: DEMONS COME TO PLAY

"Find out what's going on," Angus ordered the men. "I'll stay here with the horses."

The hunter gave another silent nod and motioned for the others to follow him. Watching them disappear into the trees, Angus remained still until he heard noises from somewhere in the thick.

Tuning the chaos out, Angus looked into the trees as he let his thoughts drift. The usual unwavering, steady beat of his heart changed. Now it was a staccato, his pulse rising for the first time in what felt like the span of forever. Time became nothing to him but murky waters, and he was nothing but a stone at the bottom stuck in a pile of trash and shite.

His entire life wove in and out of the trees ahead of him. Ghosts of his past coming to revisit him, haunt him, and drag him down into an undiscovered cave never to be found again. Sweat was pouring out of his skin making it damp and clammy. His clothes were clinging to his back and chest. Longing to be free of their confinement, Angus started removing them layer by layer until he could feel the cool air against his flesh.

I never wanted to be this way. How many times did I pray for Death? But Death found me and discarded me like everyone else in the world. Even my own mother and father.

Angus looked down at his hands. Once steady as the earth beneath him, they began to tremble now.

All I wanted was someone beautiful to see me, and to love me back. Everything I touch becomes tainted. No matter how hard I try to preserve them as they were ... they never stay.

Behind the doctor, a voice was calling out, but Angus was somewhere far away. His mind was either protecting him or devouring him as he sank further and further into its depths.

All those women smiling. All making empty promises. All of them nothing but dirty, filthy liars. Their smiles nothing more than the jagged teeth of jackals, gnashing and snapping at the tender underbelly of my vulnerability. No matter how hard I try to see their beauty, beneath the flesh, they were all the same; black, vile, and rotted.

Falling to his knees in the dirt, Angus stared at his trembling hands. The dirt on his palms was shifting and transforming. The hallucinations crept in making him believe insects crawled under the skin of his arms. Panicking, he began scratching at them until he drew blood.

All along it was me! His inner voice whispered. *I poisoned the flowers until they bent and wilted. I plucked the petals away, discarding them when they shriveled ... no longer beautiful and full of life.*

I thought I could save Her, my rose in Hell. She was going to leave me, too! Angus was sick to his stomach with the infestation of self-deprecating thoughts and doubled over as if in physical pain. *I thought if I could piece her back together and return her to the way she was before—maybe she would learn to love me.*

From one of the trees, the ghost of Angus' father stepped into plain sight. He looked the same as he did the last time Angus saw him. Across his neck, the large gaping "smile" glistened. Fresh blood was pouring down the front of his shirt, staining the fine fabric. He tried to speak but nothing came out, only the sounds of gurgling air.

You! Angus growled. *If ever I was a monster it is because you created me!*

The doctor crawled toward the vision, spitting in rage. He'd kill him again. And again. Every single time his father appeared, Angus would relive the murder until the one who created him was finally dead. Before he could reach his father, another body, this time a woman, stepped from behind a different tree.

You? But why?

This became too much for Angus who began to feel his brain burn with the flames of transgression. Falling forward, he curled his fingers grabbing fistfuls of his hair. Tears wet his eyes and he looked up once more.

Mother, please.

Another wave of pain burst inside his head and he cried out, reaching for the ghost of his mother.

Was I so repulsive you would leave me as soon as I was torn from your womb Oh, that you have seen the disgrace I have become. That I could crawl from this darkness, cold and brutal, back into you where, at least for nine months of my dreadful life, I felt loved. Felt warmth. Mother, please.

"Please." He muttered aloud, pulling himself through the leaves and mud, reached toward her with an outstretched hand.

His mother did not speak. She stared at him in silence.

There is always silence! IF there was a God, he would know I've been shunned and cast out the moment of my crowning. If I could hear her heart just once more ...

He stopped suddenly. He *could* hear it! Angus stopped moving, and tilt his head to listen harder. To his right someone else appeared. Looking to see who it was, Angus hissed.

Enuk!

Growling, the pulsing pain in his head grew. He began pounding his fist against his temple to beat it away. The force of the hits made his vision blurry.

Stop it! Cast your gaze away!

The leaves rustled and still more faces appeared until Angus stood, turning in circles, the tops of the trees spinning in unison above him.

All around him, the men who sexually abused him, his father who beat him and treated him like livestock, his mother who he was told killed herself just after giving birth (though he suspected was murdered by his father), the prostitute, the women whose children he took from their wombs, Analyn, the Herald's cousin, Girl One and Girl Two. They were all there and closing in. Their mouths opening to speak, but words never coming.

Something buried in the leaves caught Angus' attention. He looked to see the stolen infants crawling toward him, writhing naked and still covered in afterbirth.

Recoiling and shuffling backwards to put as much distance between him and the dead, his mind was starting to short circuit. *What? What is this?* Blinking his eyes, he tried to shake the illusion before him. *This ... this cannot be real. Am I in Hell?*

Angus screamed, shoving himself away until his back hit something. Too afraid to turn around, he looked down where his hands were resting. What was beneath it was hard and cold, just like whatever his back was touching. Lifting his fingers, he turned. Starting from the ground, he trailed his gaze until he saw toes, and those toes were attached to a woman's foot.

Morrigan?

He knew that foot. He knew every inch of her. The way her ankle tapered and led to the swell of her calf. How small her knees were and how long he had to search for one close enough to match. He knew the firmness of her thighs and the flare of her hips. He'd memorized the shape of her backside and the way it

curved into the dip of her lower back; just above her pelvis were two dimples.

The doctor felt the weight of fear on his chest before icy fingers were gripping his hair so close to his scalp he could feel her fingernails scrape against it. With unnatural strength, he was pulled up to his feet where all sense of composure left him, and he fought against the body of the one he once coveted.

Even as he spun around, the fingers would not give up their grip. He used his arms and legs to shove himself away but he was lifted upward until he was face to face with the one he called "Beloved."

"God, no!" Angus cried out when his eyes saw her.

He no longer saw the façade of her veiled in beauty. Her true face was staring at him, inches from his own. One eye clouded, the other bulging with fluid. Maggots slithering behind the thin membrane. Her once beautiful smile was now nothing more than narrow lines of puckered skin pulled tightly over her broken teeth. Her breath was rank and smelled of death and decomposition, making his bowels liquefy.

Once a man callous and cruel, he was now crumpling into a sniveling heap of cowardice. Angus' reaction confused Morrigan. In a forest of ghosts, she was real and standing there before him. She tried to draw him to her chest, but he punched at her and fought to get free. Angus could feel the bile rising in his stomach when he saw the weeping bobules full of her pestilence.

"Let me go!" He shouted, still fighting her grip.

Angus' world was unraveling around him. What had he done? What had he created?

Morrigan's confusion quickly escalated to frustration and then to rage. This was her creator. She recognized him as that. He fed her. He washed her. *He loved her.*

Now he was repulsed and kicking her away like a dog in the street. Around them were the bodies of the dead that had risen and followed the villagers, what was left of them, into the woods. She'd watched the others like herself set on fire, some walking as their parchment-thin skin blazed on.

No, Morrigan did not understand. He did not return to feed her like he always did. When hunger took over, she attacked the girls and feasted on them until her fingers were caked with blood and tissue.

Morrigan tried to call out for Angus with her primitive grunts and growls, but he did not come to clean her and touch her like so many times before.

She was careful when she came out of their home; the light was so bright, but all she could feel was the openness of the world without walls. The wind made her skin hurt, and she grew frightened at the strange smells. Morrigan heard the sound of something in the distance ahead of her. It had a heartbeat, but it was not Angus or Marshall. When she followed it, she heard screaming and then pain as something hit her in the temple.

When she stumbled to the side she was knocked the other way by an animal. Perhaps it was a cow or horse. Her brain had long forgotten by then. Another blast of pain and the screams grew louder with more voices joining in. Rocks were being thrown at her from all directions.

With Angus gone, those who had been captive were now turning on the ones left behind to care for them and roaming free toward the village in various states of decay. The villagers who survived the Plague were still cleaning up their dead when they witnessed the figures coming down the road. Some of them recognized them walking toward them as those who had died. A chorus of mass hysteria rose among them. Many ran for the

woods, but the others who were more brave began picking up torches and large rocks and hurling them at the walking dead.

Morrigan had only one cognitive thought, if you would call it such. As she endured the abuse, she was driven by the desire to find Him. He would save her. He would protect her.

She looked down at *Him* now as he bucked against her to free himself, then gave him a shove back so hard the wind was knocked from his lungs when he hit the ground. Angus' head landed on something sharp, and he began to bleed. The bodies of those standing in the tree line began to shuffle toward him at the first hint of his scent on the wind.

The doctor tried to stand when the first hand grabbed at him; it was Enuk. Angus jerked away, and the former nursemaid's shoulder made a soft popping noise when his arm became disjointed and fell useless to the bed of leaves beside him.

Angus rolled away and tried to get to his feet when he ran into his dead father. His scalp was falling away from his skull. The older man lurched toward his son and snapped at the air with his teeth in a blind fury. His eyes had long ago been removed and sewn shut by Angus.

The others took their cue and closed in, ready to devour the one who made them. Blood was more powerful than any emotion that would have died long ago with their soul.

"I made you! I made every single one of you!" Angus shouted through tears.

He was trying to run again, but the bodies continued to close in. Angus searched the ground and found a large branch. He picked it up and swung it left and right. The end of it made contact once, then twice, knocking one of them to the ground. He didn't look to see who it was; he only cared about getting out

alive. Another swing and there was a cracking sound of bone, and another body fell. He finally had the opening he needed.

Dropping the heavy branch in lieu of being slowed down, Angus took off running. He made it just past the line of trees before nearly running into a blade of fire with flames so high they enveloped the large oak tree in front of him. It took a moment for the doctor to process the entire scene. Trees engulfed in fire, smoke billowing into the sky, and the figures that were emerging all around him.

I shouldn't have dropped that bloody branch.

Backing up a step at a time, Angus saw shadows turning into masks. Had he finally lost it so completely?

The long masks made the figures look like large birds. The lenses reflected the orange and red light that danced around them, and the very end of their beaks exhaled a fragrant steam.

The heat lapped at Angus' skin, and though he held his arm up to shield himself, these figures were emerging and multiplying. Two bodies turned to four, then six, then ten and so on until he lost count.

A muffled voice called out from behind his mask, "Strike them all down!"

The others nodded in unison and turned into the forest Angus ran from. When they disappeared, there were others in equal numbers to replace them from beyond the wall of flames.

The cries of his creations carried over the roar of the wall of fire. In all its fury, the wall growled and consumed the large oaks, which groaned and creaked with the heat. Angus was trying to breathe, but it was too hot. His skin began to blister on the arm he used to shield his face. and he pulled it down into his coat.

Before him, the masked man who gave the orders approached. There was nowhere for Angus to go. All he could

do was stare into the reflection of the lenses heading toward him and watch as the beaked one's arm cut across with a harsh swing of his cane knocking the physician unconscious.

CHAPTER 25: CAN'T SEE THE FOREST FOR THE TREES

Morrigan stood as Angus ran. The others were fighting amongst each other to get to the source of blood from the doctor's fresh wound. The sound of his heart rate clamored in her ears when he ran past her only to grow faint again the further he went into the forest. She could track him with ease by the sound alone. He'd taught her to be patient, so when the others rushed toward him she remained back. Because of this, she avoided getting entangled in the fray.

There was a change in the direction of the wind and on it was the scent of others. The chorus of their heartbeats coming closer piqued Morrigan's curiosity. She'd never been around more than ten people since her new senses came alive. Turning, she head in their direction. She could tell they were following Angus. A sense of warning came over her.

Swiping at stray branches, Morrigan pushed through the foliage, giving little mind to the scrapes and lacerations they caused her legs and bottoms of her feet. She barely felt them. Her primal instincts of rage still functional, she drew nearer to the crowd surrounding Angus. She was about fifty feet away when the heat from the fire washed over her cold skin. It growled, drowning out the sounds that led her there. She had to shield her eyes from the blinding light produced by the heat pattern.

With the cover of the trees around her, she was still well hidden from the man who was setting a line of oil on fire, deliberately. He did not see her, but she saw him.

It was the perfect opportunity, and Morrigan was about to attack him when a familiar heartbeat fluttered from her right

side. His voice was muffled, but she *knew* it. Somewhere in her mind's dwindling capacity to catalog and store memories, this voice moved forward to the front of the line. She tried to focus and recall who it belonged to, but the memory was distant and out of reach. She needed to know who it was.

Moving closer with caution, Morrigan watched from behind the cover of a large tree trunk. She could see no faces, only silhouettes. Lifting her chin, she tried to catch his scent on the wind but all that came toward her was the smell of burning wood, leaves, and pine needles. The voices stopped when the men heard the snapping of a twig from Morrigan's direction.

The two men peered into the shadows, but could not see anything.

"What is it?" he asked.

"Probably the animals running from the fire," the first one answered.

Continuing their task of lighting the path of oil with their torches, the two headed back to camp. Morrigan picked up more voices, and when the two men left, she tracked them at a safe distance until they reached their destination. There must have been three or four dozen of them all dressed the same. Their masks and coats were similar to the ones worn by the men who were treating the others afflicted with the sickness, but these were much more frightening.

The long cloaks were coated with some kind of substance and it seemed to repel the fire around them. Morrigan was picking up the scent of what it was. A reddish-brown dye called *Alum.*

Memories were starting to come back to her. She'd seen the imported dyes and the process of coloring clothing with it in the market place just after trade began from the Silk Road.

I ... I remember.

The more she was exposed to since coming out of the dungeon of Angus' lair, the more the nerves in her brain worked, the more she *learned*. And she was *learning fast.*

Mesmerized by the chaos she stood in silence watching the figures that looked like "Bird Men" work. She watched as Angus came from the path behind her and ran straight into their circle. By now, the flames had begun to reach their black and amber fingertips into the darkening sky, winding around the tall majestic trees that had been here for hundreds of years.

She listened as the Bird Man up front spoke to her creator. Morrigan felt an odd sense of protectiveness for him. He had held her captive, fed and bathed her on command, and by all accounts did as he would according to his whim … but she felt *something* for him. An inner battle waged within her and memories flickered in and out in small puzzle pieces she could not decipher. They were simple flashes of images. Faces came and went in the blink of an eye, each one familiar but lost inside the decrepit rooms of her memory. Each one beyond her reach, and lost deep in the basement of her mind. Emotions began to pair with each face and suddenly Morrigan was overwhelmed with unexpected grief. Grief turned into mourning, and mourning turned into rancor.

The discussion between Angus and the strange man ended and the strike of the figure's cane to her Master's temple severed her tie to the internal battle. Morrigan unleashed a cry and flew forward with a fury out of some primal instinct toward them. The other men caught sight of her and screamed at the hideous creature coming at them. To fend her off, they swung their torches at her, and some of them scattered in fear when she got too close.

Morrigan looked like a pale statue that had somehow come to life. Her arms were outstretched with her fingers

splayed, and she took awkward rigid steps which made her zig-zag as she locked in on them. A few of the men came toward her and tried to stop her, but she grabbed them one by one, sinking her teeth into their necks. Fighting against her was futile. Her strength was that of 5 men. Her cold limbs held them close to her as they flailed. Dropping them to the ground, they gurgled and choked on the blood that formed in their broken necks. Morrigan trampled over them and continued on her path of Hell.

An unleashed well of emotions heightened her predatory instincts, and she could hear the slaughter of the others. They were like her only dumber and slower. Angus never gave them the attention he gave her. She was different because he taught her, having the intentions of making her his bride, to be like him.

Reaching the Bird Man who had struck Angus, two others flanked him, thrusting their torches out at her. Morrigan recoiled, attempting to lunge at them from other angles unsuccessfully. The nerves in her brain were still flickering and lighting up inside her skull like a tiny galaxy of stars. She opened her mouth and …

"Mi!" she screamed, trying to say *Mine!*

The men lowered their torches only a few inches in shock before one of them muttered, "Dear God."

"Do not let your guard down!" the head Bird Man shouted.

Morrigan growled at them, baring her teeth in warning like a wild animal. The men did not move, but she could hear their hearts fluttering. With the torches blinding her, she turned her face away before crouching close to the ground. She slid her hands under Angus' armpits and took small, cautious steps, backing away from the mob.

Another man fought his way through the crowd, dodging the torches. The outlying ring of fire had gotten out of control.

"Let me pass!" he shouted.

The men were rooted where they stood like the trees still burning around them, not daring to move. The man coming through physically shoved them aside to gain passage. When he got to the front of the others, the first Bird Man reached out to hold him back.

"No, son! It's no longer her!"

The man who broke through stood, staring in disbelief at Morrigan in her current state. His eyes narrowed, hardly recognizing the girl he once loved and cared for. "Morrigan?"

When he said her name, she tilted her head like a confused dog. Her limited thought process was jumbled and disoriented. She could only see him from the side, the lights from the torches still stinging her eyes with their brightness. Robert, still watching her, motioned for the men to back up. They did so with hesitation, shuffling one step at a time. When they had moved back far enough to give her some room, he gestured with his hand for them to lower the torches. This time they weren't as cooperative, but they held them low enough to get the girl to turn her head.

Like an ape hovering over the unconscious body of Angus, she bared her teeth again. Her gums were dark purple and her lips, torn and brittle, pulled back tight across her incisors. Her eyes were ringed with a shade to match her mouth. Vermillion clouded the sclera of her eyes and pieces of her skin hung like parchment that had been dried in the sun. Most of her fingernails were missing. The ones that remained were black and cracked from trying to claw her way out of captivity. The two locked eyes, and Morrigan's mind reeled with an influx of *knowing*.

Her scream was the most unholy thing Robert and the men had ever heard. It made all of them lift their arms to shield them from an invisible blow.

"N—No!" she cried, lowering her eyes to her hands. She was seeing what had been done to her … what had happened to her … now that her consciousness showed signs of *life*.

All the strength had drained from Robert's body, and he fell to his knees in front of her. His own anguished cry found its escape as he saw what she had become.

Morrigan flinched and pulled her arms into her sides, ashamed. Her mind had gone through too much. Robert's repulsion to her short-circuited her logical mind, and she began to pant. *Can't breathe,* she thought. *Words! Why can't I speak what I want to scream?* Her face contorted, her mouth hung slack as she tried to articulate her words. *Please, my God, please. I'm in here!*

Robert hung his head and looked away from her. All that came from her mouth were grunts and groans. *She's gone,* he resolved to himself. *She belongs to the Doctor. I was too late.*

Oh God, he hates me! I'm … I'm a monster! The shame of her condition and the exposure of her vulnerability crept under her skin. Her body was dying, she could feel it. *I will never have another coherent moment—alive.* Lifting her eyes to Robert again, Morrigan hissed with a slow, exhale like any cornered animal would. She did not move or attack him. When Robert reached a hand, the other men let out a collective exhale of surprise and tried to hold him back. Morrigan snapped her teeth at him in warning. *Let me go, Robert!*

"Come, lad," the other man tried to urge.

From the ground, Robert lowered his head and pulled down his mask to the shouting protestations of those around him. His face, revealed fully to her now, shot through Morrigan like a

frozen spear. The sudden influx of emotion paralyzed her and forgetting about Angus, she allowed him to slip from her hands. Her head was on fire. All of it was too much, and the stabbing sensation was excruciating. Her hands now free of Angus' body, she began to sob. Falling to her knees in front of Robert, tears fell from her eyes.

Robert ... His name wouldn't come out. It was lost on her tongue forever.

"Ruh!" she cried, trying harder.

Robert's face twisted in sadness, and his own tears fell down his cheeks, making long lines in the dirt and soot. *She's really gone,* he repeated to himself. He knew he was only convincing himself. The beautiful girl he knew and loved before was now hideous and revolting. She was patched together, stitches tugging dead flesh together like a quilt. Donors were used to make her whole like a child's worn and discarded doll.

Watching Morrigan reach out for him and try to enunciate his name made his stomach churn until he saw something glinting against the firelight; a small gold band on her implanted finger.

The monster created a monster, he thought, his lips pursing. *His autopsic bride.*

Morrigan followed Robert's eyes to her hand and began to shake.

No! I can't ... This isn't real! I'm in here, Robert, please! Get this off me! Her inner voice screeched.

When Robert could no longer bear to look at her as she was—when he could no longer watch her be imprisoned within the jigsaw body of foreign pieces—he stood and reached out his hand. The other man stepped forward handing him his torch, before stepping back again.

"We ... we were too late. I'm sorry, Robert," he said.

"Thank you, Marshall," Robert whispered back.

Taking a step toward the woman, Robert choked back his sobs and waited for the leader—the one who led the Bird Men—to give his nod for him to deliver her final rights.

The man was Robert's uncle. The old ship merchant had been awaiting the arrival of Robert, Alexander, and Morrigan. He lowered his beaked mask and let out an exhausted sigh, and with the burden of the mask removed, he prayed for Morrigan.

"Oh merciful God, whose blessed Son went about doin' good; uphold with thy strength and grace those who do service to the wounded and the sick."

The old grey-bearded man looked at Robert, placing a hand to his shoulder in comfort. "We beseech thee to protect and bless them in all dangers, anxieties, and labors, through Jesus Christ, our Lord."

Turning to face Morrigan, who was rocking back and forth on her knees chanting her abbreviated version of Robert's name, he continued, "I commend you, my dear sister, Morrigan Kingsley, to almighty God, and entrust you to your Creator."

"May you return to Him who formed you from the dust of the earth. May the holy Virgin Mary, the angels, and all the saints come to meet you as you go forth from this life." Robert grit his teeth as his uncle prayed, growling in despair beside him. "May Jesus, who was crucified for you, grant you His mercy and His peace."

Goodbye Morrigan, Robert said to himself knowing what was to come.

"May Christ, who died for you, admit you into His heavenly kingdom. May the Blood He shed be your salvation, and may He forgive you of all your sins and set you among those whom He has chosen. May you see your Redeemer face to face and enjoy the vision of God forever."

Robert stared at Morrigan with red-rimmed eyes as the men prayed. He saw no use in praying for any of their souls. He was about to murder this young woman, who he once loved. He could not save her. Angus could not save her.

Not even Almighty God could save her.

She was walking in her own Hell, trapped in a body for as long as the flesh held out.

And then what?

Robert could not bear to answer that question. His hand trembled around the torch, his knuckles protesting, burning white from the grip he had on it.

You're not mine, anymore, he thought.

Robert never felt the burning torch leave his hand until he heard Morrigan scream. Robert couldn't bear it and shut his eyes tight against the tears. Morrigan flailed and rolled on the ground as her flesh caught fire. Her skin was thin and caught quickly. Seeing Robert close his eyes, she crawled on the ground until she found Angus' body. Locking her arms around him, his skin burning woke him to the nightmare around him. Morrigan was like a demon, straddling him with her hair aflame. Her arms, like two matchsticks pulled him toward her until they were both screaming together.

To the writhing, burning couple before him, Robert whispered up toward the ash, "Till death do you part."

CHAPTER 26: MORRIGAN … THE END?

I felt the fire consume my flesh and enter my veins carrying its purification of the sickness from whatever it was I'd become. I remember looking up at the sky and watching all the brilliant colors lighting up the blanket of darkness behind it. Glowing embers were floating upward, turning grey and fading before ever coming close to Heaven. Every memory of my life … my childhood, my mother and my father … Robert … spiraled away into the void.

And with each labored breath I could feel my soul slipping into the void. There was a serene sense of relief. Freedom from the prison of Angus Wulfe. Freedom from the prison of my dying body and freedom from the pain of losing Robert, forever. I don't know how long I had been lying there. Time was no longer tangible. The sun rose and fell. The leaves drifted past my eyes.

What's happening? Why am I still here? Why am I still conscious? Wait! I hear someone.

There was a sound of shuffling and boots crushing the earth right next to my head. Lying there paralyzed, I was beginning to understand. My soul had not left this charred, husk of a vessel. *NO! I'm still here!*

The man standing above me was looking down into my eyes. He wrinkled his nose and looked up at someone else. "Shame about this one, aye? I heard they burned her and the others alive." He gave a shudder and motioned for the other one. "Come on, help me get her into the ditch; it's almost dark."

Help me … I don't want to be here, forever.

ABOUT THE AUTHOR

By design, Lisa Vasquez creates horror with vivid, dark, and twisted words and images that not only drags the reader in between the pages, but onto the covers that house them, as well. When she releases her grasp, readers are left alone to sort through the aftermath those images leave behind; each one becoming a seed that roots itself within the soft confines of their psyche. She takes this passion for writing horror and uses it to mentor other authors and volunteers as the Publisher's Liaison for the Horror Writers Association. In January 2016, Lisa took her commitment to the next level and opened an independent publishing house, Stitched Smile Publications.

Her work can be found in several anthologies, and her upcoming, full-length novels will be released in 2017. For more information and updates on Lisa's work, you can find her at: www.unsaintly.com or on Facebook (facebook.com/unsaintlyhalo), Twitter (@unsaintly), Instagram (unsaintly)

MORE FROM STICHED SMILE PUBLICATIONS

In the best of times, loneliness is difficult. At the end of time it can be deadly. Hank Walker is alone and struggling not just with

the undead but with depression that threatens to swallow him. Searching for the family he sent away at the beginning of the rise of the dead, Hank is left to deal with loneliness, desperation, and his own memories that haunt him. The dead are everywhere. The few people still alive are scattered, and the ones Hank comes across may be more dangerous than the biters. With an unlikely traveling companion, Hank's search takes him across the state of South Carolina and to the depths of darkness like nothing he has ever experienced before. Can Hank find his family and survive the biters? Or does he completely unravel in the world of the dead?

Also Available on Audible!

CPSIA information can be obtained
at www.ICGtesting.com
Printed in the USA
BVHW080823220719
554058BV00007B/267/P